# THE RIGHT WAY

# TO BE WRONG

## TRACY A. BALL

ISBN: 978-1-61296-610-6

PUBLISHED BY BLACK ROSE WRITING

www.blackrosewriting.com

Printed in the United States of America

Suggested retail price $17.95

*The Right Way To Be Wrong* is printed in Garamond Premier Pro

# Littles Ripples Make Big Waves

Matthew – You make everything possible: my life, my plans, my love. You are my happily ever after. I am the least deserving, yet most rewarded dreamer in history. I'm smart enough to know it's all because of you and selfish enough to like it that way.

Kelly – Just when I think you've hit your ceiling of excellence, you break it. The only thing I know of that's larger than your brain is your heart. I am truly in awe of you. Every good thing in my life has something to do with you. Being your mom is my greatest attribute.

Ramses - Every parent dreams of the perfect son-in-law: someone who is hard-working, smart, generous, kind, funny and above all, good. Thank you for making my dreams come true. We'd be incomplete without you.

# Special Thanks

You are who you are before God and no one else.

Mommie: You make every day an adventure.

Aunt Barbara: Nobody cheers louder than you.

Debi, Brian, Leon, Ronny, Wayne, Kevin, Pam, Mary, Jennie & Sue: You impact my writing the way you've impacted my life.

The Buggors- John & Carol: Love, loyalty, honor, courage, humility- when I need to see the image of Christ, I look at you.

Nicole, Sam, Spencer and Amanda:
You told a better story on the cover than I did in the book.

Covenant People: We are who we are because you got us there.

Kay: Just knowing you're near means everything to me.

I humbly thank you all.

# THE RIGHT WAY

# TO BE WRONG

# PROLOGUE

"What are you doing here?"

"Hey, Gwen." Cherry would have never called her Gwen before. Her nickname was Peaches or Peach. But these days, Gwendolyn Brookfield was anything but peach-like. Cherry didn't expect her sister to be happy to see her. Gwen was never really happy to see her. Gwen was never really happy.

"I'm a little early, I know. I hope I'm not intruding." She glanced around the dingy apartment seeking evidence of company.

"I'm alone. Come on in." Gwen opened the door wider. "Fifteen minutes before my next client."

*Client. A nice word makes it all clean.* "I came to say good-bye."

"Good-bye? I thought you weren't leaving until tomorrow?" Gwen was half dressed. She had piles of laundry scattered around the living area. She threw articles left and right looking for something to wear.

A vehicle with a siren sped down the street. Even though she heard it at least once a day, the sound was still a distraction for Cherry. "It's just one more night." She cleared off a chair and sat down. Rummaging through the nearest stack of material, she pulled out a red top with a plunging neck. Cherry wasn't sure about Gwendolyn, but Peaches always looked good in red. "Try this one." She tossed it across the room. "I figured, I could get an early start and you wouldn't need to cancel your night. Unless you already cancelled."

"No. I can't call nobody. I have to wait for them to show up." She accepted the top. "I want to hang out, but Lee is one of my favorites."

Cherry had nothing to say about that.

"Did you get to see the girls?"

"Yes." Cherry thought of Adora and Ahava, her adorable nieces.

Toddlers, both of them. They didn't know her any better than they knew the foster family who had taken them in. Still, they were all smiles and giggles. Happy just to have food.

"I don't get to see them." Gwen tugged the top down and pushed her boobs up. "I have to work. I always have to work."

Cherry had nothing to say about that.

It was hard to talk. It had been a long time since they had anything in common. Cherry didn't know how to fix it.

"Do you think you'll like your new school?"

"I hope so," Cherry said. "It has a great curriculum. The campus is really cool."

"It's out in the boonies somewhere isn't it?"

"No more remote than Aunt Sid's."

"That ain't no place I'd want to be either. How long are you going to be home?"

"A few weeks. There's not much time before the semester starts."

"Make sure you tell them I said, hello."

"I will."

"Do not give Sidney my cell. I don't want her calling me every day, telling me not to talk to strangers."

*Talking to strangers ain't what you do.* Cherry laughed a little. "That's exactly what Sidney would say."

"I know. She says it every time she calls the house. What does she think about you changing schools again?"

"Ummumm." Cherry shrugged. "She didn't want me to transfer in the first place. She probably thinks I don't like school."

"I don't think you like school."

"No. I~"

A loud knock interrupted them.

"That's my client." Peaches fluffed her hair on her way to the door.

*I like school. It's the rest of life I don't care much for.*

# THE BEGINNING

# CHAPTER 1

"E is the absolute worst letter of the entire alphabet," Cherry told her dashboard as she changed the radio station. The song, *Come on Eileen* – the reason for her attention to the letter E and subsequently her gas gage – ended, with it her desire to hear 80's music. She stopped at a Tim McGraw classic. "When in Rome, listen to Country." Checking the empty road around her, she changed lanes and pulled into the Sheetz gas station. She got out of her little blue Toyota, stretched and made a quick inventory of her surroundings. It was too dark to be impressed. According to her GPS, she was less than five minutes from her destination. However, she did not feel like being there yet. Besides, the dreaded E was before her, promising to see her stranded. She should have filled up while she was in Maryland. Yes, the Toyota was great on gas, even better when it had some.

The hand written sign on the pump read: Please pay inside. Her legs needed a stretch anyway. A worker stocked the beer cooler and another cleaned the counter with Windex. She looked up when Cherry walked in. "Hi there. Are you coming or going?"

The cashier had the whitest blond hair Cherry had ever seen. "Pardon me?" The lady seemed nice enough, but Cherry couldn't think past the hair. She didn't know what the woman was talking about.

"Your plates are from out of state. Are you going to the racetrack? Or on your way home?" She pressed some keys on her register and waited for Cherry to swipe her card.

"Neither." That was all she wanted to say, but felt compelled to add,

"I'm on my way to the University."

"Oh. Shepherd. My daughter goes to Shepherd. You just getting started?"

Cherry wondered if her daughter had super-bleached blond hair too. "Yes and no. I transferred." She signed the receipt.

"Well good for you. You stick with it. That's what I always tell my daughter. She hates school, but I tell her to stick with it. West Virginia is nice. I like it here, but I don't want her to end up with a life like mine. Two jobs. I work here and over at Martins. I'm trying to get on at the track. That takes so long..."

Cherry's cell phone blared, sparing her further details of the cashier's life. "I have to answer this. Thank you."

"Good night. Don't use the phone while you're at the pump."

Cherry nodded and talked into the phone at the same time. "Yes, Aunt Sid?"

"I was worried about you. You didn't call me. Is everything all right?"

"Everything is fine." She moved toward the door. "I told you I would call you at nine."

"I know. It's five of. I was scared you might get into trouble. You shouldn't be there anyway. Running. That's all you do. It's not going to make you happy. Running never does."

Cherry's eye rolling was a natural response. However, this time she stopped mid-swirl. Someone was holding the door open for her. "Thank you." She forced herself to walk past without staring...overmuch.

"Are you listening to me? Who is that? A man?"

"Oh yeah." Cherry snickered into the phone. "He was a hot cowboy. Hat and all. If they grow them like that around here, I'm planting a garden."

"I told you not to talk to no strange men. You have to be more careful. It's men like that you have to worry about. Most con-men pretend to be handsome."

"Pretend? How does one pretend to be handsome?" Cherry's flip-flops smacked the pavement on the way to her car.

"You know what I mean."

"No one is going to con me. In fact, in a national survey, four out of five con-men agree, they have better things to do with their time, like pre-tending to be handsome."

"Don't be flippant. Girls like you end up on the news all the time."

"I've got to go. I'm at a gas station."

"You wouldn't have to go if you weren't always on the run."

"Yes, I would. I'm at a gas station. Besides, I'm not on the run."

"What do you call it? You ran up to New York when your brother got in trouble. Now, you're in a whole new state just because you found out something else you don't like. What's that? Running?"

"That's having my own life."

"Whose life have you been having? Lordy girl. You can look all you want. You ain't going to find no over the rainbow."

"Why are we having this fight, Aunt Sid? I came here to finish school because of the curriculum. That's a good thing. Besides, I'm almost here. What's the point in arguing?"

"What's being in a new place going to do for you?"

"Earn me a full night's sleep," she muttered. She was louder when she said, "Everything. I adore new places. Because they're so new."

"Well, Miss New, call me when you get to your hotel. I'm going to wait up."

"No. Don't wait up. I'm going to eat some dinner~"

"Where are you eating at?"

"Uhhh..." Cherry scanned the area and named the first place she saw. "Applebee's. It's right here. Then I'll check into my hotel. I'm here. You worry too much, Aunt Sid. I'll call you in the morning."

"No. I'll~"

"I've got to go. I'll call you in the morning. Love you. Bye." She hung up, shaking her head. As she reached for the pump, she caught sight of the person on the other side. It was the hot doorman. *How did he get there? He just went inside a minute ago.* She hadn't noticed him come back out. *Oh well. Aunt Sid was enough to snatch anybody's attention.*

Covertly, she snuck another glance. His t-shirt was deep blue. *Weird.* At the door, it looked gray. His hat was different too. *Must be his face. After looking at it, your eyes can't focus properly.* His hair -what she could see of it- looked to be in that chestnut to chocolate-brown color range. Apparently, he missed his last appointment with his barber. A shadow of a beard dusted his jaw, like he had more important things to do than shave today. Compared to her five foot four inch frame, he was tall. And lean. And his t-shirt hung just right. She could tell, he was ripped. *Like that vampire guy from Mystic Falls.*

Aunt Sid's gibe resounded in her mind. "Wouldn't run from that. Just saying." She tore her eyes away from his earring. "Sidney would die of a heart attack if she knew what I was up to." She grabbed one last eyeful, then got in her car and had another last eyeful. Finally focusing, Cherry drove off. She made a left on a road called Flowing Springs.

. . . . .

By the time Eric returned to the truck, Holden was in the cab waiting. "Do you feel like hanging out a little bit?"

"I don't care." Eric opened the door and swung himself in. "Where are we going?"

"Applebee's."

"Cool. Do you want me to call Wyatt?"

"I don't care." Holden pulled off, his eyes several hundred yards down the road.

"What's at Applebee's?"

"A deposit."

Eric cocked his head to the side. "The hot mixed-chick in the blue Toyota?"

"Yep."

"All for it. I wonder if she has two personalities to go with her races."

"One for each of us."

"Who are we withdrawing?"

Holden could see the parking lot from the light. Her car was right...there. "You can decide. Although, my vote is for Melvina. She's getting clingy."

"Christine has been spying on us. I say we cut them both. I'm bored with them anyway." Eric speed-dialed their eldest brother. "Yo, Wyatt. Turn around. We're stopping at Applebee's...Holden wants to hunt...yeah, it should be interesting."

# CHAPTER 2

Cherry wanted the bacon cheeseburger. She wouldn't get it, but she wanted it. The grilled chicken sandwich wasn't looking too bad either. The restaurant was fairly full, not bad for a Tuesday. Even though the room was chilly, the lighting at her booth - halfway between the bar and the door, was dim - perfect for her mood. She could sort her thoughts and contemplate her life in relative peace.

The waitress set her drink -water with lemon- down. "Are you ready to order?"

"Ummm. I can't quite decide."

"I'll give you a minute."

"A minute would be good. Thanks." The waitress moved and Cherry froze, momentarily stunned. Twins. He. They. Were there. Waiting to be seated. Twins. Wow. Double yummies. One of them - the doorman one - with the gray t-shirt was crowding the hostess. Not, that she seemed to mind. She'd have to be blind to mind. The other one was searching the room intently. His eyes found hers and held them...and held them...and held them.

A shadow passed in front of her. A body cut off her vision. Cherry released a breath she hadn't been aware she was holding. She looked up at the man standing in her way. Tall, dark and handsome could describe him if it were synonymous with gothic beanpole with patches of orange hair. He had a thin chain traveling from his nose ring, through two cheek rings, to his spiked dog collar. She had an urge to touch her face.

"You are too beautiful to eat alone. I'm going to sit with you." He sat across from her and smiled.

He was missing three very important teeth.

"Ummm...uhhh...ummm..." She wasn't sure if she was more appalled by his appearance or his nerve. "I'm sorry. You...can't...join me." No way was she eating with that.

"Why not? You need some company. I'm Boston. What's your name?" He reached for her water, took a swig and spit it back in the cup. "Ugh. I thought it was Sprite. Name?"

"You're in my seat."

Cherry looked up, this time relieved and a little excited to see the twins standing beside her table. Next to Boston, they looked like the Sun and the Sun.

"What?"

"You are in my seat," Blue-shirt Sun said.

Half a beat later, Gray-shirt Sun said, "That means you have to get up now, dawg."

Boston didn't move. "She came in by herself. She didn't tell me she was with you. I can sit anywhere I want."

Gray Sun laughed. Blue Sun cocked his left eyebrow. He looked at Cherry. "Do you want him to stay?"

"I was here first. I'm not leaving."

Cherry concluded that Boston was stupid. "I don't know him." She didn't know them either, but that was beside the point.

Blue Sun said something quietly out of the side of his mouth to his twin. Then, he focused on Boston. "Last time. Get up."

"No."

Cherry shifted, uncomfortable.

Two more cowboy types appeared. It was enough to prompt the manager to join them. "Is there a problem here?"

"Not at all," Blue Sun said. "We're just switching tables." As fast as that, things were in motion. "Let's go." He reached for Cherry's hand and pulled her out of the booth.

Gray Sun slid into the booth beside Boston, effectively pinning him in.

The other two cowboys filled the space opposite them.

"Hey~"

That was all she heard Boston say. Blue Sun was leading her across the room, presumably to the booth that was originally his. She slid in, not really sure of...anything.

"I can give you back if you want. I was under the impression he was disturbing you."

"No," she said a little too fast. "That. This. Nothing like this has ever happened to me in my life. Ever."

The waitress came over. It was the same one. "Are you ready to order now?"

Cherry didn't know. She didn't know anything.

"What about you, Eric? Or is it Holden?" She winked at Cherry. "They're one hundred percent identical. Trust me."

"We'll start with the mozzarella sticks, Zina. Amaretto sour for the lady, rum and coke for me."

"Be that way then." Zina scribbled down their order and disappeared.

"Friend of yours?"

"No. I took a guess with your drink. Was that a good choice?"

"I wouldn't know. I've never had a... amaretto...whatever it is."

"Do you want something different?"

"No. I've never had any of it. Just beer."

He arched his left eyebrow.

She thought that was cool.

"Tell me you're old enough to drink?"

"Not yet. But that's all right. I'm positive this is one of those drinking moments."

"I'll order you a Coke anyway." He picked up his menu. "Do you know what you want?"

Cherry decided to go with it- whatever *it* was. "Pepsi. Coke gives me headaches. I'm feeling like a burger tonight. I'm going to get this." She pointed to the bacon cheeseburger.

"That a girl." He nodded. "This isn't a night for any wussy salad stuff. We could be here a while." He returned to his menu, missing her look of incredulity.

Their appetizer and drinks arrived. He ordered their meal and her Pepsi before pushing the plate toward her.

"Thank you." She picked up a mozzarella stick, wondering how she was supposed to eat in front of him.

He wasn't bothered. "I'm Holden," he said, dunking a cheese stick.

"I'm Cherry." The absurdity made her laugh. "I'm not an expert but introductions usually come a little earlier. Don't they?"

"You've got a nice laugh, Cherry. It suits you."

"The name or the laugh?"

He briefly contemplated asking her about her race, then decided she was part goddess and nothing else mattered. "They both suit you."

She sipped her drink, trying not to notice how intently he watched her. "This is good." It was.

"It seemed like amaretto would suit you too. Don't drink it too fast. How old are you?"

"I'm a few months short of twenty-one. You?"

"Twenty-three."

There was boisterous laughter from the direction of her former table.

Emboldened by the alcohol, Cherry dipped a second mozzarella stick in the marinara, accidentally touching the tip of hers to his. "What would you call this? Are we somehow on a date or something?"

"It would make me happy to call it a date." Holden finished off the last one. "I saw you watching me at Sheetz."

She squeezed her eyes shut so he couldn't see her flush. "Did you really?"

"Oh yeah. Aunt Sid is going to have a thing or two to say to you."

She cracked up. Her hair fell in her face and she pushed the coffee colored strands back behind her ears, unmindful that he studied her movements. "Her real name is Sidney. She's my great aunt."

"You've got an awesome laugh," he said. "We followed you here. That guy—"

"Boston."

"Boston." He snorted. "I had just found you when *Boston* got in the way." He made sure she was paying attention. "I don't let anything get in my way."

His eyes were a mysterious blue-green. Like the ocean. They were smoldering.

Cherry wasn't chilly any longer. In fact, it was getting kind of warm.

Holden pulled out his cell phone. "Before we go any further, may I get your phone number?"

"My phone number?"

"Aunt Sid's not the only one who wants to talk to you."

"I feel like the Cheshire Cat." She tried to get her smile within a normal range.

"Number?"

"Really? You want my number?"

"Number?"

"Wow." She took a deep breath. "It's 421...I don't think so. This is too weird."

"Be brave." He flashed a row of bright white, not quite even, teeth. "It's just your phone number. If you tell me not to call it, I won't." His thumb hovered over the pad.

It would be paranormal for someone to tell him not to call. Besides, she was as brave as they came. "421-996-6996."

He arched his left eyebrow again as he keyed in the last digits. "Is this your real number?"

"Yes, it's my real number." She sipped her amaretto. "I couldn't think of a fake number that fast."

A moment later, her cell phone rang.

Now, he was the one wearing the Cheshire grin. "You might want to get that. It could be important."

She laughed at her screen. "It's an unknown number. I don't answer those."

"You may want to. Just this once."

She talked into the phone while staring straight at him. "I'm sorry, but I'm on a...date. Is this is important?"

He stared back while talking on his own device. "It's very important. I wanted to make sure you had my number, because I want you to call me. Frequently."

*He sounded like... ooh...* "You were checking to be sure I gave you the right number."

"And now we know you can't think of a lie that fast."

"I'll try to work on it." *Yeah...ooh.*

"No, you won't."

"No, I won't."

"Hold on for a second. My waitress just came over."

"Mine too!" Cherry's pretend excitement made them both laugh. It became even funnier when Zina's puzzled frown went back and forth between them. She refilled Cherry's Pepsi and moved away without comment.

"We have to hang up." Cherry tried to catch her breath. "People are going to think we're crazy."

"They're jealous. But, you should get back to your date. Can I call you tomorrow?"

"I hope you do." *And sound just like that when you're talking to me.*

"Count on it. Can I see you tonight?"

"I think you should." She was done with warm. It was starting to get hot.

· · · · ·

Three-quarters of a bacon cheeseburger, a side of fries and half a slice of chocolate cake later, Cherry was still warm. Holden was the most thrilling thing she'd ever come across in her life. Having grown up on the beachy shores of Eastern Maryland, she had no idea this type of excitement came in country packages. And, Holden was one stampede away from a John Wayne movie. Her evening was perfect and steadily improving.

At the other table, Boston had become friends with Holden's family. They were having an impromptu party of sorts.

"How much longer before you finish school?" Holden had been

peppering her with questions all evening.

"A year and a half. Give or take a credit or two."

"Where were you before?"

"My first year was in Salisbury. I did a year online. Then I transferred to NYU."

"Did you get homesick?"

"No." It was so definite, she felt obligated to explain. Only, she couldn't.

"Why didn't you stay? Not that I mind. I'm just curious."

"I...uhhh...ran into a problem. So I left."

"How long do you plan on being here?"

"Until I have to leave."

"You could be here a while."

She raised a polished nail in the air. "Hold that thought. I'll be right back." He nodded and she slid out of the booth.

. . . . .

Cherry was alone when she went into the ladies' room. Besides the amaretto and the Pepsi, she needed a moment to collect herself. Country-boy was hot. No doubt about it. But, relationships were not her thing. Not right now, anyway. There was school. There was money. She needed to be making money, and focusing on school to land a job to make lots of money. She had to get her nieces back and she didn't have time to waste. Holden's middle name was probably Distraction. You could no doubt lose a day or three counting the rips and cuts hiding beneath that blue T-shirt.

Two women were at the sink when she came out of the stall. One checking her hair while the other leaned against the counter waiting. They stopped when Cherry came over.

"Are you with Eric or Holden?" the first one asked. She had dark hair with blond streaks on the top and fuchsia in the back.

Cherry wondered if this is what would happen if the Sheetz lady and Boston procreated. "Pardon me?"

"Don't get in a snit," the second girl said. Her hair was without any flamboyant color, but her lipstick was a nerve popping gold. "We just want to know which one he is. That's all."

This wasn't good. "Maybe you should ask him." She removed the suds and waved her hands beneath the towel dispenser.

"You must be new." Golden lips adopted an air of superiority. "I told you she was new."

Flaming hair said, "Word to the wise. You can't tame a Latche. Don't try."

"Now, why would anybody want to tame a Latche?" A tall thin girl with shiny brown hair and eyes that reminded Cherry of something came in. "Cherry, Right? The boys were concerned about you being harassed. Low and behold, you are." She turned on the others. "Quit antagonizing. The economy sucks. War is hell. My radiator overheated and I didn't get the item I wanted off of eBay. In the scheme of things, the fact that you're not positive which twin you slept with is not relevant to those of us who are smarter than that. In other words, get over it."

"This doesn't have anything to do with you, Amy."

"Sure it does." Amy dismissed them. "A real word to the wise, Cherry. Women scorned are a pain in the ass. Ignore them." She held the door open.

The open door was just what Cherry needed. "Thank you. I think."

Holden was finishing the last of his peanut butter pie when she returned. "You okay?"

"I believe I've had enough entertainment for one night, if that's what you mean." She laid a twenty on the table. "Thank you for dinner, but I have to get going now."

"Are you assuming there's the slightest chance you'll be getting rid of me? I followed you here. What's going to keep me from following you to your hotel?"

She had already been the center of two scenes and was unwilling to have a third. With that in mind, she slipped into her seat for a minute. "The police for one thing. Stalking is illegal." *Wouldn't run from that. Just saying...* What made her think of that? She gave herself a mental shake. "There are at least three girls in this room watching us. I'm willing to bet you'll be occupied before I get my key in the ignition."

"I doubt it." Holden inclined his head in the direction of his brother's table. All three of her restroom companions were gathered there. "I came here for you. I'm not interested in anyone else."

*He was so cute. But still.* "I really need to go."

"Can I call you?"

"If I say no?"

"I won't let you go."

He was so cocksure of himself, Cherry was tempted to disappoint him. Tempted. "And, if I say yes?" Apparently, it was a thought to smile about.

Apparently, he agreed. "In that case, as long as you pick up your money, I'll let you walk out of here without a commotion."

"I'll pay for mine~"

"No, you won't. Aunt Sid would have a fit. Besides, my momma raised me better than that."

The other twin sauntered over to their table. "Evening."

Cherry watched him touch his hat like the cowboys did in the movies.

"Eric, Cherry. Cherry, my brother, Eric."

"Hi."

"Cherry. As in, on top?" Eric kept a straight face, but his eyes, identical to Holden's, danced.

"Knock it off." Holden kicked out at him.

Eric stepped out of the way. "We're going over to the casino. Do you want to come?"

Holden seemed to read Cherry's expression. "Go ahead. We don't know what we're doing yet. I'll call you."

"Check. See ya later, Cherry." Eric touched his hat again and strode off.

Holden walked her to her car and made her promise to call him once she was settled in.

She agreed, silently deciding her life hadn't officially begun. Technically, he wasn't a distraction. Yet.

# CHAPTER 3

"Why am I on the phone with you?"

If her question came off as strange, Holden gave no indication he noticed. "Why indeed?"

"Because I'm not actually sleepy and I find you intriguing. Not," she injected before he could reply, "because of the hotness factor or anything. I'm interested to understand why three women would be confrontational and slightly hostile, I might add, over manipulations, no doubt, engineered by you and/or your twin. Then, at first opportunity, party with one of the afore mentioned beasties. Why would women do that?"

"Why indeed?"

"That's not an answer."

"Were you expecting one?"

"I did propose the question."

"I'm sure it's a question worthy to ponder, but I'm not the twin with the answer. Besides, my attention is focused elsewhere."

"Your attention... Are you even interested in this conversation?"

"The conversation? Not really. I'm interested in your voice. I don't care what you say as long as you continue to talk."

Cherry made a face. That was sweet. He excited her, but that was a secret. "What are you doing right now?"

"Do you want me to come up?"

"It wasn't an invitation. I was merely curious about your current activity."

"I'm hanging outside your hotel, waiting to see if you're going to invite me up."

"You are not."

"I'm parked right beside your car. One of your hubcaps is loose, by the way. I'll adjust it in the morning."

Cherry darted from the bed to the window. Beside her Toyota was a White Silverado. A cowboy sat on the hood with his back propped against the window. His hat was pulled low but apparently it did not obstruct his vision. He waved.

She'd been warned. Aunt Sid did say con-men pretend to be handsome. Opposed to being righteously offended, as she knew she ought to be, she took the juvenile giddy route and waved back. "Are you a stalker?"

"If I were doing that, I'd have come up to your room."

"You don't know the number."

"328."

Now, that worried her.

He sensed it. "I wouldn't have told you if I intended you any harm. My point is to get you to see the extent of my interest. I want to see you again. I'll wait all night if I have to."

"You are so out of my league. Let me just make that clear right now. I have no idea what to do with this. Or you."

Something about her admission went straight to his heart. He had a feeling drinking wasn't the only thing she hadn't tried before. She was too innocent to hunt. "You may do whatever you like. I'm not going anywhere."

"What's that mean? You're not going to sit out there all night."

"I will if you don't invite me up."

"I'm not letting you come up here!"

"Do you want to come down?"

*Yes.* "No."

"It's a beautiful night. Lot of stars. The moon's all fat and happy. Definitely a night for romance."

"I don't do romance."

"Maybe you should. It is the world's greatest pastime."

"I think I have the answer to my question." She was breathless, and they both knew why.

"Which?"

"Why those girls behaved the way they did."

"Why don't you come down here and tell me about it. Or, I could come up."

"No. See, you're lethal. They can't control themselves. If you come up here, I could possibly end up doing something incredibly stupid just because you look as good as you sound." There was a long pause. "Are you there?"

"Are you always so honest?"

"I try to be. What'd I say?"

"You think I'm handsome?"

"The number one reason I'm staying away from you."

"You can't stay away from me. I'm your best friend."

"You're my b~"

"The best friend you have in West Virginia."

"So far. You also happen to be the only friend I have in West Virginia."

"That makes me the best. Come on down. I'll buy you some ice cream."

"What is wrong with me?" Cherry came away from the window. "I'm allowing myself to be bribed with ice cream. I know better than this." She stuck her feet into her flip flops and grabbed her room key.

He chuckled with her, feeling victorious. "You won't be sorry."

"Who are we fooling? You are trouble and this is a mistake. I'm already sorry." *And I'm closing the door behind me.*

"I only have your best interest at heart."

"And where do you have my worst interest?"

"It's a secret. But if you want to search me, I won't stop you."

"I am in the elevator, on my way to spend time with a bona fide player. I know better. I have no excuse for my behavior. If I'm going to be an idiot, I should at least get a root-beer float."

"I'm a dying man. You are rescuing me. For that, you can have whatever you like."

·  ·  ·  ·  ·

TRACY A. BALL

Holden and Cherry lay side by side in the bed of his Silverado, watching the stars. His ice cream and her float were long gone and still they hadn't run out of things to talk about.

"Horses," she said. "No cows?"

"No cows. But a few of our neighbors have cows. So we have to keep the fence line intact."

"Pigs?"

"Right now, two. We don't raise them for profit."

"What do you raise them for?"

"Meat."

"Eww."

"You don't like pork?"

"On the menu and in the grocery store. Not what's been running around the backyard. Do you name them?"

"They're not pets."

"Okay. What else?"

"Crops. The pigs and chickens are for food and the horses are a side business Eric and I have. Most of my work is farming crops."

As she listened to him talk, her eye was drawn to his mouth. He had a strong jaw, covered with stubble. She liked textures. The thought of touching it made her fingers tingle. The hair on his chin would be a different texture than his lips. She wanted to touch them too.

He watched her watching him, liking the way her body went soft. He promised himself he would be good, but whatever she was thinking was turning him on. He flipped on his side, facing her and fingered a lock of her hair. It was as enticing as a rich cup of espresso with caramel shot through it. In the moonlight, her skin was smooth like creamy peanut butter. He was hungry, but not for food.

"How do you do that?" she whispered.

"Do what?" He twirled the strand around his finger, not sure of the topic, not sure he cared.

"Make a girl want to agree." She didn't know what it was. The warm night. The excitement of feeling a little bit naughty. Maybe it was just him.

*Damn.* He knew he was grinning like a sixth grader, but he didn't care.

Her eyes were soft pools of misty-gray that he was sure would linger in his dreams. Slowly, he closed the space between them, feeling like he was falling into those pools of misty-gray. "I want to kiss you." His voice went low. "I won't if that frightens you or gives you the wrong impression." He could feel her breath.

"I am so out of my league." She licked her lips.

He almost lost his control.

"I...I think I might let you. What does that make me?"

"Amazing." He captured her mouth, pressing against her softness, drinking in her moan, mingling it with his own. From just her conversation, he assumed her dating history was close to non-existent. Even so, tasting her first real kiss rocked his universe. Now, he had an addiction.

Wanting more, yet not daring to take it, Holden pulled back, enchanted by her dreamy reluctance. Eyes closed, lips partly open, she leaned forward trying to follow his mouth.

Holden was a sexpert. Deflowering virgins, illicit affairs, one night stands; he and Eric had been at it since they were twelve. When it came to women, there wasn't much he hadn't tried. The Latche twins had a knack for conquering females. Since they reached maturity, their success rate was a steady one hundred percent. But something was different about this one. One kiss, one touch and he knew. Something was off.

It didn't take him an hour to get her outside. He didn't even have to manipulate the circumstances to get that kiss. Getting her into bed would be a challenge, but not beyond his abilities. The thing was, he didn't want it...he *did* want it...but it didn't stop with the physicality. He wanted...he wanted... he didn't know what he wanted from her. He wanted to see her in the morning. Maybe take her to lunch and hang out with her. He wanted to talk to her on the phone, not avoid her calls. He wanted to protect her from men like him. He wanted to kiss her again. And again. He wanted to make love to her...No, he wanted to f... *Hell*. He did want to make love to her.

He watched her eyes flutter open as she floated back to earth. The misty-gray sparkled under a film of gloss. Her mouth was kiss-swollen and juicy sweet. For the first time in his life, Holden Latche was lost.

# CHAPTER 4

Where was she? Cherry knew she wasn't in her room before she opened her eyes. She lay still waiting for her memory to catch up with her. She was in West Virginia. Right. She had transferred to Shepherd University. The semester was about to begin. Right. She was in a hotel...because...Oh. She couldn't check into her dorm until later today. Yeah. Got it...NO! Don't got it. Cherry sat up as the rest of her memory returned. Holden. The cowboy straight out of a dream. She remembered him walking into her life, yet had no recollection of him leaving. She checked the other bed and her state of dress, in that order. He wasn't there, but all of her clothes were. That was mostly a good sign.

After making-out for half the night in the back of his truck, the security guard threatened to have them arrested. She had no choice but to invite him up to watch a movie. But how could she have fallen asleep with a guy in her room...On her bed! Was she insane?

Regardless, he wasn't there now. She wasn't positive of how she felt about that. It was certainly a surefire way to combat the nightmares. However, spending the night with a man in any sense was more than her little mind could handle.

Her eyes fell on a folded note.

*Cherry,*
*Call me when you get up.*
*I would like to meet you for breakfast or lunch.*
*Holden*

A knock at her door made her lay the note aside. Expecting house-keeping, Cherry was startled to see her handsome cowboy standing in the hallway. "Holden."

"Good morning, Beautiful."

Cherry thought his smile was made of sunshine. She opened the door wide enough for him to enter. Impressed with how not shy she felt around him, she covered her mouth with her hand. "Sorry, I just woke up. Let me go brush my teeth."

He sat in the chair and clicked on the television. "Don't worry. My plan is to get used to it."

Her hand wasn't large enough to hide her grin. She grabbed her suitcase. "I might as well get ready. I'll be right back."

"I'll be right here."

He waited until he heard the shower before he retrieved her phone from the nightstand. He picked up the discarded note and read it as he dialed.

"Good morning."

"Hey, Sugar. My morning voice is a little deep."

There was a short pause before Holden could speak. "What the hell are you doing with her phone, Eric?"

"Calling you. I'm waiting for Cherry to get out of the sho-wer so we can get some breakfast. Any suggestions?"

"Take her to IHOP. We'll make the switch there."

"Switch? Don't you want to sleep in?"

"I'm not splitting this one, Eric. She's not going into the account."

"No fair. I've been anticipating."

"Too bad. Find your own."

· · · · ·

Cherry couldn't get over how lighthearted and playful Holden was. Apparently, mornings were his thing. At the restaurant, he took his time, enjoying a full cup of coffee before he excused himself.

Holden was in the restroom, pacing. "Anything I need to know?"

"You promised her a million dollars if she'll commit to wearing that top every time you meet. She looks like one of those Geisha girls. Hot as hell."

Holden didn't appear impressed with Eric's assessment. "Anything else?"

"She got a phone call from some guy she claimed was her brother, but she had to go outside to talk to him. Might want to check into that."

"Really?" Holden's left eyebrow went up.

"Really." Eric nodded once. "And she has to call her aunt soon. You said you'd remind her."

"Will do. Give me your shirt." Holden pulled his own shirt over his head.

"Why? Nobody ever pays attention to the clothes." Still, Eric worked on his buttons.

"I'm not taking any chances."

"Uh oh. You sound serious. Must have been some night."

"That's an understatement."

"Well then, don't screw it up. Because I'm already jealous."

· · · · ·

Holden paused at the table, staring.

Cherry was studying the menu. "There you are. I ordered you more coffee." She glanced up. He was still staring. "What?"

He shook his head once as if to clear it and claimed his seat. "Did you decide on anything?"

"This one." She showed him the picture. "Or this one. Or possibly this one."

He chuckled. "I take that as a no."

"Can't help it. They all sound good. Why are you staring at me like that?"

"Like what?"

"Like you haven't seen me in weeks."

"Technically, I haven't. Regardless, you're an eyeful. Can't think of anything else I rather be seeing."

"What do they put in the soap around here? After all that sweet talking you did at the hotel, you should be out of compliments by now. And here you are, starting fresh. How is a mere amateur supposed to keep up?"

"Except it. You're a Muse." The flush in her coloring was provocative. "For the record, nothing I've said this morning can hold a candle to the things I'm thinking right now. Except my opinion of your top. Would you wear it forever, if I upped my offer to two million?"

Her deep and rich laughter ended when her cell phone rang. "I'm not answering that one. She can wait."

"She?"

"Yeah. She. You want to see?" Cherry turned her phone in his direction. The name on the screen said Terry.

"Could be a guy." He tried to look stern.

"With a little pink ballerina icon. I doubt it."

"Your other call was a guy."

She struggled to keep the bubbly expression on her face.

He hoped he hadn't given himself away.

"I am sorry. I'm usually not that rude."

He didn't comment.

She could tell he expected something more. "My brother's schedule is such that he can only call me at certain times. We can't plan it so I have to take his call whenever he can get one in."

"What's he do?"

Cherry had her answer ready. "He works for the government." *Cleaning highways and making license plates, I think.*

·   ·   ·   ·   ·

Holden wished she would stop. Mona had her tongue in his ear. Generally speaking, he was a fan of the female tongue. He liked the places they put them. He knew from experience, Mona was exceptionally good with hers. But, he wasn't in the mood. It wasn't Mona. He wasn't in the mood with Karen or Bridget either. In fact, his last three turns had all been busts. Eric was going to hate being called in again - as much as a guy can hate being called to have sex he didn't have to work for with a beautiful woman.

Mona was beautiful and sexy as hell. She just wasn't Cherry. Holden wasn't in the mood for anybody but Cherry. He wouldn't even be at Mona's apartment if it weren't for the business. The twins regularly enjoyed five to six women between them. In order to be successful and to keep up their charade, Holden had to take his turn.

Only he didn't want his turn. Eric could have Mona, Karen and Bridget. Eric could have them all. Holden wanted Cherry. He wanted her like he never wanted any woman in his life. He wanted to do the work to get her. But he couldn't with Mona's tongue in his ear.

· · · · ·

The Latche Farm was four generations old. The bunkhouse had been around at least that long. The two-story building currently served as a way for the adult males to be bachelors and still live at home. Eric ambled in and tossed his jacket across the chair.

"I've got to go," Holden said into the phone. "I promise to dream about you tonight and apologize for my behavior in the morning." Whatever Cherry said made him chuckle. He hung up and waited for his brother's rant.

"I don't like doing two girls in one night," Eric said by way of greeting. "Takes the edge off. Makes me not want it."

"I know. It's a real hardship."

Eric plopped down on the couch next to his twin. "Contrary to the image, I'm actually not two people. You are jeopardizing the business."

"I can't help it. These days, I'm all about Cherry."

"No shit. I think you should go on moratorium until you either get her worked in or worked out of your system. This double duty is wearing me out."

"That's what I was thinking...It's what I told Cherry, anyway."

"What?" Eric had been leaning back. Now, he sat forward. Telling any girl anything was a strict no-no.

"No details," Holden said. "I only told her what she already knew.

Having an identical twin who is a dog makes it seem like I'm one too."

"Because you are."

"Not anymore. I'm dating her exclusively."

"We date them all exclusively."

"I'm not lying this time."

"She's reduced you to honesty? Be careful or you'll be in love before you know it."

"I wouldn't know. Never had that happen before."

"Happened to me once," Eric said. "This girl I saw at Sheetz. She's mixed. Hot. Drives a blue Toyota~"

Holden hit him with a sofa pillow.

"What is she anyway?"

"I don't know." Holden hunched his shoulders. "Don't care. Never think to ask."

"When it comes to Cherry, I'm noting, you don't think a lot." Eric caught the second pillow and propped it behind his head.

# CHAPTER 5

From the corner of his eye, Holden assessed his favorite shotgun seat decoration. "You look nervous."

"You think?"

"Why? It's just my family."

"That would be why." Cherry glanced over at Holden's cool profile. Black was certainly his color. Well, every color was his color, but the black shirt- unbuttoned to reveal his white t-shirt- and black jeans worked everywhere on him.

"We've been seeing each other for a month~"

"Thirty-four days." His smirk made her add, "not that I'm counting."

"Do you know how many hours?"

"What time is it?" Ogle-worthy. The man was sooo ogle-worthy.

Holden shook his head, thoroughly enchanted. "They're going to love you."

"What if they don't?"

"They will."

"What if they don't?"

"They'll have to adjust."

"Have you ever had that problem before...or the opposite?"

"A girl they don't like? Probably. What do you mean by the opposite?"

"What do you mean, probably?"

Holden pondered how best to respond. So far, the truth had been working well for them. "You're the first one I plan to be around long enough for it to matter." His favorite dimple came out. "What do you mean by the opposite?"

"Any girl so special, I won't be able to compete?"

"Not in any galaxy I know of."

"You know, you have a habit of saying sweet things to me. How do I know you're not just being nice?"

"I'm a guy. I don't know how to be sweet. All I know how to do is tell the truth."

She couldn't answer. He took her breath away. '*Wow*,' she mouthed without vocalizing.

He turned off the road and her euphoria evaporated.

"Now, you're back to nervous."

"I can't help it, we're here."

Holden stopped the truck. "Cherry, this is not a test. You've already been approved." He took her hand in his. "Everybody in that house wants me happy. You make me happy. They want to show you some gratitude." He kissed her fingertips.

The euphoria returned. "Okay, now I can't function properly. What are they going to think when they see this goofy grin I can't get rid of?" She tried to fan her blush away.

"That perhaps I make you happy too." He slid out of the Silverado and went around to open her door. He held her hand as they walked up the steps to the massive farmhouse. The porch was easily eight feet wide. Thick pillars, a rainbow of zinnias and morning glories, old-fashioned rockers and a huge porch swing. Surrounded by open space and the Blue Mountains hovering in the background, it was something out of an oil painting.

She took a deep breath and he opened the door.

· · · · ·

The house was a wonderful mixture of old and comfortable. There were antiques galore but nothing shabby. Polished wood, big cushiony chairs and more pictures than she could count hung everywhere. Holden's house had a lived-in, loved feel to it.

"Hey, Holden," Hunter called out from the TV room where he was playing a video game. The lanky twelve-year-old was all arms and legs. "Cory was riding Music-man."

"Where is he?"

"He's stacking the feed. You were supposed to do that."

"Which is why he got to ride Music-man. Try minding your own business. This is Cherry. Cherry, this is my nosey little brother, Hunter."

"Hi, Hunter."

"Are you his girlfriend?"

Holden gave him a look. "No. She's a new filly for Music-man. What do you think?"

"How should I know? You don't bring girls in here."

Cherry's smile was immediate.

He guided her toward the living room. "He's going to want me to pay him for that comment."

"She's smiling," Hunter called out. "That's got to be worth five or ten bucks."

"Oh, hello." A plump woman with round hazel-green eyes and strands of elegant gray highlighting her hair came down the hall. "I'm Claire, Holden's mother. You must be Cherry." She enclosed Cherry in a slight embrace. "I'm so glad to finally meet you."

Cherry exhaled. She passed the mother test. Now, she could relax. "Thank you for having me, Mrs. Latche."

"Call me Claire." She led Cherry over to the sofa. "Dinner will be ready shortly. Holden, why don't you get her a drink. Tell me, Cherry, how do you like West Virginia so far?"

"It's the best place I've ever lived. Of course, that could be because of Holden."

"He's a good man. It's nice to see him so happy. For the last few weeks, it's been 'Cherry this' and 'Cherry that.' I wouldn't have made another day without meeting you."

"Okay, now you're embarrassing me." Holden returned to the room carrying a Coke. He offered it to Cherry. When she reached for it, he pulled it back. "You have to pay me for my services." He leaned in.

Cherry colored over with embarrassment.

"Don't tease her, Holden," Claire said.

Holden chuckled and straightened up. His bold emerald shirt accented his coloring and worked everywhere on him. Then it registered. "Hello, Eric." Cherry pursed her lips.

"You'll get used to it." His grin was golden.

"Don't pay any attention to him." Claire tapped her son. "He's a rogue."

"Don't hate because you're the only mother on the planet who doesn't recognize her offspring."

"It's not my fault you and Holden practice deception daily." To Cherry, she said, "They habitually switch seats, clothes, trucks, chores. They've got it down to a science. You can't trust your eyes."

"Must be our upbringing."

"You're right. Your father didn't beat you nearly enough."

"He didn't have to. *He* can tell us apart." Eric offered Cherry the Coke and snatched it back.

"It's amazing," Claire said. "CW, my husband, has never had a problem telling them apart."

"What's his secret?" Cherry extended her hand trying to grab at the soda.

"He won't tell. He's as bad as the boys."

"Eric, you are...something. May I have my drink, please?"

He moved it in and out of her reach again. "Not unless you pay me for my services." He took a big gulp.

"You're not offering her any services." The real Holden came in carrying a second Coke-a-cola and two Pepsis. He gave his mother the Coke and Cherry one of the Pepsis. "I let him do that to get it out of the way."

"It took me a good second. You'd think the clothes would register a lot quicker."

"They never do." Eric winked.

"Which is why I gave you a clue." Holden held up his can and sat on her other side.

"Oh." Cherry cut him a sheepish grin. "I should have realized."

"What?" A tall slender girl with a shiny brown ponytail bounced into the room.

"Coke gives her headaches," Eric answered.

"This is Amy," Holden told Cherry. "One of my annoying sisters."

"We've met. What do you mean, 'one of'? I've been the reigning champ for the last nineteen years, dude." Amy nodded in Cherry's direction. "At Applebee's. Same night you met them." She flicked her finger between the twins. "I need one of you to look at my car. It's making a funny noise."

"I fixed it last week," Eric said. "I replaced your radiator."

"Now, you need to replace something else. It's making a funny noise."

"You didn't tell me she was your sister." Cherry waited for a reason not to be annoyed.

"I was distracted."

*Okay. That worked.* To Amy, she said, "Thank you, for that."

Amy shrugged. "They were Eric's mess."

Eric grinned.

A second girl came in. This one was older, shorter, more curvy and less happy. "I have hungry children, in case anyone is interested. Are we getting dinner tonight?" She rolled her eyes at Holden.

"That would be Missy," Eric said. "Yet another annoying sibling."

"But not the champ," Amy said.

Cherry snickered.

Missy scowled.

"We have a minute." Claire pointed to some chairs. "We're chatting." She raised her voice. "Hunter, put that game away and run down to the bunkhouse. Tell Wyatt and Bruce, dinner's ready. Where is Cory?"

"Stacking the feed." Hunter got up to do as he was bidden. "He has to. He was riding Music-man."

Missy called attention to herself. "Do you do any work on this farm anymore, Holden?"

"Do you do any work on this farm at all, Missy?"

She ignored him. "So you're the college-girl who's keeping him from his job."

"Nope." Hunter came out of the TV room. "She's the new filly for

Music-man."

Cherry laughed outright. "He's adorable."

Hunter took a bow.

Holden concentrated on Missy. "Why are you interested in my work-habits? Are you suddenly paying me?"

"Touchy," Missy addressed her brother but stared at his girlfriend. "The fact of the matter, Holden, is we can all see that little-Miss-thing here has got your nose open. Instead of breeding your horses, are you going to sign up for college and take classes with her?"

"Do you have something against post-secondary education?" Cherry's eyes were the coolest they had been since she met Holden.

"No. I have something against people who think they're better than everybody else because they go to college."

"Pardon me?"

"Par-don me." Missy mimicked Cherry but watched for Holden's reaction.

It wasn't long in coming. "Shut up, Missy. Now."

Eric's 'knock it off,' Amy's 'Mis-sy,' and Claire's 'that's enough,' were muffled under Cherry's response. "Seeing as you don't know me, you have no reason to assume I think I'm anything. Not, that it would be any of your business anyway." She stood up. "But whatever the problem is, it's going to have to be yours." She faced Claire. "I'm sorry if I've been rude or disrespectful in your home." She turned to Holden. "I need to go."

"He's not taking you anywhere," Eric told her.

"No, I'm not," Holden said. "You were invited and Missy is going to reel it in right now." His stare was cold when he addressed his sister. "You need to apologize."

"Are you threatening me, Holden?"

"Did you hear me threaten you?"

"He didn't," Eric said. "But I might."

Missy sneered. "Paying Tabby's tuition doesn't mean I have to kiss your butt."

"I paid Tabby's tuition because Bruce ain't good for shit~"

"Watch your mouth, Holden." Claire's correction was automatic.

"—because Bruce isn't good for anything. Nor am I going to punish her because you're being a bitch~"

"Holden!"

"—because you want to attack Cherry."

"No you didn't~" Missy's façade dropped.

"That's enough, you two." Claire stepped between the siblings. "This is no way to behave in front of a guest."

"I should leave." Cherry stepped back.

Claire put a soothing arm around Cherry's shoulder. "We're sorry for making you uncomfortable."

Amy came forward, taking Cherry by the hand. "You are so not taking away my fun. Come on." They went into the kitchen. "Holden has been ready to whack Missy all week. If he'd do it, and get it over with, she could feel better and get on with her life. Here." She handed Cherry a stack of plates. She, herself carried a basket of flatware.

"Should I ask why?" Cherry followed her into the dining room. They circled a large table, setting the places while Amy chatted.

"Missy feels guilty because she had to get money from Holden. She's big on biting the hand that feeds her."

"And Holden?"

"Holden is very generous. Usually, he lets her rant. But apparently, he does have an un-crossable line."

"What would that be?"

"You." Amy tucked a runaway strand of shiny brown hair behind her ear and continued laying out the utensils. "Dudette, he called his sister a bitch. Obviously, nobody is allowed to pick on you."

"Don't you have anything better to do than gossip?" Holden brought in an armload of glasses.

"Nope," Amy quipped. "Not a thing."

Eric was right on his tail with a second armload of glasses. "We've already traumatized her. After tonight, she'll probably never want to come back."

"She'll be back." Holden shot Cherry an assured glance.

"I know that." Eric shot Cherry an assured glance. "But she probably won't want to."

"I'm too overwhelmed to know what I think." Cherry didn't mind these two of Holden's siblings. They behaved as if her presence in their midst had always been.

"Then don't think." Missy brought in a large bowl of green beans. "Eric, can you get the gravy?"

A slightly shorter, slightly stockier brother whom Cherry had seen but had not been introduced to came in carrying a platter of sliced beef. He sat it in the center of the table. "Thinking won't do you no good around here anyway. Wyatt." He nodded.

"I'm Cherry."

"I know."

Missy swung around to face Cherry. "I'm sorry if I offended your delicate sensibilities."

"That's not an apology." Cherry set the last plate in place. "That's sarcasm intended to cover up your embarrassment at having to apologize. Let me do you a favor. Don't apologize to me when you don't mean it. Because I don't need it."

"I don't know what your major is." Missy placed a hand on her hip. "But, do I look like I need a psycho-analysis from you?"

"Business and yes."

That made Amy laugh.

Amy's laughter made Cherry smile.

It took Missy a moment to regroup. "Well, I don't."

"Quit acting like you do." Holden nudged his sister with his elbow.

Missy relaxed and let the argument go.

Wyatt whispered to Eric, "She got some fire in her."

"Oh yeah." Eric leaned in. "Did you see Holden's dessert?"

"No."

"He called it Cherries Jubilee. You add some brandy and light a match." The brothers laughed.

"I thought it was appropriate." Holden added to their humor.

Eager to show her spirit, and her acute hearing, Cherry said, "I didn't know you could cook, Holden."

That got them going. Even Missy was eager to comment on Holden's culinary excellence. They fondly reminisced about the time he fed them wild boar bacon and wondered when he would do so again. They debated the difference between shallots and scallions. They told of his extraordinary birthday cakes and the crème brûlée he made for Amy. They added their personal favorites to his list of kitchen accomplishments. According to his siblings, there wasn't anything Holden couldn't make delicious.

THE RIGHT WAY TO BE WRONG

# CHAPTER 6

The evening was a huge success. Witty banter went back and forth across the table almost as fast as the mashed potatoes. Cherry was included in and teased as if she belonged. Holden's entire family was there: his parents, CW and Claire; his siblings, Wyatt, Missy, Eric, Amy, Elizabeth, Cory and Hunter; his four-year-old niece, Tabby; his two-month-old nephew, Brucey; Also, his cousin Eli, Missy's boyfriend, Bruce and Wyatt's girlfriend, Roslyn.

Roslyn was overweight; not obese, but heavy. However, she had intelligent eyes and the sweetest disposition Cherry had ever been exposed to.

"You've got to have some more." She sat a second serving of dessert in front of Cherry. "It's not going to last so you better get it now."

"Thank you, Roslyn. I'm almost embarrassed to be getting seconds. You guys weren't joking. This is delicious."

"Don't be embarrassed. When Holden cooks we all get seconds. Call me Pattycakes."

"You look like you get fifths." Entertained with himself, Bruce tilted his chair back. No one found him amusing. Eric hooked his foot around the chair leg and yanked. Nobody paid attention to his cursing as he got off the floor.

Bruce's hooked nose and uneven mustache held no appeal for Cherry. She decided not to pay attention either. "Pattycakes? Didn't see that one coming."

"Wyatt started calling me that when we were in third grade and it stuck. But I like it."

"Pattycakes it is."

"How did you get Cherry?"

"Cherry is not a nickname. My mother couldn't tell her children from produce."

Everyone found her amusing.

"Tell us about your family." Claire refilled her glass with lemonade.

"It's microscopic compared to yours. My parents died when I was younger. I was raised by my great aunt. My sister and her children live in New York. And my brother... lives...in Jessup, Maryland." She waited to see if the name held any meaning for them. "I have an uncle, a couple of cousins and that's it."

"That is small by comparison."

"Yep, and we all have food-names. My brother's name is Benjamin, but instead of Ben, he got slapped with Beany. They put Gwendolyn on my sister's birth certificate but started calling her Peaches before she left the Hospital. My parents didn't even bother with giving me a real name."

It was obvious those memories were good ones for Cherry.

"Since we're on the subject of you." Elizabeth captured Cherry's attention with all the tact expected from a fifteen-year-old. "Exactly, what color are you?"

"Elizabeth!" CW and Claire said together.

"I can't figure it out and I'm tired of trying and it's better to ask than assume and Wyatt and Bruce and Eli have a bet and I get twenty dollars for asking so I'm asking."

It took a heartbeat for Cherry to respond and when she did it was with vivacious laughter. When she could breathe easier she said, "Before I tell you, why does it matter?"

She included all of the culprits in her stare.

"Nosey," Wyatt said.

"Curious," was Bruce's response.

"I don't know." Eli hunched his shoulders.

"It's a twenty-dollar question." Elizabeth didn't flinch.

Doing a visual roll-call around the table, Cherry didn't get any more responses. "Why didn't you ask Holden?"

"I did," Elizabeth said. "He told me to mind my own business. He tells everybody but Eric to mind their own business."

"What did he tell you, Eric?"

"He didn't know."

"And?" Holden spoke up.

"He didn't care."

Cherry wasn't concerned with the rest of the clan, but Holden's opinion mattered. "Is that what you said?"

What mattered to him was her dimple. It was showing. "Have I ever asked you a thing about your race?"

"I figured you thought you knew."

"No. I don't care."

That uncontrollable euphoric haze washed over her.

Amy had the antidote. "Dudette." She snapped her fingers twice. "When you get done swooning, you'll find that we're waiting for an answer. I'm with Wyatt. Nosey."

Amy was on her way to becoming Cherry's favorite. Amy was sooo...Amy. "What are the bets?"

"Hispanic."

"French."

"Half black."

"Half black and what?"

"White."

"Pocahontas!" Tabby added her opinion.

"Asian."

"Hispanic."

"Half Hispanic."

"You people are idiots." Holden leaned back, draping his arm across the back of Cherry's chair. "Of course, she's half something. If she wasn't mixed, she'd be what she is and you wouldn't be having this retarded debate."

"Tabby is the closest," Cherry announced.

"Yay!" The preschooler bounced in her seat. "I always get it right. When I say he's Uncle Holden and he's Uncle Eric," she pointed to her uncles in random order, "I guess right. And when I say he's Uncle Eric and he's Uncle Holden," she repeated the same pattern, "I'm right again."

"Yes." Missy calmed her down. "You're the only one who always gets it right. Now, let Miss Cherry talk."

"Actually, I'm not half. I'm quartered." She studied the confused faces. "My dad and both of my grandfathers were military. I guess that's one of the few ways something like me could happen. My mother was a black Korean. My dad was a white Comanche. My brother looks mostly white and my sister looks mostly Korean, given the right clothes, I can pass for anything."

"So you're the perfect mutt." Eric reached over to muss her hair. "And you ought to know how to fight."

She gave him a peek at her dimple. "Don't learn that the hard way."

Cherry participated in the after dinner clean-up process. She liked that they expected her to behave as if she belonged. She was only mildly tense when Missy picked up a second dishtowel and helped her dry.

"I'm sorry for attacking you. Believe it or not, I was in rare form."

Cherry looked around and noticed the other women were conveniently out of the room or occupied. "I don't know what form you were in, but you seem sincere. I appreciate it."

It was enough for both of them.

After a few minutes of silent wiping, Missy said, "I am jealous of you."

"I have no idea why."

"Look at you. Pretty and free and I wish I could go to school."

"I would kill for your eyelashes. And your hair." Cherry pointed to Missy's natural waves falling past her shoulders in thick dark layers.

"You're sweet." Missy brushed her hair back, pleased with the compliment.

"Why can't you go to school?"

"Humph. Did you see those two little monsters in there? The one drooling and spitting up milk and the one wearing more food than she ate. Yeah, they would be my kids."

"So? People with children take classes. Did I mention, no one would believe you just had a baby with that figure?"

"I am fond of the baby-boobs." Missy stuck her chest out. "Too bad I won't get to keep them."

For the next several dishes they took time to actually get to know one another.

· · · · ·

The next day, Cherry got an official tour of the Latche two hundred fifty acre farm. The following day she went horse-back riding with the Latche siblings. On the fourth day, they put her to work.

She liked hanging out there anyway. Now, she was getting paid. Plus, it increased the amount of time she got to spend with Holden. For Cherry, it was all very good.

# CHAPTER 7

Very rarely did Holden push Music-man to his limit. But he was testing it today. The sky was a clear azure, but his mood was rainy gray. He didn't know why.

He did know why. That one woman could be so vexing was knowledge he was happier without. Cherry was, Cherry was... She was everything, damn it. He had no idea how that happened. Almost eight weeks with no sex. How was that even possible? Can you be mad at a tease for being a tease if she didn't know she was a tease? How could she not know? These days, his erection was a constant.

Holden used his legs to drive the horse faster. Last night, they weren't slow dancing. He could feel her nipples rubbing against his chest. Her ass was in his hands- his busy happy hands. He was grinding hard enough to make her climax. She probably did for all he knew. The only thing she didn't do was yield. She let him hold her, and touch her, and rub her. But she wouldn't let him undress her. She did not yield. Even now, he could taste her kisses, feel her warmth, remember those soft gray eyes and allow it. Why the hell was he allowing it?

Up a hill and across a wildflower meadow, the land was still theirs but wilder, more rugged. The Latche land was just like the Latche sons: decisive, obstinate and prone to doing whatever they damned well pleased. So why wasn't he doing what he pleased with Cherry?

They'd been dating for the better part of two months. Holden didn't wait two days. The pleasure had to come first and often. He didn't waste his time or his money putting up with a nuisance –make no mistake, women were a nuisance – if he wasn't getting some pleasure out of it.

Cherry wasn't a nuisance...well, kind of. A daily hard on was a nuisance. But Cherry was something else. She fit. She fit his life. Her thoughts were important to him. She listened when he talked. She was fascinating to watch and soft to touch. Her hair and skin and eyes were perfection. She had a sultry smile and a dimple he was addicted to. She trusted him. That was big. He wasn't the type of person to instill trust in a woman, but he wanted Cherry's trust. She made him feel strong. And grateful. He was a better person because of her. She had become so much a part of him, he could close his eyes and smell her perfume.

Holden didn't close his eyes. If he conjured her perfume, he'd imagine the scent wafting up from her cleavage and he would no doubt, get a hard on. Holden didn't want a hard on. He didn't want to be sexually frustrated. He certainly didn't want to think about the fact that he was falling in love.

...And the woman he was falling for was more than likely cheating on him.

It was going to rain. It didn't matter that the sky was cloudless and azure. He could feel the rain. It was in Music-man's pull. The big animal wanted to turn back. It was in the hush across the meadow. The birds and insects had already settled in. It was in his heart, dull and heavy, full of rain.

· · · · ·

Eric and Hunter were playing two on two football against Cory and Eli. Bruce nursed a beer and watched from the back porch. Wyatt was missing. Presumably, the bunkhouse was occupied. The whole world could be occupied for all that Holden cared. He led Music-man around the far side, choosing to enter the barn from the back, hoping his presence would go unnoticed.

Mechanically, he removed his saddle, bridle and blanket. He checked Music-man's feet and retrieved his favorite brush. Normally, the long slow strokes had a tranquil effect on both man and beast, but not today. Holden couldn't keep a rhythm. His strokes were choppy and uneven. Sensing his master's disquiet, the big black horse shook his mane, side stepped and nudged Holden's shoulder impatiently.

Out of patience himself, Holden snapped at him. "Knock it off."

"Looks like you started it." Eric approached with a second brush in hand. He took up a position on the other side and went to work. "What are you pissed about?"

Eric and Holden shared every twin connection known to man and a few that were unknown except between them. Holden couldn't hide anything from Eric. Holden was Eric. "The list is short, but exhausting."

"Did you and Cherry have a fight?"

"Not yet, but it's coming."

"Obviously. Will it be resolved once you get laid?"

Holden sighed. There were times when that connection was less than convenient. "No, but that would help."

"What exactly is the hold up?"

"She's a virgin."

"You have the cure."

"She's not aware it's an illness."

"Enlighten her."

"Working on it."

"Shall we double your efforts?"

"Stay the hell away from her, Eric. She's still off limits."

"Obviously. Or you wouldn't be all bent out of shape."

Holden threw down his brush. "She's cheating on me."

Eric ducked under the Horse's neck and went to work on that side. As suspected, Holden had done a piss poor job. "No, she's not."

"The evidence would suggest otherwise."

"Of course, it does. But the facts are undeniable." Eric worked his way down from head to flank in smooth easy strokes. "If you ain't getting it, nobody else is either. If someone had gotten it, you would definitely be getting it."

"Cocky, but true," Holden admitted.

Eric grinned and continued his line of reasoning. "She doesn't have it in her. Besides, when and with whom? At this point in life, most people know it isn't worth the trouble to fuck with us. If she's not at school or off with you, she's here. Speaking of which, I haven't seen her today. Where is she?"

"Not here." Holden's nostrils flared. "She's got something in her, but I can't figure out what."

"Sounds ominous. Do tell."

Holden busied himself with filling both the water and feed troughs. By then, Eric was done. They left the barn together.

"I got an early morning text from her telling me something came up and she was going to be out of touch all day. Not long after, I got a call from Shontae Diggs. Do you remember her?"

Eric nodded. "Red curly hair, not on her head."

"Yep," Holden said. "She's in Cherry's class. She was trying to take advantage of the situation."

"Did she happen to tell you what situation that would be?"

"As a matter of fact, she did. Cherry pre-arranged to miss that class. She needed to go to New York."

"New York?"

"The professor knew about it three days ago but she hasn't mentioned it to me yet."

That was enough information for Eric to know they'd be happier at a bar. "Want to get a drink?"

"A lot of them." Holden followed his twin to Eric's Dodge Ram.

．　．　．　．　．

Cherry had been crying for so many hours, she forgot she was doing it. The meeting was terrible. She hadn't expected it to go well, but she hoped. She hoped Peaches would straighten up and do what she needed to do to get her girls back. She hoped the child authorities would decide Adora and Ahava would be better off with her, their aunt, than with their current foster family. She hoped her job at the Latche farm and the promise of an apartment would offset any concerns about a college student raising children. She caught the train to New York with a lot of hope. All she returned with was reality.

But Holden was waiting for her. Holden. If not for him she wouldn't have come back. She always wanted to go to California. She saw a postcard from Oakland once and the image stayed with her. She could live in Oakland and be very happy. She wouldn't have to think about the bad things New York did to people. If he wanted, Beany could come and live with her when he got out of prison. He'd like that. It was beautiful in Oakland. Even the name was beautiful. Oakland didn't have any bad memories. But Oakland didn't have Holden either. And Holden was everything. She couldn't wait for him to hold her and make her forget this nightmare of a day ever happened.

· · · · ·

Ik its 18. I dnt wn2 disturb U bt I wtd 2 tel u I'm bk +I luv u. C U n d AM. Nite. Three minutes after she sent the text, Cherry's phone rang.

"Where are you?"

It was soothing just to hear his voice. "Aren't farmers supposed to turn in early?"

"Aren't girls supposed to share their plans with the man they're involved with?"

"I plan to go to my dorm, crawl into bed and sleep like the dead."

Holden was in no mood for games. "Where have you been?"

"Maybe I should just let you go to sleep."

"Maybe you should tell me what the hell is going on."

That she was taken aback was a surprise to him. He could hear it in the catch in her voice.

"Going on? I-I told you. Something came up. I'm back now. I don't know what your problem is but sometimes things happen and schedules have to be changed."

"You know what. Keep your damn secrets. It's late. I think I am going to go to bed. Good night."

"Holden?"

"Good night, Cherry."

"...Good night..." For a long minute, she listened to the silence on the other end.

. . . . .

He picked up on the second ring. "Hmmm?"

"Holden. Are you asleep?"

"When?"

"I'm sorry. I'll call you in the morning."

It was going to be morning in a few minutes. "I'm awake now. What's going on?"

"I'm sorry. I feel bad for the way we got off of the phone." Cherry sniffed.

Holden didn't feel bad. A few hours ago he was mad. Now, he was just sleepy. "Where were you?"

She went through an hour of hurt feelings and another hour of indignation before she admitted to herself, she owed him some sort of explanation. "I went to see my sister." That was true.

"Why did that have to be such a mystery?"

"It wasn't a mystery. It's just something I had to do. It wasn't a fun visit. I went. I helped her. I came back. That's it."

"I would have gone with you."

"I know. I would have invited you, but Peach isn't the most sociable of people these days. *Unless you're paying.* I didn't want to make things any harder than they were."

Holden pondered a moment. It wasn't Cherry. It was the sister. He breathed easier and let the relief come. Cherry had been in an awkward position because her sister was obviously unfriendly. And, they were rather new. If one of his siblings were unapproachable, he'd smack them in the back of the head. But his family was different. He had to remember that.

Twenty minutes of sweet talk and a promise to be there in time to help him feed his horses and Holden's world was back to good. They hung up and he drifted off to sleep mildly curious about Peaches and what help Cherry gave her. When he tried to think about it, he found he was too tired to care.

# CHAPTER 8

It was Thanksgiving.

"We're almost there and you've yet to mention which side of your family we're visiting."

"You never asked. My mother's father's family."

Holden beckoned for some more information to come forth.

"What do you want to know?" Cherry watched the scenery roll by, noting with satisfaction they were coming up on Berlin, MD. The town thrived on being old fashioned. It was made for strolling and antiquing. The look, the feel, the values; it was small town, USA. It was Cherry.

Their early departure and Holden's driving would put them at her uncle's house almost a half hour earlier than she expected. Of course, no traffic on the Bay Bridge always helps.

"I want to know who I am going to be meeting and what I should expect."

"Mostly everybody. Expect them not to concern themselves overmuch with either of us. Today, corncake and stuffing are top priority. Make a left at the light."

Holden put on his blinker. "When it comes to your family, I'm noting, you're not big on sharing." He wanted to ask her which race he would be seeing. She did have four to choose from.

She made a face. "Not everybody has a family like yours, Holden. There just isn't that much to tell."

He had the sense that backing off would be good. "I'll guess you'll be happy to see your sister?"

Cherry looked out the window. This time, the scenery wasn't what she was seeing. "Peaches won't be there. Beany either."

The car ride turned quiet while Cherry scowled. A short minute later, she came back to herself. "My cousin Terry will be there. She's famous."

Happy that whatever had gripped her was gone, Holden jumped into the conversation. "Famous? What is she famous for?"

Cherry giggled. "Well, have you ever heard of Woodrow Rich? Played for the Texans? They call him the Flatliner."

"I know who he is."

"Terry tried to give him her number once."

He laughed outright at that.

"I think she's still waiting for him to call her. And do you remember the movie, Runaway Bride?"

"I didn't see it. Was she in it?"

"Oh, much better. There's a scene where one of the stars walks by the high school bleachers. Her cheerleading squad's practice spot is on film."

"That's a lot of fame. How does she cope?"

"Lots of selfies. We're here. It's the brown house, right there, on the left."

If the old woman in the rocking chair on the front porch was any indication, her mother's father was black. "What's your family going to think about you being involved with me?"

"Nervous?"

"Curious."

"Being the byproduct of a couple of interracial relationships, they're not even going to notice. Besides, unless I marry Beany, I have to intermingle. The Mutt-club is sparse."

"Elite." He put the truck in park and set the emergency brake.

The elderly woman stood up slowly.

As Holden helped Cherry down from the cab, she whispered, "Aunt Sid. Brace yourself."

"Cherry? Is that my baby-girl?"

"Hey, Aunt Sid. I'm home!" Cherry raced up the steps to embrace Sidney.

"Look at you! Look at you!" Aunt Sid touched her face and Cherry leaned downward to receive a kiss on the forehead. "Aunt Sid, I want to you meet Holden."

Aunt Sidney reached for Holden's hand. "Holden, you're a right handsome young man, aren't you?"

"It's nice to meet you, Ms. Brookfield."

"No, no. You call me Aunt Sid, you understand?"

"Yes Ma'am."

"Good. Good. Let me tell you, Holden. I'm glad you came. Maybe you'll be the one to pin our little bird's feathers to the ground."

"Aunt Sidney."

Sid ignored her great-niece. She took Holden by the arm. "You come on in and meet everybody." She led him toward the house, but stopped short at the door. "Before you get too comfortable, let me tell you now. Y'all ain't sleeping together. Not in this house."

"Aunt Sid~"

Sidney waved Cherry silent and shook her knurled finger at Holden. "I mean it. Get a hotel if you can't control yourself, but I don't care how hunky she thinks you are, that ain't happening here. Do you understand me?"

Aunt Sid was a slight woman, her gray head barely came to Holden's elbow, and yet she scared him. "Yes ma'am. I understand. That's not going to happen."

"I knew I could trust you."

He held the door for them both and wiggled his eyebrows at Cherry above Sidney's head.

"All the same," Sidney continued. "Cherry, you'll be sleeping down at the house with me. Holden can sleep here in Cork's room."

· · · · ·

Thanksgiving with her family, Christmas with his and New Year's all by themselves. For Cherry, it had been the perfect holiday, the perfect winter, complete with snow, ice-skating and Holden. In those few short months, they became set in stone. Their first holiday as a couple exceeded their expectation of what makes magic. Unfortunately, it was coming to an end. Classes were due to start and it was going to be a tough semester. Cherry was going to have to dilute her daily diet of Holden with studying. It wasn't a thrilling prospect.

"Don't worry about it." She trudged across the frozen mud, muttering to herself. "When it's time, you'll get through it." She opened the door to the storage shed. "Summer is coming. We'll go to the beach." Cherry flicked on the light and stopped. "Oh! Pattycakes. You gave me a heart attack. Why do you have the light~"

Pattycakes turned her tear-streaked face toward Cherry.

"What's wrong? Are you hurt?"

She shook her head, sniffed, then let out a long wail.

Cherry wrapped her arms around the crying woman. "Shh...shh...What is it? What happened?"

"I...h-hate...m-m-my...myself..." Pattycakes clung to Cherry, weeping on her shoulder.

"No, you don't, Pattycakes. You're awesome."

"I'm fat...and ugly and... nobody likes me..."

Cherry was dumbfounded. "You are not. Where is this coming from?"

"Look at me...I am..."

"You are not." Cherry didn't offer more. Pattycakes' short strawberry-blond hair was usually layered in neat curls around her soft round face. Now, it stood out in clumps, as if she had been yanking it. Cherry smoothed the strands and rocked Pattycakes from side to side. Pattycakes was five years older than Cherry, however, at the moment, she was clearly the wounded child.

When her outburst had quieted into broken sobs, Cherry picked up the conversation. "Now, what is going on with you?"

Pattycakes took a few deep breaths. She wanted, needed to talk. "I come in here to cry. Sometimes, I can't take it." A hiccup and another deep breath.

"Look at me. I'm so ugly. I'm such a nobody."

"Is that what Wyatt thinks?" Cherry thought she had a good angle.

Cherry was wrong.

"Yes."

"He does not."

"He never said it, but I'm not stupid."

As far as Cherry was concerned, Pattycakes was not someone who should be nursing deep hurts. She locked the door. "Why don't you start from the beginning?"

Pattycakes wiped her face, seemingly heartened by the comradeship. "Wyatt and me have been together since elementary school. I gave him my virginity when I was thirteen. I practically live here—"

Cherry nodded after each statement.

"—Do you want to know how many times he's been unfaithful to me? Eleven times that I know of. Eleven. That's almost once a year."

"Good Lord, Pattycakes. Why are you still here? Why are you with him?"

"What else am I going to do? Where am I going to go? Who in their right mind would want me?"

"Lots of people."

"I doubt it."

"You're behaving like you don't believe Wyatt wants you. So why put yourself through it?"

"Because. Because...I love him. I want him."

"Pattycakes. You can't live like this. Living off somebody's crumbs. You're better than that."

"Am I?"

"Yes. God made you. He didn't make you to be less than. He certainly didn't make you to be cheated on."

Pattycakes took a long time to absorb Cherry's words. It was as if she didn't know what to do with them, as if she didn't know what to do with herself. "I don't know how I got this life. I don't want it."

"So get a new one."

"It's not that easy."

"Yes it is."

"I don't know how."

"That's why I'm here."

For the first time, the weeping girl smiled. "That's why you're here? I'd bet it was more of a, you-needed-something-from-the-shed thing."

"Divine providence."

"How are you going to help me get a new life?"

"First, we figure out exactly what you want. Then we can work on getting it."

A few remaining sniffles and a wicked wipe at her face. "I don't know what I want. I know I don't want this."

"Do you want to break up with Wyatt?" Inwardly, Cherry crossed her fingers.

"No."

*Damn.*

"But I want...I want...I don't know. I want him to treat me better. Like I matter."

"If you want his respect, you're going to have to earn it."

Pattycakes swallowed.

"Earn it by respecting yourself. If you don't, nobody else will."

"I'm a fat, stupid cow. Who's going to respect that?"

"Oh yeah, heap on the insults. That's going to make you feel loads better, I'm sure."

Pattycakes snickered.

"Start focusing on what you do like about you and whatever it is you don't like, change."

"That easy, huh?"

"That easy...to say. I'll help you with the doing part."

"I don't like being fat."

"Why are you?"

Pattycakes paused, unsure how to proceed.

Cherry went on, steady. "What I mean is, how you look and feel is totally up to you. Your weight is only a problem if it's a problem to you. Nobody else has a right to care. Now, if you don't like it, do something about it."

"Dieting and all that stuff don't work."

"B.S."

"Excuse me?"

"You heard me. I said, B.S."

"It doesn't. Every time I try, they mess me up and they can't wait to see me fail."

"That's your own fault."

"Excuse me?"

"If you tell somebody who isn't helpful or encouraging, don't expect them to be helpful or encouraging. Did Holden mess you up?"

"No, no. Not Holden. I never talked to him. Or Eric. Amy either. It's mainly Bruce and Wyatt and sometimes, Missy. But Wyatt is usually showing off in front of people. When we're alone, he's always sorry."

"Oh, he's sorry all right." Realizing Pattycakes is in love, Cherry left off her focus on Wyatt. "See, if you would have told some real people, you may have gotten some real help."

"I guess."

"So when do you want to join the gym?"

"I can't do that."

"Because you want to keep the weight you don't want?"

"No." Pattycakes sighed. "If I go to the gym, the whole town will be joking about it."

"Underneath all that low self-esteem, you're actually vain. Did you know that?" Cherry scoffed. "I'm sure the whole town has better things to do than make fun of you."

Pattycakes was un-offended. "It's possible, but I doubt it."

"All right. Problem solved. Two problems, in fact."

"Do I know what we're talking about?"

"We're going to register you for school."

"Underneath all that selflessness, you're actually weird. Did you know that?"

"This is a great idea."

"Feel free to share it."

"You ought to take a class. Something fun, just for you. It will do much needed wonders for your self-esteem and..." Cherry held the note. "It will allow you to use the gym at the university. The best part is it will only be you and me. No one will know. If it works, they'll see the results. If it doesn't, who will care?"

Pattycakes didn't answer. Fear was written plainly across her face. Something was stirring in her. Something deep. Something she hadn't felt since she was young. A good idea. A hope? "You...would help me? Go...with me?"

"Do you think you're bad enough to keep me away?"

"I'm not smart enough to go to college."

"You are so. That's a myth anyway. College isn't about being smart. College teaches you how to get things done."

"So I'm going to go and learn to get things done?"

"That's the plan. See. I told you it was easy." Cherry's cell phone fired off a tune. "Ummm. Pattycakes, I have to get this. I'll be right back."

She slipped out so quickly it made Pattycakes wonder if the phone call wasn't the reason she had come to the shed in the first place.

# CHAPTER 9

Week 1:

Missy stuck her head through the bunkhouse door. "Hey, Wyatt. Is Pattycakes in here?"

"She's at her mother's."

"Again?"

"Yes, Missy. Again. That is where she lives."

"She's over here more than she's over there."

"Not today."

Week 2:

"Hi." Cherry wrapped her arms around Holden's waist and turned her face up expectantly.

"Hey, Babe." He willingly obliged her with a kiss. "You just get here?"

"Almost three minutes ago. I had to stop and admire the butterfly Tabby drew."

"What did you do today?"

"Went to Business. Went to Political Science. Came here." She finally released him. "Was there something I was supposed to do?"

He smoothed her crinkled forehead. "No. I was wondering about the time. It's after two. I thought Wednesday was your early day. Your classes are done by eleven thirty."

"Forty minutes at the gym and then I made the mill run with Eric."

"Oh. Why?"

"Ummm. I'm feeling a little fat. The gym is good."

"Yeah, you're fat. In all the right places." He gave her backside a smack. "But that's not what I meant. What made you do the mill run with Eric?"

"Mostly because he's an idiot, partially because I'm a goober. He was just about to pull off when I got here. He told me to come on and I jumped out of my car and into your truck not realizing you weren't driving your truck."

"You're right. He is an idiot and you're a goober."

Week 3:

"Wyatt." Amy climbed up the side of Wyatt's truck and stood in the center of the bed. "Did you and Pattycakes have a fight or something?"

"If we did, I don't know about it."

"Maybe it's me, but she seems gone more than she's here."

"Hmmm. She's here every night. That's all I care about."

"You're a pig. You know that, don't you?" Amy jumped down on the other side.

"Wouldn't it have been easier to walk around it?" he called after her.

"And miss an opportunity to annoy you? Not a chance."

Week 4:

"Whoa." Eric tugged Pattycakes' ponytail. "Since when did you start wearing your hair up?"

"Since I started letting it grow and it got long enough to get in my face."

"I like it. It makes you look eighteen."

"Aww. What a sweet thing to say. You made my day."

He studied her. "There's something else too. I can't put my finger on it...yet."

Pattycakes beamed. "Don't give up. You'll figure it out."

"Whatever it is, it sure has you in a good mood."

"You have no idea, Holden ...or Eric..."

"Don't give up. You'll figure it out."

"Not likely. Nobody else does."

Week 5:

"I bet she's seeing somebody."

Wyatt scowled. "Shut the hell up, Bruce. Pattycakes isn't seeing anybody."

"She's doing something. She looks different. She's acting different. She done glued herself to Cherry. Look at them." Both men looked out across the yard from the bunkhouse balcony. Pattycakes and Cherry were at the picnic table, huddled together over a book. "You need to watch Cherry. She's a bad influence. Pattycakes is up to something and I bet Cherry put her up to it."

"Something like what? They get along. They're reading a book."

"You should check with Holden. I bet he thinks they're up to something."

Week 6:

"Why don't she spend time with her own family? Don't you find it odd that Cherry and Pattycakes are always together?"

Holden didn't look up from his work on Amy's car. "No, Bruce. I don't find it odd. I'm happy they get along." Cherry didn't like to talk about her family and he respected that. He struggled for a moment, tightening a cable. "Cherry and Amy are inseparable. I don't have a problem with that either. Cherry and Missy joke around a lot. She's babysat Tabby and Brucey twice so far. She went shopping with Mom yesterday. That's all good news to me."

"Yeah, but Pattycakes."

"What about her?"

"She's been acting all different. She's not as nice as she used to be. She looks different too. Something ain't right."

Holden was pleasant. "By different, do you mean because she told you to kiss her ass on at least three separate occasions? She's finally realized nobody puts up with your shit, Bruce, and she doesn't have to either."

Bruce did not have a comment.

"Do you want to know what's up with Pattycakes?"

"Yes. I do."

"You're a moron. That's what's up. She's losing weight. She's hot and she knows it. If Cherry had something to do with it, I'll be proud."

"I think she's cheating on Wyatt."

"That's because you're a moron."

Week 7:

"She's cheating." Wyatt threw back a shot.

"She's not cheating," Eric said without turning around. Currently, he was watching a waitress sashay between tables.

"I bet she is." Bruce watched the waitress too.

Holden nursed his beer. He didn't feel like being there. But Cherry had study group tonight and Wyatt was in need of a pity-group. "She's not doing anything wrong."

"The evidence says she is," Bruce said.

The waitress made eye contact and licked her lips. Having attained his goal, Eric faced his family. "What evidence?"

"New clothes. New hairdo." Bruce finished his shot and refilled his and Wyatt's glasses. "She's trying to get somebody's attention."

"She lost weight." Holden sighed. "That would require new clothes."

"She didn't sleep with me last night." This seemed to be the catalyst for Wyatt's mood. He threw back another shot. "She told me she wasn't getting any sleep this week so it was better for her to be home. Bullshit."

Holden paused as his brother's words washed over him, feeling familiar. Cherry had used that exact phrase. It was mid-terms. "When did Pattycakes start changing?"

"I don't know. Last month. Give me that bottle, Bruce."

Bruce slid the bottle over. "It was longer than that. It was right around Christmas or not too long after 'cause I was hoping that with Cherry not around so much, things could get back to nor~" He stopped.

"You have a problem with Cherry?" It was Eric's cold tone addressing him.

"No. No. I don't have a problem with...hell." He was sitting between them. "Cherry's trouble. That's all I'm saying."

"You are going to say a lot more than that." Holden's tone was just as cold.

"Fine." Bruce had another shot. "You asked. You just ain't the same anymore. You don't like hanging out. You don't want to be here now. For what? You haven't been with a girl since you met her. And we all know you ain't getting none. Every time she stays over, she sleeps in your room and you sleep in the bunkhouse. One day Missy came out and asked her. And you know what? Cherry told her that she was a virgin, like it was normal. You used to screw Lilly every other week. She said you haven't called her since before the last rodeo. That was in August. That was when you met Cherry. What's up with that?"

"And your reason for discussing me with Lilly would be?"

"Her brother lives with my sister," Bruce snapped. "Seeing as we're practically family, we do talk." Now that he was on a roll, Bruce let it all out. "And another thing. Who gave her the right to run around owning the place? Everything she does is all right with everybody. She's got an opinion about everything and she's got every woman on the farm agreeing with her. She's worse than Amy with her wild ideas. Cherry talked Missy into applying to some stupid beauty-school. Missy won't shut up about it. I bet she put Pattycakes up to it- whatever she's doing. Probably with some guy in her class." One more shot. One more comment. "I've seen her studying Eric. If you ask me, the reason she won't screw you is because she wants the other brother."

Bruce flew out of his chair and slid three feet across the floor. It wasn't certain which brother got to him first: Holden and Eric were both on their feet, fists balled, huffing. Bruce saw stars and his jaw hurt. More than likely, the twins tagged him at the same time.

"Pattycakes is cheating on me." Wyatt threw back another shot.

# CHAPTER 10

As a rule, most college campuses were cool. But Shepherd's quirky combination of artsy, quaint and Wi-Fi, made it was a hard place to hate.

"I can't believe how tough that test was." Pattycakes chatted happily as she and Cherry made their way over to the gym.

"It's your own fault." Cherry nudged her shoulder lightly. "I told you to take one easy class, not two hard ones. Besides, you know you did fine."

"I like the creative writing. And I love the accounting."

"That's because you are crazy."

"I still like it." They walked close together, hunched against the February cold. "Did I mention how awesome and eerie it is to see you like this?"

"It's the jewelry." Cherry brushed her hair out of her face. "Whenever my hair is straight and I pull out the Indian jewelry, it takes people right to The Last of the Mohicans."

"It's wild. In one sense, you don't even look like you."

"Wait until after mid-terms. I'm going to braid my hair and wear my big gold hoops."

"Are you serious?"

"You haven't seen it, but Holden has." Cherry grinned at a memory. "He likes my thug appeal."

"He likes your everything."

They looked for traffic and stepped off the curb together. "Hey, what did you tell Wyatt you were doing last night?"

"I didn't tell him anything. I said the same thing I heard you tell Holden. I wasn't sleeping too well." She made a funny face. "He thinks I stayed at my mother's to get some rest."

"Ummmm. I don't think he thinks that anymore."

"Why not?"

"Because, unless I'm seeing things, Wyatt and Holden are walking toward us and Eric is leaning on Wyatt's truck talking to those girls. That better be Eric."

"Oh crap."

"I know."

Pretending to be braver than they felt, Cherry and Pattycakes stayed still, waiting for Holden and Wyatt to catch up.

"What are you doing here?" Wyatt said by way of greeting.

"I was~" Pattycakes broke off. "What are YOU doing here? That's the question, Wyatt."

"Looking for you. Now answer mine."

Holden stared at Cherry half amused, half not. *Somebody that attractive should not get into this kind of trouble.*

"What?" Her misty-eyes widened; further proof of her guilt.

"Don't 'what' me. You know exactly what." It was hard not to smile-because he wanted to. He was mad, but he was having a hard time trying to remember that.

"Cherry and I are done with classes for the day and now we're going to the gym."

"Gym?"

"Yes, Wyatt, the gym." Pattycakes pointed to the Fitness Center.

Holden pulled Cherry a few feet away. "What are you up too?"

"Class. Gym. What's the big deal?" She knew what the big deal was. She just wasn't ready to admit it...ever.

He responded with silence. Cherry was where she said she would be, doing what she said she would be doing. Technically, he didn't have a problem. Still, her intentional secrecy was bothersome.

He was better at being stubborn than she was.

"Do you want to go somewhere and talk?"

"What do you think?"

She inhaled. "Gym's out, Pattycakes. Do you want to go to the cafeteria? Or better yet, let's go to the Ram's Den."

"Okay. But I'm still going to the gym." It was Pattycakes who led the way.

· · · · ·

Aromas from the Bistro and the heat from the fireplace made the room feel cozy. Unfortunately, it didn't touch the atmosphere surrounding them. Three soft drinks and two waters were the summation of comfort to be found at the Latche table.

"Who wants to start?" Wyatt cut his eyes from one female to the other. They lingered on Cherry.

"I will." Pattycakes was notably cheerful. "What did you think I was doing, Wyatt?"

"I didn't know. You neglected to tell me, Roslyn."

"You came up here hunting me down. You must have thought something."

"We came here hunting Cherry down," Holden said.

"I knew you were up to something. Holden figured Cherry knew what." Wyatt cut his eyes to Cherry again.

"Wouldn't it have been easier to ask me?" Pattycakes stared at Wyatt unflinchingly. "I'm taking classes and working out. There's your big news."

"Why the secrecy? All the sneaking around?"

"What secrecy? Because I didn't tell you doesn't make it a secret."

"Why didn't you bother telling me?"

"Like you care. That's the thing. I'm not doing anything you couldn't have known about, Wyatt. If you cared to know. You just haven't bothered to be concerned with me or my life."

"If I didn't care, I wouldn't be here."

"Maybe this should be private." Cherry almost stood up. Almost.

Holden's hand snaked out to pull her back down. "You're not getting away that easy."

"Chicken." Eric smirked.

"I'm trying to give them some privacy." She rolled her eyes at both of them.

"Chicken." Eric smirked.

"You lay off of her." Pattycakes pointed her finger at Holden. "Cherry is the only one who did care. She is the only one who paid enough attention to see how sad I was. She's the one who helped me. She changed her whole schedule for me. I asked her not to tell anybody and she didn't. She's been supporting me. If you're mad about that, too bad."

The twins eyeballed each other. This side of Pattycakes was unnerving. Unnerving, but technically not unpleasant.

"Calm down, Pattycakes. Nobody is attacking Cherry." Eric mashed his lips together, trying not to laugh.

Holden turned to Cherry. "I don't give a damn what she says, you're not off the hook yet."

Cherry had been biting her nails. She stopped long enough to roll her eyes again. "I'm not on the hook."

Wyatt waved them all to silence. "Can I get an answer?"

Now that Pattycakes was riled up, she let loose. "You're only here because you thought I was doing something wrong. That's why you rolled in with your posse." She flung her arm out to include the twins. "What? Did you assume I was seeing somebody else? Were you going to interrogate Cherry to find out who?" She didn't need a confirmation. "Wyatt, mid-terms are this week. Mid-terms. That's half a semester I've been occupied. You never asked me once what I was doing with my time. I'm down a half size because I've lost twelve pounds. Not that you've bothered to notice. Amy noticed. One of the twins noticed. But not you. You haven't complimented my hair." She puffed it. "You haven't told me I looked nice. Nothing."

"Pattycakes~"

"What you did notice was that I didn't sleep with you last night." Again, she didn't need a confirmation. "The second you were inconvenienced, then it's what the hell is Pattycakes up to? She must be screwing around. No, Wyatt. That's your department. I don't mess around. But let me tell you this, there is a guy in my accounting class who did notice my hair. And my clothes. And that I've lost twelve pounds. Perhaps you should be concerned about that."

There was a long silence.

Holden turned to Cherry.

"It wasn't my secret to tell," Cherry said by way of explanation. "In the beginning, we wanted to keep it quiet until we knew if she could do it. After that, whoever asked got an answer. You never asked."

Holden didn't waste a second. "I'm sorry, Pattycakes. I did notice the changes, but A- it wasn't my business and B- how you look and what you do is always all right with me."

"Ditto that," Eric said. "If it helps, we never thought you were doing anything wrong. Just mischievous."

Pattycakes' mouth turned up at the corner. "You did compliment me once. One of you did."

"Me," the twins said in unison.

Now it was Wyatt's turn. "I'm guessing a simple apology won't work for me."

"No. It won't."

His eyes lit up appreciatively at her sassiness. "I am sorry, all the same."

"It's a start." This was Wyatt. For Pattycakes, it was enough.

"Who else knows?" Holden asked.

"Amy," the girls said together.

"Anybody else?"

"Missy knows," Pattycakes said.

"And your mother," Cherry added. "She's been trying to cook healthy when Pattycakes and I have dinner over there."

"How do you think I lost those last two pounds?"

"That veggie lasagna was so good."

"I know. My metabolism is finally starting to kick in."

As the girls moved into effortless chatter, the guys breathed easier. The smells from the Bistro and the warmth from the fire reached their table.

"Hey." Eric suddenly remembered something.

They all looked up.

"What time are your classes, Pattycakes?"

"Monday, Wednesday and Fridays eight-fifty to nine-fifty and ten-fifteen to eleven-fifteen. Why?"

"We need to know what time to kick the accountant's ass."

# CHAPTER 11

Bruce walked through Wal-Mart not caring to pay attention. There wasn't any point in paying attention. The store had been rearranged again. He wouldn't be able to find anything even if he did care. He kept walking. He would eventually come across something he wanted. Right now he wanted the Latches to blow up. All of them. The house. The farm. Everything. None of it meant anything to him anyway. They could all go to hell and he wouldn't shed a tear.

TV's. They were fun to mess with. He adjusted the sound on the nearest flat-screen. Missy could afford to buy him a new Ultra HD. But no, she was way too selfish for that. That's what the Latches' were, selfish. Every last one of them.

He turned the sound up on a second television, louder than the first.

Did CW care that he, Bruce, did more work than all of his sons put together? No. Did CW care that he knew more about running a farm than they did? No. Is CW paying him more than he's paying everybody else, even though he has to raise CW's grandkids? No. Is Bruce going to inherit anything when CW finally kills over? No. Of course not. But his children will. His girlified sons and his rejected nephew. *They* will inherit while he has to raise CW's grandchildren living off of their crumbs.

A third television got turned up.

Sure, Missy would be taken care of. Amy too, although he didn't know why. And Elizabeth. Somebody ought to backhand that brat. She was the worse one. No. Amy was the worse one. Talking down her nose at him.

Treating him like he wasn't qualified to be dirt. He ought to screw her brains out.

He switched the channel then turned the volume up.

No. He wouldn't screw Amy. She didn't deserve him.

"May I help you, sir?" A pimply teenager in a blue vest stood beside him.

"Uh-uh. I'm just looking." Bruce walked away. It was too noisy over there. A few steps later he was in the automotive aisle.

The worst part of all was those dingbats. Pattycakes had been there longer than mold. She'll marry Wyatt, take all his money, and get her fat fingers on some of what CW leaves behind. *If* the man would kindly go die. How is that fair? Here he is, doing all the work on that farm and Pattycakes gets money for no other reason than she's a girl. A fat, ugly girl. Wyatt could do so much better.

Cherry.

The bottle of windshield wiper fluid slipped from his fingers. He jumped back, away from the splash, cursing. She ruins everything. EVERYTHING. Chicano-nigger-chink-spick-whatever the hell she is. Does she even belong? Does she know anything about a farm? Does she know anything? Yeah, she knows how to wreck people's lives. She knows how to interfere in other people's business. She knows that. And she's going to get the biggest piece. He knew more about breeding horses than Holden and Eric put together, but did they give him a cut of that thirty-five thousand dollar purse they took last year? No. If she doesn't take her greedy claws out of Holden will she get a cut? Probably two. She's a damn whore. A dumb-ass whore who shouldn't be getting anything. All she does is hang out with Amy causing trouble. He should screw her. He should screw Amy. What's Amy going to say about her battery cable being fried? What kind of funny sound is that going to make?

Bruce left the automotive section- there was a big mess on the floor. The power tools were two aisles over. He'd go look at them.

*Speak of the devil.* Not that seeing Cherry in Wal-Mart was any kind of omen. Nobody ever went to Wal-Mart without seeing somebody they knew. He walked right up on her. "What are you doing here?"

"Hey, Bruce. What are you up to?"

"That's what I'm asking you? Ain't you supposed to be in school somewhere?"

"Not today. I need a few things, but I'm heading out to the farm in a little while.

"I bet you are. Is Holden paying for it?"

His odd question made her pause. "Pardon me?"

His eyes narrowed and then widened innocently. "I was teasing you. Since Holden is all in love, hopefully, you're spending all of his money."

Cherry looked away. If Bruce thought he was being funny, far be it from her to enlighten him. "I don't want to be in here too long." She shifted her weight. "I better get moving."

"I only need a few things myself. I'll shop with you." He stepped to the side and waited for her to move.

Without a choice, Cherry pushed her cart forward. There was an awkward minute while she made a mental list of things she was not going to pick up with Bruce there.

They passed two sales associates debating the location of some out-of-stock merchandise. Bruce nodded in their direction. "Do you know why they hate each other?" He didn't wait for Cherry to guess. "Because of Holden and Eric. Mainly, Holden."

"Do I need to know this?"

"They thought they each had one, but it turned out he was screwing them both."

Cherry ignored him.

Bruce didn't notice. "To this day, they blame each other. They'd both come running if Holden called them."

"How do you know which twin it was?"

"Everybody knows who it was."

Cherry made a sound of disbelief.

Unhappy with her response, Bruce changed the topic. "How long are you planning to be here?"

"Not too long. I don't have that much to get."

"No. I mean in West Virginia?"

"Oh. I don't know. I haven't thought about it."

"Why not? When you get done school don't you have plans? Some kind of life you want?"

"I did. But that was before Holden. Now it all depends on what kind of life we're going to want."

Bruce made a humorless sound. "Cherry." This time, his eyes went from wide to narrow.

"Yes?" She picked up an off-brand detergent.

"What type of life are you and Holden ever going to have?"

An off-brand bottle of bleach went into the cart next. She went forward. "I don't know yet. That's why I don't have any specific plans."

"Are you serious about him?"

"That's a ridiculous question. Of course, I'm serious about Holden."

"You think he's serious about you?"

"Have you been drinking?"

"I don't want to see you get your feelings hurt." His expression was sincere. "But I thought you were smart. College girl and all."

"Smart about what?" Cherry priced the Kleenex, unwilling to look at her companion.

"Come on. You know Holden. You don't think he likes his life the way it is? Do you think he's going to settle down? Get married, have kids like they do on TV? You think Holden is that, I don't know, desperate?"

"Getting married is an act of desperation?" She threw two boxes of tissues in the cart.

"No. More like stupidity if you're a Latche. They already have everything. Jobs. Money. Property. Whatever they want. Whoever they want. Women want them, they know that. Look at Pattycakes. Wyatt's got a wife with no strings attached. And there are about twenty other women wishing they were her." They stopped in front of the toilet paper. "Don't get me wrong, darling. You are without a doubt Holden's favorite. He'd rather be with you than anybody. But..." He grabbed the twelve-pak from the top shelf, she was reaching for. "What logical, intelligent, sane reason would Holden have to change his life? Hell, he even has somebody to be him whenever he doesn't feel like it. Or, he can be Eric anytime he needs to be somebody else." Bruce was careful not to look at Cherry. He did not want to have a reaction to her reaction.

. . . . .

Holden leaned against the stall, holding the phone to his ear with his shoulder. "What do you want, Amy?"

"Why are your horses making so much noise?"

"Because my nosey sister called. I'm actually working now. What do you want?"

"You should be nicer to me."

"I bought you a phone for Christmas. What else do you want?"

"A million dollars to start. In the meantime, I thought I would give you a heads up. I got a text from your girlfriend."

"Isn't she here?"

"Yeah, dude. She's right behind you. Turn around."

"Where is she?"

"She's not coming over today. She asked if I could pass the message on in case she missed you."

"Did she mention why she wasn't coming?"

"Dude. You're a dork. She's mad at you about something."

"Mad at me? Why?"

"You tell me."

"What makes you think she's mad?"

"Duhhh. Let's see. She's not coming over and she obviously doesn't want to talk to you~"

"What do you~"

"Please. Pass the message on," Amy repeated. "Is it so hard to hit speed dial? You do have voice mail. It's number one on your keypad. She didn't want to take a chance and have you pick up. You made her mad."

"I haven't seen her."

"Not prerequisite for making her mad."

"Thanks, Amy. I'll call her."

"Better say you're sorry."

"I haven't done anything."

"Not a prerequisite for being sorry."

# CHAPTER 12

"Where are you?"
*

"Why aren't you answering my calls?"
*

This is my third text.
*

"I've been calling and texting all afternoon. Is it so hard to get back to me?"
*

"Now, I'm getting pissed. Where the hell are you?"
*

"Hi. I'm sorry, my phone was turned off."

"Where are you?" Holden started counting down. He'd give her thirty seconds to explain.

"I'm at home."

"I thought Amy said you weren't coming over."

"I'm not at your house, Holden. I'm home."

"What?"

"Aunt Sid's."

"You're where?"

"My house. I'm at Aunt Sid's."

"You drove all the way down to the Eastern Shore?"

"Yeah... that's why I had my phone off. I didn't want to talk while I was driving."

"What the hell are you doing on the Eastern Shore?"

His incredulity was no match for her attitude. "I live here."

*This isn't good.* "I thought you were coming over."

"I changed my mind."

"Obviously. Why didn't you call me?"

"I left a message with Amy."

He wanted to ask why she didn't leave a message with him, but moved on to less annoying topics.

"Why did you decide not to come over?"

"No reason."

Holden frowned into the phone. "What's wrong?"

"Nothing."

"Cherry."

"Yes."

"You're on the Eastern Shore. For no reason, according to you. What's wrong?"

"Nothing. I just wanted to come home."

"Why?"

"No reason."

"Are we going to do this all night?"

"Do what?"

"You're testing my patience."

"I'm not testing your anything. If you don't want to be on the phone, you don't have to be. You can hang up anytime you want."

"I wouldn't have to be on the phone if you were here, but you're not, so I do have to be on the phone. The question is why are you testing my patience?"

She huffed. "Why are you taking that tone with me?"

"What's wrong?"

"What's wrong is your attitude."

*Huh. Amy was right. Doing something is not a prerequisite for being sorry.* "I'm sorry if I am upsetting you. But, you've left the state without telling me a damn thing. All I'm trying to do is find out what is going on. Something is wrong. Why won't you tell me?"

"What makes you think something is wrong?"

He didn't answer.

"Holden?"

"Are you coming back tonight?"

"Tonight? No. I'm not coming back tonight."

"All right. I'll drive down there as soon as I wrap up here."

"No. No. You can't drive down here. You do whatever you were planning to do tonight. I want to be by myself."

"I was going to spend the evening with you. I'm still going to spend the evening with you. If it means I have to drive three hours to do it, so be it. I'm on my way."

"No."

"No? Tell me what's going on?"

The silence felt longer than it really was.

"Cherry?"

Without warning, she blurted out, "Holden, we shouldn't be together!"

Now, the silence was his.

"Holden?"

"Where did that come from? It's bullshit by the way."

"I think it's better if I leave you alone."

"Better for whom?"

"Better for you...and eventually, it will be better for me."

She was crying. He had no idea why she was crying, but he could tell she was crying. Hormones? Insanity? What was he supposed to do about that? He got comfortable on the ground with his back propped up against the stall. "Cherry, I don't know where this is coming from. I don't know what's wrong with you. But I wish you would talk to me."

It was the desperation in his voice. She was causing him pain. She never meant to do that. "I guess I got the wrong impression about us. I'm sorry."

"What impression do you have?"

"That we might be something we're not." She sniffed.

Her logic was baffling, but at least she was talking. "What do you think we are?"

"I don't know."

She sounded so tiny. Sad. It broke his heart. "I'm in love with you." Into the silence, he said, "Did you hear me, Cherry? I'm in love with you."

"Really?"

"I don't lie to you."

She was crying again, if she ever stopped. "I love you too Holden and I'm so scared that you really don't love me because your life was perfect before we met and I might be expecting too much from you and I'm going to push you away so I left because you deserve your freedom but I want to be with you forever."

She got all that out in one breath. Hormones *had* to be involved.

"The only thing wrong with my life is you're not here. Honey, if I love you and you love me, who has the wrong impression?"

"Maybe I'm smothering you. Maybe I believed we were going to be all happily ever after and you're thinking something different. Maybe, you don't want a happily ever after with me."

He banged his head against the stall. "Of course I want a happily ever after with you. That's all I dream about."

"Maybe you're as happy as you're going to get with me. Maybe you're going to get bored and wish you weren't with me."

"That's a lot of maybes. Where is this craziness coming from?"

"It's not crazy."

He could tell she was pouting. No way was he going back to that. "Did somebody say something, or do something to mess you up?"

"It's not important."

"You're important. I don't want you upset. And I damn sure don't like it when you're not here. So please, tell me who said what?" Regardless of whatever she'd heard, he knew for a fact, for once in his life, he was completely innocent. Not a thought, not a word, not a look. He had done nothing to jeopardize their relationship. He just needed to wait for her to cry it out so they could get to the bottom of it. Then, she could come home and he could kick somebody's ass...

• • • • •

Holden looked at the roof of the tree house. "I have to get up in about ten minutes."

Cherry snickered. "I guess you better hang up and get to bed. I've been up all night too. Plus, I've been driving so you don't get any sympathy from me."

"It's your own fault. Driving to the other side of hell because of Bruce."

"I know. I'm an idiot."

"Don't be talking about my girl. I might have to give you a spanking."

"Empty threat."

His heart fluttered at the imagery.

It was after four a.m. Holden and Cherry had spent the entire night on the phone. Once he put her at peace about Bruce's comments and took her to task for not coming to him in the first place, it was wonderfully amazing how long they spent talking about nothing. Their conversation had taken him from the barn, to the bunkhouse, to the tree house without a break. After the whole night of hearing her voice, he couldn't wait to see her.

"How much longer before you get here?"

"I don't know." She yawned. "About twenty-five minutes give or take."

"Speed."

"No." He'd been making that suggestion since she started driving. It made her want to. "It's not like I'm going to see you anyway. At least not right away."

"Yes, you are. You're coming straight here."

"No. I look a mess. I'm not going anywhere near that farm. I have to clean up first."

"You know what?" He sat up, inspired. "To hell with this." He had a need and she was going to fill it. He wasn't going to argue about it. "Meet me at Harpers Ferry. I'll pick up breakfast."

· · · · ·

A long hug and a deep kiss was the first order of business, followed by coffee and McGriddle sandwiches- her favorite. Still, they hadn't run out of things to say. They walked through the predawn shadows to the outlook where the rivers meet and watched a flock of ducks paddling by.

"This is never going to happen again."

Cherry was all about honesty. "It might."

Her fingers were clasped in his. Holden tugged her to a halt. He shook his head.

"I would leave you alone before I would ever do anything to hurt you. If you fell out of love with me, I'd leave."

She tried to pull away, but his reaction was quicker. By now they were close to the river's edge. Two steps and he had her pinned against a tree trunk. He pressed into her because she couldn't stop him. He kissed her savagely because he was tired and aggravated, and she was completely mental, and he wanted her more than he wanted anything in his life. "It's crazy for you to think I'm ever going to get tired of being with you."

"Holden." The syllables carried on her sigh.

"We've got at least forty or fifty years before we've gone through my preliminary list of things I want to do with you."

"Holden."

She was soft and delicious, and there was her dimple, begging for attention. He complied by lightly licking the tiny indent and whispering into the wetness, "I will always want to be with you."

She met his ardor with fervor. Holden didn't want to think of anything other than kissing her thoroughly.

Cherry wasn't thinking of anything at all. He had removed her ability to think.

• • • • •

Holden whistled as he walked through the barn. Music-man came to the front of his stall. He shook his ebony mane expectantly. Holden passed him the apple he had brought for his prized-pet. He rubbed the silken muzzle affectionately. Ritual complete. "I know who is getting your next filly."

"I was coming to open up." CW came in behind Holden. Fifty-one years of farm life had been good for CW. He was strong and active. Rough hands, laugh lines and white hair at his temples were the only giveaways to his age.

"Hey, Pop. I was just getting ready to take care of it."

"Good man. You just getting in? Were you with Cherry?"

"That's right."

"She wasn't over here yesterday. Is everything okay?"

"It is now."

"What was her problem?"

"Bruce. I'm going to knock him on his ass and that should solve it."

"That boy has got a mean streak I hope Brucey won't inherit."

"We won't let that happen."

They turned on lights and opened bags of feed, scooping even measurements for each of the barn's inhabitants. The horses whined and nickered, ready for breakfast.

"Is she over it? Feeling better?"

"Yep. Made sure of that. She'll be over in a few hours. Going to do some work in the garden, I think." Holden tossed the appropriate number of feed bags on to the utility trailer attached to the four-wheeler they would use to tend to the animals outside. His movements were graceful and fluent, as if the fifty-pound bags were weightless.

"As long as she's happy. That's all that matters."

"That's what I think."

"She's a good woman."

"That's what I think."

"I mean it. She's a real lady."

Holden nodded.

"Are you treating her like a real lady?"

"I have to. I wouldn't consider marrying a woman who was less than a real lady." Holden watched his father's face for a reaction.

CW beamed with approval. "Good man."

Music-man shook his mane in agreement.

# CHAPTER 13

Cherry could hardly contain herself. A rodeo. A real live rodeo full of dust and people and noise. She thought they were only held in Texas and Oklahoma- certainly not in Maryland. Yet, here she was, sitting at the J Bar W Ranch for the exciting two-day event. All the guys participated, but rodeos were Eric's domain. Several times he had been solicited to join the professional rodeo circuit. According to the Latches, there was no one better.

The entire Latche clan went. Cory and Hunter grabbed any chance to hang out with the big boys. Elizabeth grabbed any chance to see boys. The rest of the girls went because it was Cherry's first rodeo. They wanted to share in her excitement and to keep her company when she got bored. Cowboys and boy-cows. She had a boyfriend already. *Of course* she was going to get bored.

The guys signed in and prepared. CW and Claire wandered through the crowd, greeting old friends and business associates. Tabby rode on Cory's shoulders as he and Hunter bought hot pretzels and Elizabeth flirted with the cashier. The girls found seats, good ones.

"So, what should I do?" Missy returned to an earlier conversation.

"What can you do?" Pattycakes asked.

"Kick him out." Amy pulled at a piece of cotton-candy.

"Give him an ultimatum," Cherry said, "and then kick him out."

Amy snickered.

"He is the father of my kids," Missy declared. She shifted Brucey from one arm to the other.

"Exactly why he needs an ultimatum. Tabby and Brucey deserve a better father." Cherry reached for the baby.

Brucey came willingly, eager to drool on her shoulder and bat at her earring.

"Bruce is a good father."

Amy snickered again.

"He's not a good father if he can't be better to their mother," Cherry said.

"I agree." Pattycakes pulled off a piece of Amy's cotton-candy. "Keep that away from me. I tried on the dress I wore to your graduation and it slid off my shoulders." She pulled another piece of the sugar-concoction.

"Good," Amy said. "That dress is hideous."

"You picked it out."

"What was I thinking?"

Missy talked over them, directing her question to Cherry. "What does one have to do with the other?"

"Missy, your happiness is conducive to your children's happiness. The same way you suffer with them. They may not be able to understand or express it, but they don't feel good when something is wrong. They can't. When is the last time you were actually happy in your relationship?"

"Sometime before it was a confirmed relationship," Amy moved her cotton-candy out of Pattycakes' reach. "Back when she thought he was somebody he wasn't."

"Shut-up, Amy." Missy pulled at the cotton-candy, offering a pinch to Pattycakes.

"Missy, I love you," Cherry said. "But you're no better than Bruce if you let him screw you over like he's been doing. You deserve better. Tabby and Brucey deserve better. Is this the life you want Tabby to have? Is he the kind of man you want Brucey to grow into?"

Each of Cherry's words brought Missy's tears closer to the surface. She didn't hide them. They were sisters. She was safe. To answer Cherry's inquiry, she shook her head.

"Don't forget." Amy wrapped an arm around Missy. "That is *your* house. That is *your* farm. There is no reason for *you* to be unhappy." She offered up her cotton-candy.

A minute later, Cherry's phone vibrated. "It's Beany. I've got to grab this." She passed Brucey to Pattycakes and skipped down the bleachers.

Amy followed her movements. "Does anyone else think that's strange?"

"What?" Pattycakes shifted the baby to a more comfortable position. "He's her brother."

"Exactly," Amy said. "Whose brother is so important you have to go hide just to talk to him?"

"Not any of mine. That's for sure." Missy licked the candy crystals from her finger.

· · · · ·

The first Latche event was the calf roping. Eric came in first, Holden third and Eli, sixth. Wyatt and Bruce finished lower, but still in the top twenty. Eric and Holden shared a runaway victory in the team roping.

Then came the first day of the rough-stock competition: Bareback Bronc Riding and Bull Riding. Eric was the reigning amateur champion of both sports.

Bruce didn't last the eight seconds needed to qualify. Eli scored a sixty-eight. Wyatt did better with a seventy-five. The twins were the heavy favorites. They did not disappoint. They earned an identical score: a record-breaking ninety-six. There was some speculation as to whether the same twin had ridden twice. Holden did confess that while they both rode, Eric went first, as Holden. He, Holden, had no choice but to be Eric, imitating his brother in all movement.

"That's why we tied," Eric joked. "Doing it my way is better."

Later, when they were alone, Holden admitted to Cherry, "I had to tie or beat him. He's determined I should win this year. I've determined all the Rodeo trophies will have Eric's name."

"I know most twins are close, but you and Eric have reached a new level of unhealthy."

. . . . .

It wasn't until the Bull Riding was underway, the next day, did Holden give any merit to Cherry's statement. Eric, having entered as himself this time, again beat his record from last season. Fighting-Fire, the feisty bull he'd been assigned, snorted and tossed his head as Eric leapt from the mighty beast's back. He skirted out of the rodeo clown's path and climbed the fence to wave his hat at the cheering crowd. He made eye contact with Cherry...and held it.

Cherry felt the jolt and the accompanying heat. For a moment, she thought he was Holden. And for another moment – a tiny one – she didn't care. The man riding the fence had ridden a bull. No, controlled a bull. She could not look away. He was all sweat and muscle and determination and desire. Her body tightened. An invitation played around her lips.

Tabby jumped up and down, waving her arms to get Eric's attention. Cherry caught the movement in her peripheral vision and gave herself a mental shake. No, he wasn't Holden, but he was...Eric.

Eric waved at Tabby, refusing to dwell on what happened, what he thought happened. *Did that just happen?* He didn't know and it was too scary to touch. Cherry? *Damn. Did she think I was Holden? That had better be what that was. She shouldn't be looking at me like that. I damn sure shouldn't want her to. Cherry?* Damn. That a moment- probably confused- could mess with his head was troublesome and too scary to think about.

Further down the fence, near the bucking chute, Holden had been watching Cherry- he was always watching Cherry. He saw that look, identified it. It was the look she gave him two seconds before he got aroused. His thoughts ran parallel to Eric's. Only where Eric was confused, Holden was uneasy and agitated. *She thinks that was me.* Deciding that was the sum of the exchange, he let himself breathe.

. . . . .

The rodeo ended as expected with Eric as the big winner. Being Eric's partner and assisting him with his training proved to be beneficial to Holden as he added to the celebration by snagging a few awards of his own.

The hour and a half ride home was broken up with a victory dinner at the Outback steakhouse in Frederick. Cherry imagined, as they pulled into the parking lot - a one, two, three, four succession- they had to be the perfect image of redneck. Of course, she amended, when Holden lifted her out of the truck, he made the image quite appealing.

"You must be outside your mind!" Bruce slammed the door to Missy's Honda. He pocketed the keys.

"I'm done. I'm not doing this anymore." Missy focused on the back seat. Tabby sat with wide fearful eyes. Thankfully, Brucey was asleep. "Come on Baby, it's okay." She released the child from her car seat.

Bruce walked ahead, not bothering to help with the children. He didn't stop until he was in front of Cherry. "What did you do this time?"

"Pardon me?"

"Oh, don't give me any of that stuck-up crap. What~"

Holden stepped in front of Cherry. "Do you have a problem, Bruce?"

"This ain't about you, Holden. This is~"

"I asked you a question. I won't ask again."

"Look, I don't have~"

"Why are we having a display in the parking lot?" Eric's tone was light. He took up a position next to Holden, his stance aggressive.

"Now what? Are you going to double-team me? Like always. You don't even know what the hell she did!"

The family converged on them. All except Amy. She collected Brucey, then herded Tabby, Cory and Hunter into the restaurant, leaving the others to fend for themselves.

Elizabeth followed with a full running commentary. "Nothing Bruce does is surprising...We're going to be squished with this many people...I'm getting a good seat..."

"Is this something that can't wait until we get home?" Wyatt asked.

Bruce pointed at Holden. "You better tell your girl to leave other people's business alone."

"Why don't you quit being a bully, Bruce?" Missy squeezed in between Bruce and her brothers. "Blaming Cherry for your mess won't make it go away."

Eric grinned down at Cherry. "You get into more trouble."

Cherry raised her hands in surrender. "I swear. I don't know what's going on."

"This isn't about you, Cherry," Missy said. "Bruce has an aversion to truth. He's lashing out. That's all."

"He's not going to lash out at her." Holden was deadly serious.

"That ain't all. This~"

"Is going to have to wait." CW overrode Bruce's objection. "Whatever the problem is, it has to go on hold. That's all there is to it." He was the patriarch, the father, the boss. There would be no further argument.

Bruce took a reluctant step back. The circle broke up and they headed for the door.

"Oh, wait." Missy stopped them. "I need my keys."

"What?"

"You heard me, Bruce. I need my keys."

"Oh. So now, I can't drive home?"

"Not with me." She had the nerve to smile.

"Yeah. Try to take them." He turned away.

"Dude." Missy did an excellent imitation of Amy. "That is my car. If I say you can't drive it, then you can't drive it." She held up her hand to CW, halting his interruption. "I'm not driving home with you. The car seats are in that car. The kids have to ride in that car. If you don't give me the keys, you'll either have to take care of the kids yourself or force them to be unsafe." She paused a beat. "Do you want to give me the keys now?"

"They're my kids too. I'll take care of them."

Missy's grin was evil. "Good idea." She practically bounced her way into the restaurant.

Holden draped his arm around Cherry. "Anything you want to tell me?"

Cherry crinkled her brow. "I honestly don't know what I'm being blamed for."

"I'm sure you did something," Eric said from her other side.

She frowned. "Thanks."

"You're welcome."

"It doesn't matter if you did something or not." Holden brushed a soft kiss against her temple. "I don't need a reason to beat the crap out of Bruce."

"No," Eric agreed. "His existence is reason enough."

# CHAPTER 14

The intense turn the evening had taken became more intense. Bruce's brooding and Missy's goading was in direct correlation. The rest of the Latche clan tried to ignore them. The attempt was unsuccessful - Holden had to threaten Bruce twice, because of comments concerning Cherry. By the time the check arrived everyone was relieved.

$$\bullet \quad \bullet \quad \bullet \quad \bullet \quad \bullet$$

Wyatt glared at Holden from the back of the Silverado. Holden glanced in his rearview mirror and nodded in silent agreement. Before dinner, Cherry and Pattycakes rode beside them, now it was Eric and Eli. Amy was driving Missy in Eric's truck. For some inexplicable reason, Cherry and Pattycakes needed to ride with them. But, that wasn't the worst of it. For yet another inexplicable reason, Amy did not stay on highway 340 behind CW's Ford.
*

The girls laughed hysterically when their cell phones rang in unison.
"Hi."
"Hello."
"What?"
"May I help you?"
In contrast to the various tones and greetings the girls gave, Bruce and the three Latche brothers posed the same question. "What are you up to?"

*

"We're hanging out."

"We're taking some girl-time."

"None of your business."

"Don't be concerned with what I do."

*

"Hanging out where?" Holden asked.

"Girl-time for what?" Wyatt wondered. "I thought that was why you were riding home with them."

"As long as you're in my truck, it's my business. I left you in charge, Amy. I'm holding you accountable."

"Yeah, I will be. What are you going to do about these kids?"

*

"No idea. I'll call you as soon as I have something pertinent to say."

"What are you, the girl-time record keeper? Unless you have something against me hanging out with Missy, Amy and Cherry, I'll see you later."

Amy made kissing noises into the phone. "Now, go get a real life and leave me alone."

"I'm not going to do a thing about the kids. You are their father. Figure it out."

*

The guys went back to sharing the same brain: "Fine."

*

"Bye."

"Good-bye."

"See ya."

Click.

The hysterical laughter returned.

· · · · ·

Bruce was already crazy-angry with Missy for not getting into the car in the first place. He was also pissed at her brothers for not backing him up, especially Eric for giving Amy his truck. However, nobody was higher on his payback list than Cherry. Missy's attitude reeked of Cherry's meddling. He was not going to lose his job or his house and his family because Cherry couldn't mind her own business. Wyatt and Holden may be a couple of wusses, but after he got Missy straight, Cherry was going to have to go. That, to him, was a fact.

• • • • •

"All right." Pattycakes clapped her hands. "Everything. Don't even think about leaving out any details."

Missy, riding shotgun, turned on an angle to be sure everyone could hear. "Not a whole lot to it. Last night after we talked I felt, I don't know, different, released. I couldn't figure out why I put myself through so much for him. I made a list of pros and cons of living with him. I'm ashamed to admit it, but there were twice as many cons as pros~"

"Only twice?" Amy cut in. "I'll have to give Bruce more credit. I'd have thought four or five times."

"Shut up." Missy laughed along with the others. "Anyway, I tried to discuss it with him. I wanted to give him a chance, the benefit of the doubt or something."

"That was good," Cherry said.

"Yeah. No," Missy said. "He was a total jerk. He told me I was damned lucky to have him. He counted off a handful of women who wanted to screw him. And, he told me if I didn't start treating him better, *he* was going to leave *me*."

"No, he didn't." Cherry's mouth fell open.

"Excuse me?" Pattycakes' eyes doubled in size.

"Dudette. You have to be kidding."

"Yes, he did."

"What did you say?"

"What did you do?"

"What did you hit him with?" They laughed at Amy's sincerity.

Missy said, "He thought he was scaring me. Only, it had the opposite effect. Right now, he's grossing me out and I want him to go away. I told him, I thought it was a great idea. And since *he* was leaving *me*, he would

93

need to get the hell out of my house and off of my property."

"Yayyy..." Amy let go of the wheel so she could clap.

"He said he wasn't going anywhere. But I could. Can you believe that?"

"Did you remind him that his boss is your father?" Cherry asked.

"Yes."

As if working from a list, Pattycakes went to the next item. "Did you tell him CW has five sons and a nephew working for him? Bruce is more or less expendable?"

"I did."

"How about this one," Amy said. "Did you tell him, he's an idiot?"

"Several times. In fact, I was explaining that to him, yet again, when we got to the Outback."

"There's a question." Cherry asked, "Why is he blaming me?"

"Mainly because he's an idiot," Missy replied. "He doesn't apologize for anything. He never takes responsibility for anything. Not as long as he can find someone to blame."

"Oh." Cherry hunched her shoulders. "Gee. I feel honored."

"He already had some bug up his butt about you, Cherry," Amy said. "He was the one saying Pattycakes was messing around on Wyatt because of you."

"That's right." Missy remembered.

"Hmm." Cherry hunched her shoulders again. "Now, I definitely feel honored. Being on Bruce's bad side must be an accomplishment."

"Don't." Pattycakes shook her head. "I've been on his bad side for years."

"I've got you beat," Amy said. "I've never been on Bruce's good side. Not once since I've known him."

Missy snorted. "I should have been so lucky."

· · · · ·

"It's almost two, Amy. Where's Cherry?"

"Hello to you too, Holden. Are you awake?"

"Does it matter?"

"Yes. If you aren't awake, it matters where you happen to be sleeping."

"I wasn't asleep. Answer my question."

"Lucky for you, I intend to. Which is why I'm calling."

"Is she hurt?"

"Wow. I had no idea how pathetic you are. Do I sound like she's been hurt?"

"You sound like you've been drinking."

"Not that lucky, I'm the driver."

"Does this call have a purpose? Or can I talk to Cherry?"

"No, you can't. She went to the ladies'. She said it's too late for her to come home with us. She wants us to take her to her dorm. She doesn't want to disturb you."

"I'm waiting up for her."

"I would have told her that had I known how pathetic you are. Is anybody else up?"

"Eric went to bed. He's feeding the animals tomorrow. Today. Whatever. He said to tell you to fill his tank. Wyatt is still around. I haven't seen Bruce since we got home. Where are you?"

"Inner Harbor."

"Inner Harbor? You drove to Baltimore. Are you crazy?"

"We're about to leave...err...soon...I imagine."

"You imagine?"

"Missy has had more than the legal limit of fun. She's not ready to leave. But they have last call for a reason."

"Get your ass home. Tell Cherry I'll be waiting for her."

"Dude, you are so pathetic."

• • • • •

It would have been better for the male egos if the girls had attempted to be quiet when they arrived. The girls had no such notions. It was after four thirty. Claire, CW and Eric would be getting up within the hour anyway.

Holden turned off the television and watched as they filed past.

"Hey...umm, Holden," Missy guessed first.

"Or Eric," Pattycakes said.

"How about Heric." Amy giggled. "Or Eroden."

"It's Holden." Cherry tried to whisper. She came into the TV room and sat beside him.

"It better be." Amy didn't try to whisper. "If you're going to do anything with him." She led the way up the steps. "Good night whoever you are."

"Good night."

"Night.

Missy and Pattycakes followed, debating whether or not you could still call it night.

Holden waited until they were gone before giving his full attention to Cherry. "It seems like you've had some night."

"Oh yeah. I could probably sleep for a week."

"What did you do?"

"We ended up at a bar, three bars to be exact." She hiccupped to prove her point.

"Since when do you drink that much?"

"I don't and I didn't. This was all about Missy. She had a lot of frustration to unload."

Cherry's voice soothed Holden. He hadn't realized how agitated he had become. "I was worried about you."

"Aww. That's so sweet." She kissed him. "I'm sorry. I didn't think you would worry, given the company I was in." Four-thirty-something a.m. and Holden was an exciting combination. Cherry kissed him again.

Holden didn't mind indulging her. "The company you were in is what had me worried. What is this about?" He pulled her against him, marveling at how nicely she fit.

"Mmm." Cherry was only half into the conversation. She was tired and he tasted good. "Bruce is a jerk. Missy is fed-up."

Holden was less than half into the conversation. Cherry's hands were on his chest, boldly enticing him. He had no intention of thwarting her effort. "What does this have to do with you?"

"Technically nothing." She nibbled the corner of his mouth. "We were giving Missy moral support." She worked her way down his neck.

He tilted his head back. "Why does Bruce think you're involved?"

"Apparently, I'm easy to blame." Her words were muffled against his throat. "I was the one to suggest that she give him an ultimatum."

"Of course you did."

"I also suggested that she kick him out." She yawned. "You know," she talked through another yawn. "I haven't had one bad dream since I met you."

"Wish I could say the same. I'm losing a lot of sleep over you." After a silent moment he said, "You know I'm joking right?" She didn't comment and he realized she didn't know anything. Cherry was asleep.

Holden held her a few minutes longer, as it was the only enjoyment he could expect tonight. For him, Cherry was adorable and exasperating, and always at the same time.

Holden gathered his strength and stood up with Cherry in his arms. He took her to his bedroom. It was her bedroom as far as he was concerned. He let his mind play with the thought of undressing her. However, even if he wanted to -which he did- he didn't. Not only would Cherry kill him in the morning, but Missy was asleep in Eric's bed. That she didn't go up to her own room in the attic told Holden how serious his hot-headed sister was. Missy's decision to bunk with Cherry was going to be bad news in the morning. Not that Holden gave a damn about that.

# CHAPTER 15

Missy's declared war on Bruce had an immediate effect. On everybody. Bruce's shock at not seeing her before breakfast was replaced by his shock at her announcement that he had to move out of her room. He only got to deny her once.

Offering a wicked grin that was fast becoming a trademark, Missy's eyes danced around the breakfast table. She spoke to the girls first. "Let's do it." To the guys she said, "Wyatt, Eric, Holden, you have a choice to make. There is a man in my room and I don't want him there. You can either be my brothers or not. I'm leaving. I'll be back when I have a bedroom." She placed her son into his Uncle Eric's arms, tossed her hair over her shoulder and almost skipped out of the room. Amy, Pattycakes and Cherry (after blowing Holden a mischievous kiss) followed her out.

"What the shit is going on?" Wyatt asked aloud.

Elizabeth, the last female remaining, said, "That's why I'm here." She was the only Latche sibling with blond hair. She fingered it lovingly, as it was her favorite attribute.

"To tell us what's going on?" Eric asked.

"Yep. Who's paying?"

"Paying?" Bruce snorted. "For what? So you can tell us some more mumbo-jumbo that Cherry told Missy because she don't have nothing better to do than to pluck my nerves."

Holden shot Bruce a dangerous look. "I'm going to knock you flat on your ass if you don't lay off Cherry."

"Actually," Elizabeth said, "it was Cherry's idea—"

Bruce smirked.

"—but you should be thanking her Bruce, she saved your butt."

Bruce frowned. "What?"

"Pay up."

"Elizabeth, I don't have time~"

"You don't have nothing but time."

A car pulled off, followed by a second, a third and a forth.

Elizabeth grinned. "Pay up. Oh, and if I tell, I'm going to be late for school. Holden, can you give me a ride?"

"Ummhmm."

"I would have asked you Eric, but your truck just left."

"What?" Eric passed Brucey to Wyatt and went to the window. Sure enough, the Dodge was missing.

"Amy said to remind you that you put her in charge."

"That was last night."

"She said, you told her you would look at her car. She said she was staying in charge of your truck until you do. She said it's still making a funny noise."

"That's all well and good." Wyatt cut into Eric's cursing. "Dad and Eli are already out there. We have to get to work. Elizabeth, can we get on with this? Please."

"Not until I get paid. Bruce..." She held out her hand.

Reluctantly, he reached into his pocket and pulled out a five dollar bill.

"Is that a joke?"

He yanked out a second five.

"Are you trying to be insulting?" She raised an eyebrow.

Bruce mumbled something about greedy teenagers and dug out a twenty.

Elizabeth took it from him and then collected the two fives from his other hand. "Thank you."

"Now talk." Wyatt passed Brucey to Holden.

"You heard her," Elizabeth said. "Missy wants Bruce out of her room. If he doesn't go on his own, she wants you guys to move him out. If you don't, you all are a bunch of deadbeats with no family loyalty. She's not coming back here until he's out of her room, either way. All the girls are backing her up, which means, Amy and Pattycakes and Cherry aren't coming back here either. But, I'm staying because there's a lot of money to be made." She pocketed her thirty dollars.

"What about her children?" Bruce demanded. "Did she forget she was a mother?"

"No. She'll take care of Tabby. You can take care of Brucey."

"What does Cherry have to do with this?" Holden didn't want to know. He really didn't.

"The original plan was for Missy to stay with her at the dorm, but children aren't allowed. Cherry thought it would be better for Missy to stay with Pattycakes. That way Tabby could be with her." She pointed to Bruce. "You still got Brucey." Elizabeth stood up. "The other thing you should be thankful for, Bruce, is that it was Cherry's idea to move you out of Missy's room~"

"THANKFUL!"

"Uh huh. Missy wanted you off the farm. Cherry said to let you keep your job for now, and I quote: 'He might need the money for child support'. Pattycakes wants you gone and Amy wants to run over you. That's why she's keeping Eric's truck. Let me get my books, Holden." With a happy little flounce, Elizabeth left the kitchen.

Holden gave Bruce his son. "I have to get her to school. What's the general plan?"

"Figure out how to unscrew this day," Wyatt said.

"Yep." Eric turned to Bruce. "Can you move yourself or are we going to have to help you?"

"I'm not going nowhere."

"Yes you are," was uttered in triplicate.

Bruce's mouth fell open.

"Shit," Wyatt said. "Mom took the boys to the dentist, first thing. We're going to be a man down. Unless you got somebody to babysit."

"Women are evil." Eric gave a humorless chuckle. "I get the planning, but when did they have time to put all this together?"

Elizabeth came back into the Kitchen, book-bag over her shoulder. "I packed for Missy, Amy and Tabby last night. Fifteen bucks apiece. Tabby was free. Plus, Amy let me borrow this shirt." She pinched the material at her shoulder. "This gig is sweeeet."

Holden put on his black Stetson and opened the door for Elizabeth.

Eric followed them out. "Get your stuff out of her room, Bruce. We got a bunch of crap here because of you."

"Me? Because of Missy. Because of Cherry."

Eric turned on his heel. He walked until he was right up in Bruce's face. "Because of you. Missy is doing this because she is fed up with you. That ain't something you can blame on Cherry."

Brucey squirmed, catching Eric's attention. He swallowed his attitude and backed off. Picking up another Stetson, also black, Eric left.

Wyatt was slower to rise. Slower to move. Bruce was his best friend.

"This ain't right."

"I don't know what you expect from us, Bruce. Missy is my sister and Pattycakes is my girl. I want them both back. You've slept in the bunkhouse before."

"Not because Missy put me there."

"That's something you should think on." When he got to the back door, Wyatt said, "Since you have to stay home with your son, you might want to help out with these dishes and possibly lunch. That's usually Missy's job, but thanks to you, she ain't here. None of the girls are."

For a long time after Wyatt left, Bruce stood there, confused. He couldn't imagine one single thing he did to deserve this.

Brucey squirmed some more.

The dishes did not get done. Lunch did not get made. It wasn't necessarily stubbornness that kept Bruce from complying. It was more the attention Brucey required. Everything the child needed was nowhere to be found.

The Latches attended to the problem as best they could. Eli helped Claire clean up the breakfast mess. Eric made a run to Chick-Fil-A. CW played with Brucey. Holden kept working to make up for the slack, and

Wyatt helped Bruce move into the bunkhouse.

. . . . .

"You have to go? What do you mean, you have to go? Go where?" Wyatt opened the garage door. "Yeah. You better call me back. I'm not waiting up all night either. Bye."

"Any luck?" Eric said from under Amy's car.

In the background, the radio was set loud enough to even out the banging:

*I made a mistake. Yeah...*
*I made your heart break. Yeah...*

"Not enough." Wyatt pocketed his phone. "This isn't right."

"What did Pattycakes say?"

"She said they aren't coming back tonight. None of this is right. Whatever is going on with Missy and Bruce is their business. Pattycakes and Cherry and Amy shouldn't be involved. And they damn sure shouldn't have involved us."

"Cherry told Holden it was necessary because Missy couldn't do it by herself. Whatever 'it' is supposed to be."

"Holden's talked to Cherry?"

"Yes. She told him they weren't coming back tonight either. Hand me the wrench."

Wyatt used his foot to guide the tool to Eric's outstretched hand."

"Did she happen to mention why, exactly?"

"School is her excuse."

"And everybody else?"

"She said they were busy but it's possible they'll be home tomorrow."

"Busy doing what?" Bruce came in from the kitchen. He rounded the car holding Brucey like a football, looking haggard.

"Don't know. Holden went to find out. You know what?" Eric slid out so he could see the other guys. "This is the exact reason I am and will remain unattached."

The radio played on:

*I got a disease deep down inside. It's hurting my pride.*
*I can't go on without you. I got a disease...*

. . . . .

"Holden." Cherry opened her door wide enough for him to enter. "What are you doing here?"

"You know what I'm doing here." He walked into her dorm room fully loaded with the anger he had compiled throughout the day.

Cherry was grinning bigger than the Cheshire Cat. That made him angrier.

"I'm so glad you came." She threw herself at him, leaving him no choice but to grab and punish her with a kiss. She took it like a man: wrapping her arms around his neck and slipping her tongue into his mouth.

Holden's brain incinerated and his animal instinct took over. He backed her up, not stopping until she was pinned against a desk. He broke contact with her mouth only long enough to push aside some books and brochures and lift her onto the desktop. Then he reattached himself to the underside of her jaw, nibbling his way up to her ear. A brochure -an announcement for a summer trip to Senegal, West Africa- fluttered to the floor.

"Ahemm."

They broke apart.

"I'm sure you want to be alone. Unfortunately, that is not going to be possible."

Holden turned, intending to murder whoever made the noise.

"Candice." Cherry untangled herself. "I forgot you were here."

"I saw that. You're on my desk."

"Opps. Sorry."

Holden stood back, allowing Cherry space to climb down. "Could we have a minute?" Holden was normally polite to Cherry's roommate, but at the moment he was too keyed up to care."

"I'd like to indulge you, Holden, but if I were going to do that, I would have left instead of reminding you I'm here." The cheeky Korean squeezed past them to sit at her desk. "Homework." She picked up her fallen paper and slid her books back into place.

"It will only take a second."

"That doesn't sound very satisfying. Homework."

"Don't mind her." Cherry pulled him to her side of the room. "She and her boyfriend broke up. She's not in a friendly place today."

"Also, she was betrayed." Candice talked from behind a math book. "It wasn't a half hour ago you were telling me, you wouldn't get to see your boyfriend for a few days. You said he was going to be mad at you."

"That's what I thought~"

"I am mad at her, but I didn't come up here to listen to you two debate," Holden said. "We'll go somewhere else. Why don't you pack some clothes."

"I have school in the morning."

"You can still go to class if it's that important."

"I can't come to your house. Missy would kill me."

"If we don't get this worked out, I'm going to kill you."

Cherry studied Holden. "I think if you could figure out a way to kill me without actually causing me any harm, you'd probably do it."

"You'd be right." He tried not to fall into those pools of misty-gray.

She gave his earring a little flick then slid her palm lower to trace the contour of his jaw. Obviously, he had more important things to do than shave today.

One touch from her and he let himself fall.

"Ahemm. Homework."

Shaking her head at Candice, Cherry said, "I'll go with you, just not to the farm."

"Fair enough. I'll be in the truck." Holden walked out.

Candice put her book down. "Mmm mmm. He is so hot. You should thank me."

"For being rude and not giving us a second to talk?"

"For forcing him to take you with him. A man like that should not be left alone."

"Thank you, Candice." Cherry pulled out her overnight bag.

"If you were sincere, you would introduce me to his brother."

"Nope. He's mine too." Cherry wondered what made her say that.

. . . . .

Holden speed-dialed Eric. "Can you find Wyatt and Bruce?"

"They're both right here. I'll put you on speaker."

"I might be able to solve the problem."

"How?" was echoed around the garage.

"I'm going to take Cherry out of the picture for a few days. That should give you some time to work on getting your girls back. Whether she knows it or not, she is the mastermind behind all this chaos."

"I told you~"

"Shut up, Bruce." Holden hadn't lost an iota of his anger. "What she does is good. You don't like it because you can't continue to be a fuck-up. But, that's beside the point. This was a sneak attack. I'm just leveling the playing field. Whether or not you work it out will be up to you and Missy. Wyatt, you should get Pattycakes out of this crap too."

"I'm getting ready to go over to her house now."

"Are you coming back here, Holden?" Eric asked.

"Not tonight."

They all smiled while, in the background, a singer crooned about boys in the summertime. Holden hadn't been in hunting mode since he met Cherry.

# CHAPTER 16

Cherry wasn't speaking to him for driving back to the farm. She stayed in his truck and pouted while he packed a few things. He took her prolonged silence as an assent to his decision to drive anywhere he wanted to go. He wanted to go up highway 70. Then he wanted to get on 68. But it wasn't until they got to the cut in the mountain that he realized he wanted to go to Deep Creek.

She stopped being officially mad about fifteen minutes into the drive-once they were safely out of Jefferson County. They listened to the radio and talked a lot about nothing, content with the company. They were headed toward lonely places. The mystery of Heaven unfurled with each passing mile. Chemistry and osmosis made them acutely aware that something more was coming: Something big.

Holden and Cherry were going to have sex. Holden was sure of it. That could be the only possible conclusion this mounting tension could bring them to.

Holden and Cherry were going to get engaged. Cherry was sure of it. That could be the only possible conclusion this mounting tension could bring them to.

· · · · ·

It was early in the season, finding a cabin was easy. Finding the grocery store and a Red Box movie kiosk was easier. They gave no thought to spending the night together. Technically, that happened on their first date. It was finding the words to express what they were feeling. That was the hard part.

. . . . .

It was completely dark when they parked outside the tiny cabin nestled in a patch of woods between the road and the lake. Holden started a fire while Cherry made dinner: Dominoes. They knew exactly where the pizza was to be delivered.

She took a shower and prepared for bed while he paid the pizza guy and opened the wine. They had their meal on the floor in front of the fire.

Cherry's cell phone blared. The sound was rough and ominous, cutting through the tranquility.

"That's Amy." She accepted the call. "Hey, what's~Heyyy?"

Holden slid the phone out of her hand and put it to his ear. "Don't ever call this number again." He hung up on his sister and tossed the phone under a chair.

"That was rude."

"Is there another way to treat one's siblings?" He cocked his unrepentant left eyebrow.

He was too cute to be offensive. "What brought all this on?" Cherry leaned back into him.

Holden sipped his wine and decided being completely honest was going to be the way to go. "We needed the time. I wanted you to myself for a little while."

She sighed, snuggling closer. "I belong to you. What more could you want?"

*Well, not completely honest. Not yet, anyway.* "I'm good with everything you do with my sisters until it starts interfering with us."

"I wasn't~"

"Shhh." He touched her lips with his finger. They were soft, so he caressed them. "From the first day I brought you home, you've been a part of the family. And that's great. But lately, you girls have been a little insane~"

"We're not~"

"Shhh." He pushed his fingertip into her mouth. It was erotic.

She lightly nibbled on it.

He got an erection.

"I was starting to get angry until I realized my problem wasn't so much the craziness. It was more that we haven't had any quality time. I can't remember the last time we did something without my family."

"That's because you and Eric are sharing a life." She talked around his finger.

It was sexy.

"I thought you liked Eric."

"I adore Eric." She could tell he was enjoying her administrations so she let her tongue slide down the length of his finger, sucking it all the way into her mouth.

For a half-second, Holden thought he picked up something in her tone when she said Eric's name but he lost his concentration when her tongue started moving. He pushed his finger in and out of her mouth, mesmerized.

He felt her moan and jerked his hand away. A few more strokes and he would ejaculate. It was that simple.

"What's wrong?"

He grinned and pulled her closer. "Nothing. Absolutely nothing." He brought his mouth down hard on hers, replacing his finger with his tongue.

Cherry's moan was louder this time. Holden swallowed it. She slipped her arms around his neck and melted into his embrace.

Cherry's silk pajama top had three buttons holding it closed. Holden kissed his way down her neck and undid the first one. He slid the material aside to expose her skin.

She shuddered with excitement when his lips touched her shoulder. "Ohhhhh... what are you doing to me?"

He undid the second button and slid his hand inside. At the same time, his mouth moved lower. "I'm making love to you. Do you like it?"

"Yes... ummmm... don't... don't... aren't... ummmm... aren't you supposed... to ask me something..."

He undid the last button.

"...first..."

His hand curved around the underside of her breast. She moved against him, restless and needy. He brought his mouth right up to her ear, flicking the lobe with his tongue. "Please," he whispered. "Please let me make love to you. I didn't plan it, but this is right. I love you and we're perfect, Cherry. Let me make it perfect. Please." He was panting, filled with anticipation, heavy with his own need.

Lost in his desire, at first Holden did not notice her movement against him had ceased. She pulled away, staring at him with wide sad eyes. He watched her with a growing realization that something was wrong. He couldn't figure out what. Everything had been flawless.

Cherry took a minute to catch her breath and collect herself. "Holden," she said. "What do you mean, you didn't plan this?"

"I wish I had. The fact is all I wanted to do was talk. I didn't know where we were going. I had to go get clothes," he reminded her. "But being with you, finally alone. I want to make love to you. I have to make love to you. I love you. It's time." It's past time, he wanted to say but didn't. Instead, he burned her with his heated gaze.

Cherry pulled her top closed and withdrew into herself.

Holden plopped down on his back. His anger came back, intensified. He had never waited this long for a girl in his life. Enough was enough. Whatever excuse she came up with, she could forget it. Her virginity was his and he wanted it. Now.

"Holden, can I tell you about my parents?"

"You want to talk about your family? Now? You haven't wanted to talk about your family since I've known you."

She nodded her head nervously. "It's pertinent."

"Go ahead." He was still mad. He wanted her to know it.

She winced under the condemnation. "My mom died of cancer when I was in the eighth grade. My dad died two years later, in Iraq."

*And this applies how?* "I'm sorry you had to deal with that kind of tragedy. Twice." He was sorry. And he was glad she was opening up to him, but he didn't want any excuses from her and that's what she was giving him. Added to that, it took her this long to finally tell him about it. What the hell kind of relationship was this?

"May I share something else with you?"

*You never learned how to open your legs? I've been informed.* "Go ahead."

Her voice was shaky. "When my mother was dying, we hardly left her side. I missed a lot of school. That's why I apply myself so hard now. I'm making up for lost time. Anyway, the last pertinent conversation she had with my sister and me was to tell us how she wanted us to live. She told us not to play house when we grew up. She admitted she didn't love my dad...not like she should have. Not like she used to." Cherry focused completely on Holden. "You see, he never married her. He didn't have a reason to. Mommy was crazy about him in the beginning and he was a good father. He took care of his kids. But, according to her, he took her life and he didn't give her his in return. Having sex with a man who didn't love her enough to share his name eventually made her bitter."

"I will share my name with you, Cherry. When it's the right time."

She smiled a tragic little smile. "Mommy said that's what they all say." She held up her hand to stop his interruption. "She said some of them mean it. The thing is, that's still just playing house. The right time is before a man makes demands on a woman, not after. The only thing I have to give as proof of my love is myself. I don't need to prove myself to someone who doesn't find me worth his name. If I have to give the only thing I have before he'll give me his name, he's not worthy of me. He just wants to play house. I'm not going to play house with you because I don't want that for us. I don't want to resent you and love you less because you couldn't love me more."

"It's not like that for us. You know that. I know you know that." He sat up now.

"That's what my sister thought. She's been in love with four men. She has children by two of them. Peaches thought each one would love her enough, and they did. They loved her enough for themselves."

"What do you want? Me to marry you?" He didn't mean to sound disgusted. Incredulous.

"I hope someday. When we're ready for it. I'm prepared to give you that. I'll wait until you are ready. But my virginity is for sale. My life cost yours. The price of my sex is a wedding ring." Seeing the complete and total shock on his face softened her next utterance. "The last letter I got from my dad was kind of a premonition. He told me God expected great things from me. He told me I deserved a better man than he had been to my mom and that my Mr. Wonderful would come if I didn't compromise. He also told me to honor my mother and be the best person I can be. And that he loved me..." She waited for him to lock his eyes with hers. "Holden, for me, having sex isn't just about the act. If that were it, I would have jumped you the first night we met. Believe me, I wanted to. I want to every day. But, I have not one, but two parents, whose memories I have to honor. I love you enough to do it if you want to. But I can promise you, I will be spending every second thinking about how much you don't love me, and how I've let my parents down, and how I didn't wait for the man who would have loved me right. And I'll end up hating you for it."

$$\bullet \quad \bullet \quad \bullet \quad \bullet \quad \bullet$$

Holden crept back into the cabin. Cherry was asleep in the same place he left her. Her declaration had so stunned him, he beat a hasty retreat. Walking in the woods at night- not the brightest idea he ever had. But he needed the time. The space. All along, he thought Cherry was acting a part, being the prim and proper good little girl because A- she didn't know any better and/or B- she thought it would make him want her more. That she had real reasons for her old fashion values had never occurred to him. He felt like an ass. Then, he ran out, spewing some crap about needing to get some air. He was an ass.

Cherry had curled into a ball and cried herself to sleep. It was obvious from her tear streaked cheeks. From the master bedroom, he grabbed a blanket and two pillows. He returned to the fireside, added a few logs and covered Cherry up before undressing and crawling in beside her. He pulled her against him and woke her with kisses. Several kisses.

"Holden?" She wept.

"I'm sorry, Cherry. I'm a screw-up. I'm sorry." He kissed her eyelids and her cheeks, her nose and her mouth, continuing his cycle between his words. "I don't want to play house with you. When we're ready to get married, we will. And I'll wait. I want to make love to you but I want to be worthy of it."

"Holden, I'm sorry. I'm so sorry."

"No. Shhhh...shhhh...you don't have anything to be sorry about." He kissed her tears. "Tell me you forgive me and let me hold you. I swear that's all I need. I swear that will be enough for now."

. . . . .

Daylight was tricky in the woods of Deep Creek, filtering down between leaves and thick foliage, bright white in some places, warm gold in others. Sometimes, it hid behind shadows, pretending the new day had not yet arrived. Rabbits and squirrels and hikers, eager for new discoveries, moved through the thickets, each at their own skill level.

Dawn grew into morning and morning stretched into early afternoon while Holden and Cherry slept. For hours, they made love- not the carnal kind- their intercourse did not involve penetration. Instead, they gave and got intimacy. They touched and they talked, whispering their affection, learning who they truly were. Cherry traced her infatuation into his chest hairs and Holden branded her waist and hip with his palm, committing the feel of it to memory. It was tender. It was satisfying. For now, it was enough.

Holden was captivated by her loveliness. Reverently parting her nightshirt so that her beauty was opened to him, his eyes lingered, awed...and possessive. He kissed and caressed what was his, worshipping her body from the waist up.

Cherry was not ashamed. She was treasured.

They lay entwined, skin to skin. Separated only by the lace of her bra, their hearts beat the same rhythm and became one.

. . . . .

School became a non-issue. One day at Deep Creek turned into three. It was too late to ski and too early to swim, but there were long walks to be taken, horseback riding trails to be explored, movies to be watched, an open fire to cook over and all the firelight romance they could hope for.

It was late Thursday night when Holden finally dropped Cherry off at her dorm, promising to call her the minute he got home. Only then did they remember her cell phone. It was still under the chair at the cabin. Rather than be miffed, Cherry promised to call *him* tomorrow after she got back from the phone store.

. . . . .

"Hello, Aunt Sid."

"Child, where have you been? I've been trying to call you all week."

"I lost my cell phone Monday night. I just got a new one today."

"Lordy, child. You didn't have no phone all week. Was Holden with you? You could have been killed."

"I saw Holden every day this week." *Every night too.* "There were no murderers to be found."

"Don't be flip. What's your new number? Let me get a piece of paper."

"You don't need any paper. The number is the same."

There was a knock on Cherry's door.

"The same number? What if somebody finds your phone? They can call you and come and find you. It could be a con-man."

"You worry too much. No one can get my information. By now, the battery is dead anyway. I have to go. Somebody is at my door."

"You ask who it is."

"I will. Love you."

"You call me back and let me know you're safe."

Cherry pretended she didn't hear her and hung up.

Amy was at the door. "Where have you been? I've been trying to call you all week."

"I lost my cell phone. I just got a new one twenty minutes ago." Cherry shook off the déjà vu feeling.

"That's what Holden told Missy. I thought he was lying." Amy walked in and went straight to Cherry's closet. "That still doesn't cover the where have you been part?" She grabbed Cherry's jean jacket. "Here."

"I was with Holden. We went to Deep Creek. I'm surprised he didn't mention it. Where are we going?" She accepted her purse from Amy's outstretched hand.

"I haven't seen Holden. Not that I'm speaking to him anyway. We're going to the Outlets. After Holden kidnapped you, Wyatt got on the bandwagon. I swear he's trying to get Pattycakes pregnant."

"Are we shopping for baby clothes?" Cherry followed Amy out.

"No. Wedding gifts. Missy and Bruce are getting married tomorrow."

"What?"

"That's what my ten thousand phone calls were about. I was stuck babysitting while Holden was leading the divide and conquer Missy game."

"He didn't do that." Cherry shook her head. "He didn't know anything about it."

"I don't know what he knew. I don't care. Bruce is going to be permanent."

"It hasn't been a full week yet. Married?"

"I know. Missy is an idiot and we have to buy her presents for it."

# CHAPTER 17

Chicken, lasagna, barbeque, burgers, pasta, vegetables, salads, chips, dips, snacks and desserts of every kind filled the Latche kitchen and dining room. People rushed from room to room arranging flowers, laying out cards and gifts, and making last minute preparations.

Pattycakes, Cherry, Elizabeth and a few other women had the food, the house, and the yard ready by one o'clock Saturday afternoon. The new Mrs. Melissa Magagee, her husband, their children, their parents and their wedding party consisting of Amy and Wyatt were home from the courthouse by two. The reception immediately got underway.

The party was perfect. Bruce and Missy looked like they were in love. Wyatt, Eric and Holden ate more than they needed to, drank more than they should have and showed off quite a bit because they could.

Amy hung out with a man she later described as new and hot- a rare occurrence, according to her.

Pattycakes was complimented endlessly on her new look and her noticeable weight loss. More noticeable in the low-cut, high-split dress she wore.

Cherry met a wide range of Latche family and friends. She drank things she'd never heard of and danced with Eric almost as much as she danced with Holden.

Everything was wonderful, except no one but Missy was truly happy for Missy.

· · · · ·

He was drunk. Not smashed, just crazy enough to try it.

Cherry leaned against the fence, feeding Music-man a carrot. The wedding reception was still in full swing, people were everywhere. She came down for a quick moment of quiet. Only it wasn't altogether quiet. Somebody was laid out by the back fence and she was sure there were at least two, possibly three couples in the barn. *Deep Creek was so nice.* She sighed and then jumped, startled.

Holden slid his arms around her waist. "Is something wrong?"

She leaned back into him, raising an arm above her head to caress his neck. "Nothing is wrong, especially not now. I only came out for some air."

"What were you thinking about?"

"Deep Creek." She blushed.

He leaned down, placing his lips right next to her ear. "Me too."

"Were you, really?" She couldn't help the breathy rush of syllables.

"I want to make love to you again," he whispered and kissed her lobe.

Cherry turned around and pushed him hard, more humored than annoyed. "Not even if I were twice as drunk as you are, Eric. You try that again and I'll castrate you." She pushed him again and walked off.

Eric laughed until she was out of sight and then he dropped his pretense. He went to find Holden.

· · · · ·

Holden wasn't hard to locate. Coming around the corner of the bunkhouse, they almost bumped into each other, literally. "Have you seen Cherry?"

"Yeah, I tried to feel her up a few minutes ago."

"Any luck with that?"

"She threatened to castrate me."

"It's a start."

"Wyatt is going to kick your ass."

"He can try. Does he have a reason?"

"Because he lost a fifty dollar bet to Bruce."

"And I'm somehow responsible?"

"You or Cherry. I don't know who he'll blame."

"What was the bet?"

"That he did the animals twice, I made the mill run, and Eli and Bruce did all the hay because you were finally getting laid. Why did I do the mill run if you weren't getting laid?"

Holden didn't ask how Eric knew. He didn't want to know how Eric knew. "Some things are more important than sex."

"Like what?"

"Cherry."

"And here I thought she was a reason to have sex."

"That's because you're drunk and you don't know what you're talking about."

Eli and Wyatt stumbled down the path.

"Who's drunk?"

"Who's having sex?"

Eric snickered. "Not Holden."

"You've got to be kidding me?"

"You had her for a whole week and you didn't get nothing?" Eli pulled out a cigarette. "Man, are you crazy."

"Nope," Eric said. "Just pathetic."

Holden dismissed them with a head shake. "If you want to know the truth, I'm proud."

"Proud your thing is going to shrivel up and fall off from lack of use," Eli said, as if it was a possibility.

"Proud my relationship with Cherry is based on something stronger than sex."

"It has to be. 'Cause sex ain't in the equation."

Eric and Eli laughed at Wyatt's joke.

"Yuck it up all you want. I'm not ashamed. I don't want sex right now."

"Yeah you do."

"Bull shit."

"Right."

"All right," Holden corrected. "I do want it. But I'm okay with not getting it right now. Marriage is important to Cherry."

"Let me get this straight." Eric stuck a finger in his ear as if he were unplugging it. "You're not getting any tail unless you marry her? I just lost my buzz."

"He'll be screwing Lilly or somebody before the summer is over." Eli flicked his butt and stepped on it.

"He'll get to Cherry before summer starts." Eric crossed his arms.

"He'll get rid of her before we know it." Wyatt finished out the speculations.

"Why don't you bet on it." Holden turned and talked over his shoulder. "Especially you, Wyatt. You seem to have a lot of money to lose." He walked away.

· · · · ·

Cherry was taking out a bag of trash when Holden found her. He hadn't realized he was agitated until he saw her and the anxiety eased up.

"There you are. I gave up trying to find you."

"Don't ever do that." He wrapped her in his arms.

"Where were you?"

"By the bunkhouse letting my brothers get on my nerves."

At the mention of his brothers, Cherry's face lit up.

"What?"

"Nothing. Your brothers are something."

"My brothers are a pain in the ass."

"Not Cory or Hunter."

"Not Hunter," Holden allowed. "But he's only twelve. In a year, he'll be the worst one."

"You are in some mood." She placed her hands on either side of his face "This is a party. No pouting allowed." She kissed him. She kissed him again because it was pleasant. She kissed him a third time because she wanted to. By then, he wasn't pouting anymore. "That's better."

"That's what I needed."

"Anytime Soldier."

"Now." This time he led the kissing game, parting her mouth, nibbling on her lip and dueling with her tongue.

Amy came out with a second bag of trash. "Counting Missy's attic, there are six bedrooms in the house, five in the bunkhouse. You've got the basement, the barn, the tree house, the garage, the shed and who knows how many cars. Go be nasty in private."

"Can we go back to Deep Creek?" Holden's lips moved from Cherry's mouth to the underside of her jaw "Please."

"Like that will do you any good." Eric walked past, lightly shoving them into the trash cans.

· · · · ·

Missy and Bruce honeymooned at the Hilltop Inn in Harpers Ferry for one night. Bruce moved back into the attic the next day. For a week, they imitated the other lovers on the farm. And, within the month, their life and relationship was the same as it had always been.

# CHAPTER 18

Cherry scooped oats into each bucket. Feeding the horses was one of her favorite chores. They were so powerful and majestic. Thoroughbreds. Nobility in their own right. She gave each one a gentle rub on its muzzle and a few words of praise.

The sound of soft thunder outside caught her attention. She moved to the back of the barn where she could see the paddocks. Eric was in the process of breaking in a three- year-old. He gave the animal- a chestnut red- his total focus. His jaw was set and his muscles were locked. Steely determination showed in his every move. Eric Latche was as stubborn as the Red was strong.

The battle of wills between man and beast captured Cherry's attention completely. She was mesmerized.

Fifteen minutes of bucking and rearing did nothing to unseat the rider. The Red began to slow down, winded. All of the Latche horses began their training as foals. The Red didn't represent a real challenge, but Eric used every opportunity available to put his skills to use.

When the animal was calm enough, Eric walked him the circumference of the paddock, halting when he was close to the barn. "Come here." He beckoned Cherry forward.

"What?" She pretended annoyance. "Some of us have to work for a living." She held up her oat bucket.

"You haven't done a spot of work for the last two hours. Get your ass over here."

She was already in route. "What? Did the poor baby hurt himself? Want a band-aid for your bum?"

"What I want ain't got nothing to do with why I called you over here. Give him a hand full of oats. He earned it."

Immediately, Cherry went closer to the horse. She sat her bucket down and dug out a heaping scoop of grain. "There you are. You did earn it. You big, gorgeous, beautiful, baby. You're a good boy. Aren't you?"

The Red flicked his tail and accepted the treat with gusto.

"Now, go do some real work and quit making me lose my concentration. If I get thrown, your ass is mine. Literally." His green-blue stare was wickedly mischievous.

Her entire face lit up at the challenge. "Ohhh. I'm quaking in my boots. Don't blame your ineptness on spectators. It's all about your ability. Prove it or admit you don't have any."

"Is that an invitation?"

"Walking away, Eric. Walking away."

He watched her swaying hips until she was back in the barn and out of sight. He didn't have to see her face to know she was smiling.

A hundred feet away, Bruce paused to take in the scene. He didn't have to see Cherry's face either. It was all very clear to him.

·  ·  ·  ·  ·

"Hey, what's up?" Cherry picked up on the first ring. If Pattycakes was ditching the gym this morning, that was fine with her.

"I was on my way, but I got a call. There's an emergency of sorts. We've got to get to the farm. I'll pick you up in a few minutes."

"What's going on? Is somebody hurt?"

"Oh no, no, no. I didn't mean to scare you. That house is full of dogs and somebody needs their balls cut off. That's all."

·  ·  ·  ·  ·

"Okay. What happened?" Cherry clicked her seatbelt in place.

Pattycakes pulled away from the curb. "My cousin, Mia."

"Do I know her?"

"No. Before this is over, you're going to wish you never heard of her."

"Why? What did she do and what does it have to do with me?"

"Let me see. Isaiah is almost a year. So...two years ago. That's when this started. Rick and his brother John were working for CW." She watched the road, barely drawing a breath between sentences.

"Anyway, Mia lives in Brunswick, but she was always over here. She is in love with the twins." She looked over at Cherry. "Especially Holden, but she'd take either one in a heartbeat."

"Can't blame her for that."

"Yes, you can. You better."

"Okay. I hate your cousin."

"Right now, so do I. Mia is such a whore. Rick. And poor Isaiah." Pattycakes shook her head. "She and Missy were like this." She held up her crossed fingers. "I'm her cousin. She didn't like Lydia, Eric's girlfriend at the time. But still..."

Cherry didn't comment. She still didn't know what this was about.

"Mia used to come up every summer. She worked with us on the farm, supposedly, to save some money for college. We all knew it was so she could get close to Holden and Eric. Eric was with Lydia and Holden wasn't interested. Then she got pregnant by Rick. End of story."

"So, what's the problem?"

"Isaiah got sick last month. Long story short, Rick is not his father. It turns out she knew that when she said it."

Cherry could guess what was coming. "Is this something Holden should be telling me?"

"Oh, he's going to talk. They all are."

"They all?"

"My mother told me Mia finally confessed. She doesn't know who Isaiah's father is."

"What does she mean, she doesn't know? Wasn't she there?"

"Apparently, they were all there."

"What?"

"Mia screwed Rick after she screwed Holden, Eric, WYATT, Bruce, Eli and John. The whole freaking farm. She slept with them all."

Cherry's mouth dropped open. That was the only way to receive that kind of information.

"All of them. My boyfriend. Missy's boyfriend. Their brothers. Their cousin. It's a wonder the horses were safe."

"Did they know?"

"That's one of the questions we're going to ask. That and which one of them is Isaiah's father."

. . . . .

Someone had already made phone calls. Eli pulled into the Latche drive behind Pattycakes. There was activity in the house and around the yard. Lots of yelling. Missy hurled things- Bruce's things- at Bruce. His clothes littered the front porch.

"Missy, wait. I~" He ducked a well-aimed shoe.

Eric got ahold of his sister, but abruptly released her when she bit him. Wyatt grabbed at her, but stopped when he heard the car door slam. Now, he had his own fight to worry about.

In Wyatt's favor, Pattycakes was down from 235lbs to 208. However, the last few months at the gym was turning her excess weight into muscle. She came at him like a charging she-bear. The urge to run went through Wyatt, but seeing as running hadn't helped Bruce, he thought better of it. She punched him like a prizefighter. It took Wyatt, Eric and Eli to keep her from swinging again.

"Missy, stop it! Ouch!" Something electronic cracked against Bruce's head.

Cherry followed cautiously. The day had a surreal quality about it.

Holden met her halfway across the yard. "Cherry?" She wasn't swinging, but he wasn't sure of what to expect.

"Holden."

They stared at one another, three feet apart, while around them the world came to an end.

"Say something."

She shook her head slowly. "Is this who you are?"

"No. It's not even who I was. Hell. Maybe. Whatever. It's not me. Not now." He closed the distance. "Please tell me you understand. This was something that happened way before your time. Something I promise you will never happen again."

She believed him. She trusted him.

He read it in her eyes and his world righted itself. He held her, kissed her and thanked God she was his.

Pattycakes nailed Eli. He stumbled backwards down the steps. Eric jumped back, away from her next swing. Wyatt backed up fast. Hands held up in surrender, he tried to explain.

"Hey Now!" Bruce yelled. Missy found a hammer and went toward his car. He charged forward but hastily retreated when she turned on him.

Holden led Cherry into the house, away from crunching metal and flying glass. Eric followed them in. He'd had enough of females who fought. "Why are you so calm?" He went to the sink to run some water on his hand. Missy had drawn blood.

"Why wouldn't I be?" She eased herself into a chair, only then realizing how shaky she was. "I wasn't there."

"No. But this still affects you."

"This affects everybody. What were you thinking?" She looked from one twin to the other. "Any of you?"

"A freebie." Eric shrugged.

"I can't decide what appalls me the most, that one girl would sleep with an entire family or that an entire family would sleep with one girl."

"It wasn't a gang bang," Holden said. "Nobody knew what she was up to."

"Would it have mattered?" Amy came in.

"We use condoms, so probably not."

"Not to me," Eric added. "I don't care who you are, or who you're with." He slashed his eyes to Cherry. "You turn up, uninvited, in my bed at one in the morning, don't expect to cuddle."

"She got in your bed?" Cherry repeated. She and Amy exchanged the same bewildered expression.

"Mine too," Holden said. "I wonder if it was the same night."

"Naw, I tired her out."

Amy grimaced. "Ewww. This is vile on so many levels."

A thud from outside made Cherry jump. "Do they have any excuse? Do you, Eric? You had a girlfriend."

"Vile," Amy said again.

"First. I had a girlfriend. Emphasis on past tense. If I could have been faithful to her, it wouldn't be past tense. Next, Wyatt and Pattycakes have been a couple since sixth grade. He's been screwing around on her since fifth grade. But their relationship is different. I don't know what she's all riled up for. That's your influence." He pointed to Cherry. "Pattycakes knows Wyatt is getting it out of his system. That's why he hasn't made a commitment. Everybody knows, especially Pattycakes, as soon as Wyatt can settle down, she's the one. But he's got to get there."

"What a crock." Cherry waved him off.

"Is it?" Amy was interested.

"Definitely. Don't you ever buy that crap from any man, Amy. I'm glad Pattycakes is wising up." She turned to Eric. "What is Bruce's excuse?"

"Ahh, that. Missy is married to a dog. They don't come any worse than Bruce."

"And as her brothers, you allow this?"

"We're not hypocrites, Cherry."

"No, Eric, you're worse."

"And one of you," Amy sneered, "has passed that poison on to the next generation."

# CHAPTER 19

True to Latche style, the paternity tests were taken care of immediately. They made the short trip to the Hydrochem Lab in Shenandoah Junction.

After more than two hours locked away with Missy, Pattycakes, Amy and Claire, there was no point in going to class. Cherry used the wait-time doing odd jobs around the farm. She helped Claire stock the incubator. She helped CW turn out the horses, finishing the job when he complained that he thought he pulled a muscle in his chest. Then she spent the rest of the afternoon with Amy, mucking.

"Is there any guy that doesn't have creep somewhere in his blood?"

"They all have the potential," Cherry said over the stall. "But some choose not to act on it."

"How do you feel about Holden's part in this? I mean, he wasn't with anybody at the time, but still."

"I'm not sure I have a right to feel anything. I wasn't in the picture."

"I wonder if it would have made a difference."

"It had better."

"They all slept with her. But, she got in their beds. Did they have a chance?"

"I don't know, Amy. Part of me wants to understand. They didn't plan it, it just sort of happened. But, a bigger part of me knows there is no excuse for it. None. If I had been involved, I wouldn't be here right now."

"What do you think Missy and Pattycakes should do?"

"Hard to say. As I said, if it were me, I'd be gone. Missy's got children.

That's not so easy. I love her but, Pattycakes is an idiot."

"You didn't like Eric's excuse for Wyatt. Why don't you believe it?"

"Please. You either love somebody with all your heart or you don't. Wyatt's got her on hold." She mimicked, "'I'm going to do everything I want to do and when I run out of girls to screw, I'll be right with you.' Please. The idea is to make a choice one way or the other. Women aren't now-and-laters."

"He thinks he's doing her a favor. Getting it out of his system before he ties her up. Not be a dog, like Bruce."

"He should sell cars. She's already tied up. She's been waiting on him since she was what? Two? Do you think he'd go for that if it were the other way around? Wyatt isn't doing her any favors. Wyatt is a dog just like Bruce and he is stomping on Pattycakes, the woman he is supposed to love. If she leaves him, it would be the least he deserves."

"Why don't you two quit gossiping." Wyatt rounded the corner. He stepped into the stall Cherry was cleaning.

Rather than be embarrassed, Cherry leaned on her pitchfork. "Nobody's gossiping. If there's something you don't want to hear, Wyatt, maybe you should quit eavesdropping."

He was in no mood to back down. "Maybe you should mind your own business."

She flung her rake aside. "I'm multiracial. I have a lot of attitudes to choose from. Which one would you like to see?"

Amy came around to stand between them. "What's the matter, Wyatt? Truth hurt?"

"You don't know anything about me and Pattycakes. Neither one of you. So keep your thoughts to yourselves and butt out." He glared first at one and then the other. "She better not get any ideas about leaving."

"If you don't want Pattycakes to leave," Cherry snapped. "I suggest you give her a reason to stay."

Wyatt didn't comment. When the silence became potent he turned on his heel and walked out.

"I guess the boys are back." Amy threw down her pitchfork.

Cherry followed Amy out of the barn and stopped short. A beat up green neon was parked in the drive. A young woman with mousey-brown hair, pulled into a messy bun, got out. She opened the back door and leaned in, giving attention to a car seat and the baby it held. Her low ridin' jeans rode too low, offering the world a plumber's view of her backside.

"Uh-oh," Amy muttered.

"What's wrong? Who is it?" Cherry asked as if she didn't already know.

"That would be Mia and I'm guessing the baby with the multiple-father-disorder."

"Hey, Amy." Mia waved. "Do you want to come meet your nephew?"

"Sure do." Amy linked her arm through Cherry's, dragging Cherry over to the neon.

"This is Isaiah." Mia grinned, offering the child to Amy. "He's your nephew."

Amy took the baby. "You think?"

"He is. Look at him. He looks just like Holden."

While it could be argued that Isaiah had the Latche nose and his eyes were the same blue as CW's, his probable grandfather, Amy couldn't identify Holden exclusively. "If he looks just like Holden, that means he also looks just like Eric. He would bear a strong resemblance to Wyatt too. And, since Eli is a first cousin, you might be able to find him in there as well."

"Uh-uh. He looks like Holden."

Amy skipped ahead. "Mia, this is Cherry."

"Hi."

"Mia. Hi. Hi Isaiah." Cherry wiggled his hand. "You're a cutie."

Isaiah liked the game. He reached for Cherry.

"May I?" At Mia's nod, she reached for the baby.

"I didn't hear nothing about you." Mia sized Cherry up. "You work here?"

Cherry felt a sour note on the air. "Mmm. I've heard quite a bit about you." She bounced Isaiah lightly.

Amy felt it too. "Cherry is Holden's wife."

"Wife?"

"Girlfriend," Cherry corrected.

Amy said, "You'll be his wife soon enough if I have anything to say about it. And let me assure you, I do."

"How is it up to you?" Mia reached for her baby.

Isaiah voiced his displeasure at being taken from Cherry.

Having her first question ignored, Mia proposed another. "Where did everybody go?" She shoved Isaiah's binky into his mouth.

"Probably in the house." Amy led the way.

They were almost to the steps when they heard Holden.

"Cherry," he called from the bunkhouse path. "We need to talk," he said when he joined them. His eyes were sharp but his voice was gentle.

"Hi, Holden."

"Mia."

"Here's Isaiah." She offered her child to him.

"I just saw him a half hour ago." Holden took the baby anyway.

"They were at the lab too," Amy guessed.

"Seeing as he has the most important DNA, his presence was a must." He held the door open for the girls.

Eric met them in the hall. He relieved Holden of Isaiah, swinging him high in the air and sang, "Who's your daddy..."

Isaiah giggled and drooled, basking in the attention.

. . . . .

It didn't take long for the family to gather in the Latche living room, except for Missy, Pattycakes and CW. The former two had been locked in Missy's attic all day, neither willing nor wanting to face the outside world yet. The pain in CW's chest seemed to have spread. He felt bad enough to go to bed, an extremely rare occurrence for him.

The others were in equal parts cool to Mia and lovingly warm to Isaiah. Isaiah was definitely a Latche, a welcomed addition to the clan. His presence was neither resented nor regretted by anyone. Mia, however, was another story.

Thus far, Cherry had proven to be the most hospitable toward the girl. Mia rewarded her with rudeness. It was that behavior, more than anything fueling the animosity directed at her. As bright as she had always been, Mia choose to ignore the warning.

"Why didn't you tell the truth and deal with it when you got pregnant?" Claire rocked Isaiah.

"Because, I was with Rick when I found out." If Mia was embarrassed, it didn't show. "Me and Holden hadn't hooked up yet. Everybody else was with somebody. I didn't want to cause any problems so I kept quiet."

"What?" Amy made a face. "Dudette, sleeping with men who are related who have girlfriends is all very problematic, as this little powwow can attest. Missy wants to shoot you but she and Pattycakes are fighting over which gun to use. That, to me, is highly problematic."

"Humph," Mia said, "they're not going to do nothing to me. I know Holden is my baby's father."

"I thought the test results wouldn't come back for five to ten days." Cherry turned her puzzled glance to Holden.

Mia pursed her lips. "I don't mean to sound rude—"

Nobody believed her.

"—But, I don't see how you figure into this."

"You've got a one in six chance of being right about me being Isaiah's father." Holden cut into her comment. "That means there is a one in six shot this will directly affect Cherry. That's how she figures into this."

Mia didn't respond.

"Why are you so sure he's Holden's?" Wyatt asked. "Not that I mind being an uncle."

"It's possible he's Eric's, but I'm pretty sure I was pregnant after Holden and me made love."

"We never made love."

"Yes we did~"

"We had sex."

"Sex is just a crude way of saying making love."

"Sex is what we had. Love wasn't involved."

She looked wounded. He didn't understand why. None of the men understood why. To ease the sudden tension, Eric said, "I don't know, Holden. I've been studying Isaiah. He's definitely got your chin."

Holden smiled a wicked grin. "He has your chin. And your ears."

"Your ears. And Wyatt's nose."

Cherry watched Mia's countenance drop. "Why don't you all knock it off. The fact of the matter is the mother would have the best idea of when she got pregnant."

"That's because they usually don't have so many people to choose from," Bruce said loud enough to be heard.

"Of all the people in this room to pass judgment, Bruce, you should be the last." Cherry rolled her eyes.

Holden stood up. "We need to talk, Cherry." That same sharpness was back in his eyes. He held out a hand to help her up.

"Holden." Impatience tickled Mia's tone. "I'm not staying here too much longer."

He arched his left eyebrow. "So?"

"I'm about to leave."

"See ya."

"Don't you want to spend some time with the baby?"

"Eric will play with him. Isaiah won't know the difference." Holden and Cherry left.

Eric sang, "Who's your daddy..."

When they were out of hearing range, Mia scrunched her face in distaste. "Is she Mexican? Why is he with a Mexican?"

"There's a new one."

"I wonder how often she gets that."

"I don't see Mexican."

"I don't know. That girl can kill an enchilada."

The Latche clan debated Cherry's Mexican-ness until Mia interrupted. "Don't nobody care that she's not white?"

"Do we need to care?" Eric cocked his head to the side, attitude showing.

"We have more important things to be concerned with." Amy offered just as much attitude as Eric did. "For example, her reputation."

"Mexicans don't have no good reputations."

"I'd call you an expert on bad reputations." The room went quiet with Amy's comment.

Eric returned to his song. "Who's your daddy, let's make a plan~"

"Stop singing that, Eric," Mia said. "That is so rude."

"It's appropriate."

"It is not appropriate. I know who Isaiah's daddy is."

"Who?"

"Holden...or you."

"Pick-a-twin, any-twin," Amy singsonged.

Mia huffed.

Isaiah as almost asleep in Claire's arms. "You're going to have to be sure. If he does belong to one of the twins, DNA testing won't be able to reveal which one."

"Why not? The tests they do nowadays are reliable and they did the Y chromosome test thing. They told me that one is pretty much foolproof because the Y chromosome is passed straight from father to son without changing."

"Eric, Holden and Wyatt all have the same daddy." Amy shrugged. "Eli has the same granddaddy. You aren't getting a whole lot of help from that test."

Claire kissed her new grandson. "Eric and Holden are identical twins, Mia. Their DNA is identical."

"Besides having the same Y chromosome, they're clones," Amy said. "Having the same DNA is what makes them identical. So if it's one of them, Isaiah is going to get two for the price of one."

"Or neither," Bruce added. "Because she won't be able to prove it's either one."

"I know who my baby's daddy is."

Wyatt said, "Until last month, it was Rick."

"You could be right about Holden or me. Either way it will be fine." Eric leveled his gaze straight at Mia. "As long as you know, getting Isaiah a father doesn't get you a man."

# CHAPTER 20

Holden and Cherry walked along the back fence. Their footfalls landed softly, muffled by the Kentucky Bluegrass. The breeze was steady and mildly fragrant, wafting the scent of lilac and honeysuckle. Nearby, a foal neighed, impatient to latch on to his dam's teat. They kept pace. Cherry was tucked under Holden's shoulder, her arm tightly around his waist. The cool of the night did not touch her within his protective grasp. However, the cool of his attitude did.

"Did I do something, Holden?"

How exactly was he supposed to answer that? "Mmmm."

Besides missing class and mucking stalls, she hadn't done much today. *She* certainly hadn't given them a child to consider. "What's wrong?"

"Have you spoken to Missy or Pattycakes?"

"Earlier."

"Mmmm."

"Did you think I wouldn't be here for them? Honestly, Holden. I can't get over your brother. And Bruce. Don't get me start~"

"Cherry." He cut her off. "I don't want to talk about Wyatt or Bruce. I want to talk about you and what you've been saying."

"What have I been saying?"

"That's what I want to know."

"What makes you think I've been saying anything?"

"Because you have an opinion about everything. 'Don't get me started,'" he mimicked. "When you talk, all the women around here want to hear it."

"So?"

"So what did you have to say?" They paused under the tree house. Holden pulled the trap door open. He didn't bother with the rope ladder, finding it just as easy to heave himself through the opening. He reached a muscled arm down to Cherry. As soon as she grasped his hand, he hauled her up with only the strength of his right forearm.

The three elder Latche brothers had built an enviable fortress complete with electricity, mini refrigerator and sleeping bags.

"What did I have to say?" Cherry helped open the sleeping bags. Holden offered her a Ginger-ale. Three minutes later they were spread out, having a picnic. "Let me see. I don't think I said anything you don't already know. I wasn't involved so I'm not exactly in the same category." She paused to catch his eye. "If I would have been here then, we wouldn't be having this conversation, because I wouldn't be here now."

"Did you tell Pattycakes not to be here?"

"Pattycakes has a mind of her own, Holden."

"Did you?"

"No." She replied with enough pout to let him know she wasn't pleased.

"Good. Pattycakes and Wyatt belong together. Don't mess that up."

"Isn't this a conversation you should be having with Wyatt?"

"I did."

"Let me see if I have it straight. It's all right for you to be involved, but not me?"

"I'm not involved."

"You talked to Wyatt."

"He is my brother. Giving him moral support isn't the same thing as interfering."

"For you it's moral support. For me, it's interfering."

"You're getting snippy."

"You're being a jackass."

Her too serious expression made him smile. "The point is everybody knows how strongly you stand by your convictions. What you would do in this scenario is not what we want Pattycakes to do. Or Missy."

"Do you think what I would do is wrong?"

"It's not about right or wrong on the issue. It's about right or wrong as to whether they should stay together."

"Whether they should stay together? If that's the point, then it might be a good idea for Wyatt to make choices that don't jeopardize their future."

"You're right. It was a bad choice, but it was an old one. He didn't do this yesterday."

"I've never heard of a statute of limitation on messing around. She didn't find out until this morning so he gets a bye?"

Maybe it was the confines of the tree house. Maybe it was her proximity. Whatever. Her attitude was starting to arouse him. Of course, that happened about eighty percent of the time he was around her. It was either a good thing or too bad she didn't know it. He was never certain which.

She went on, oblivious. "You're all about protecting Wyatt. Do you care about Pattycakes or Missy at all?"

"Of course, I do. I don't want to see either of them unhappy. If Missy leaves Bruce or Pattycakes brakes up with Wyatt, they're going to be miserable too. They do love the men they're with."

"I guess it's too bad the men they're with don't love them in return. Did it ever occur to you, Missy and Pattycakes are already miserable?"

"That's because Mia is a slut~"

"Don't blame Mia. None of you were forced to sleep with her."

*Damn her lips.* The shiny lipstick made them look wet. "While you are protecting her, you may want to remember she doesn't like you. In fact, she'd like to get between us."

"I know that. What girl doesn't? That still doesn't make her accountable for Wyatt and Bruce choosing to hurt the women they claim to love."

He watched her throat work and felt the movement in his groin. He didn't want to talk anymore. He cut out the light. *To hell with Wyatt and Bruce.*

"Why are we in the dark?"

"So I can do this." He pressed his lips against hers. Her immediate response- to fit her hand in his hair, pulling him closer -made him instantly hard. He leaned into her, crowding her, forcing her backward. He was able to dominate her without actually covering her body. He wanted to cover her. He wanted to press into her, to plunge madly until he was buried, balls deep, not coming out until the ache he had become subsided. Perhaps, not even then.

Instead, he thrust his tongue like he wanted to thrust his member and let the images heating his brain melt one into the other.

Her answer was a needy moan. Her body was willing. Her body was wanting. But, Holden knew her mind, her heart. Cherry would only exchange her virginity for a wedding ring. To consider any other option was blasphemous.

She moaned again, pulling him closer, trusting his ability to restrain.

Holden licked her lips, nibbled at the corner of her mouth, imagining what he wanted to do while cursing the piece of his conscience that wouldn't let him do it. The underside of her jaw... the column of her throat...the back of her ear...he branded them all. With one hand, he massaged the material of her top away from her shoulder so he could taste her collarbone.

Her hands at his back and in his hair, had her breasts pressed against him. He could feel the hardened peaks. They were begging to be caressed. He would comply. Squirming beneath him, Cherry didn't know what she needed, but Holden did. He would give it to her: not everything, just enough...Enough to make her want more.

He fused their mouths together, silencing any protest before it could form. He slid his hand lower, undoing one button, two. That was all. That was enough. The cool of the night first, then the warmth of his breath as he kissed his way down her neck. Her nipples were not exposed, so she had no objection to his delicious, torturous administrations.

He slipped his tongue between the soft mounds of flesh not covered by the lace of her bra. All skin not safely hidden was fair game and he was an experienced hunter.

Of its own accord, her body moved faster. She held him to her, wanting him to do more, trusting that he would not.

•  •  •  •  •

"What else is there to say?"

Cherry stiffened and Holden cursed. He wasn't ready to stop.

"If you give me a chance, you might find out." Wyatt's voice carried across the night.

"I'm here, aren't I?" Pattycakes said. "I agreed to let you drag me out here, didn't I?"

They stopped at the picnic table, on the far side of the tree house.

"I had to beg you to listen to me for five minutes."

"And that's all you're getting." Pattycakes looked at the time on her cell phone.

\*

"What do we do?" Cherry whispered, panicked.

"Shhh." Holden knew what horrors were running through her mind. For Cherry, having someone think she had sex was almost as bad as actually having it. Not that anybody on the farm would care. He kissed her lightly, half hoping to divert her attention.

\*

There's something I want to say to you." Wyatt cleared his throat. "I've been thinking...about...about something Cherry said~"

"Don't you go busting on Cherry again, Wyatt. I'm not putting up with that. This is about what you did and nothing else~"

\*

Cherry tried to sit up.

Holden clamped his hand over her mouth, ignoring the fire in her eyes. He pushed her down and pinned her with his weight. Whatever Wyatt had to say, he was going to say it without Cherry's opinions.

\*

"Let me talk." Wyatt shushed her. "I'm not busting on Cherry. This is about something she said that I agree with." He cleared his throat again. "Cherry thinks I'm a dog~"

"You are."

"That I'm as bad as Bruce."

*

Cherry nodded but otherwise remained still. Holden felt it safe to remove his hand from her mouth. He kept her pinned just in case...and because it was pleasurable.

*

"What's your point, Wyatt?" Pattycakes checked the time again.

"My point is..." He heaved a sigh. "My point is, I think she's right."

All three listeners drew back, surprised.

"That's not who I want to be. I don't want to be like that. You deserve a better man." Now that he had begun, Wyatt let the words tumble out, exactly the way he felt them. "Cherry told Amy love was about choosing. Pattycakes, I choose you. I love you." He held her hands. "All I kept thinking about was that this was the thing that was going to be too much for you. That you finally had enough. I didn't want you to talk to Cherry because I know what she thinks, she'd be gone. I was afraid you would decide to leave me." He slid to his knees. "Probably the best thing is for you to leave me, but I'm scared. I don't know what I'll do if you go." One more deep breath. "I don't want you to go. I want to marry you, Roslyn. I want to give you the love you deserve. I don't ever want to take a chance on losing you."

"Wyatt?"

"I know. It's not what you were expecting. I don't have the ring yet. We can go get it tomorrow. Please, I want to get married."

"Are you doing this to get out of trouble?"

"Hell yes." He stood up. "I don't ever want to be in this kind of trouble again. I don't want to be with another woman. I want to get married. If I'm Isaiah's father, I want you to be his stepmother. If not, I want to have my own kids with you. I want to never hurt you again. I want to be a better man than I've been. I want to do what I should have done a long time ago. I want us to get married." He kissed her then, more in control of himself. Now that he had decided, it was a done deal. All he had to do was convince Pattycakes.

Pattycakes did not require a lot if convincing. She was finally getting what she had waited her whole life for. Wyatt proposed. What else mattered? "Oh, Wyatt..."

He had his answer. He knew it.

\*

Cherry wasn't exactly sure of how she felt about Wyatt's timing. However, seeing as it wasn't her business, she didn't dwell on it. Instead, she let her romantic heart melt with happiness for Pattycakes.

"Like I said," Holden whispered. "Everybody should listen to you." He avoided her comeback, by licking her throat.

"Mmmm." That felt too good for her to mess it up with a comment.

Four distinct ringtones sounded at once. Someone had texted them all at the same time.

"Who the hell is in the tree house?" Wyatt called out.

"Congratulations," Holden answered, reaching for his cell.

It was the same message to all of them from Amy: `Daddy is in trouble. Eric called 911.`

# CHAPTER 21

The waiting room at Jefferson Hospital was crowded with the Latche clan. CW had a heart attack. He was currently undergoing bypass surgery. There wasn't a whole lot to say or do. Just the waiting.

Bruce stayed home with Tabby and Brucey, leaving Missy free to be with her family. She sat on one side of Claire, Elizabeth on the other, and Amy one seat away. Across from them, Wyatt and Pattycakes refereed the tabletop football match Cory and Hunter were having across the magazine table. Holden and Eric were putting Cherry's identifying abilities to the test. Between the two of them they had a small collection of photos on their phones. She had gotten more right than wrong. So far, she had the best record of anybody except CW.

"How do you know?" Eric arched his left eyebrow; an exact Holden imitation.

"Like I'm going to tell you that."

Cocking his head in Eric-fashion, Holden asked, "How do you know I'm Holden? We may have been messing with you."

"I checked your driver's license."

Eric whipped two ID's out of his wallet. "This one or this one?" The same person was pictured, but the names were reversed: Eric Holden Latche on one, Holden Eric Latche on the other.

Holden pulled out an identical set. Cherry stared incredulous. As far as she could tell, the same person was in all four photos. She had no idea which twin posed. "You two are juvenile in the extreme. This has to be illegal."

"No more illegal than anything else we've done," Holden said.

"Like today," Eric added.

"What did you do today?" Amy had been listening.

"The same thing we always do when tests are involved."

"What would that be?" Cherry asked her boyfriend's brother.

Amy knew. "You switched your information on the paternity tests."

"Not all of it." Holden grinned.

"—We didn't switch the date of birth."

"—Height. Weight."

"—Eye color."

"No," Holden corrected. "I switched my eye color for yours."

"Damn." Eric snapped his fingers. "Everything is going to be messed up now."

"Watch your mouth, Eric," Claire said.

"I'm Holden."

"Sorry. Watch your mouth, Holden."

"I didn't say anything."

"You two."

The twins laughed.

"Juvenile is right." Missy reached for a magazine.

"I'm going to see if they have any information yet." Claire stood up.

"Can I go with you?" Elizabeth asked.

"Of course." They left together.

To dispel the heaviness that came with Claire's departure, Holden said, "Hey Wyatt, don't you have something you want to tell us?"

"I don't think this is the best time for it."

"I disagree. If we ever needed some good news, it would be now."

"All right." Wyatt leaned forward. "I want to announce that Cherry finally gave in. Holden got laid."

Missy's 'what?' Amy's 'huh?' Cherry's 'NO!' Cory and Hunter's 'ohhhhhh', Pattycakes' 'Wy-att' and Eric's laughter blended into a collage of chaotic sound.

"Very funny." Holden shot Wyatt a look.

Wyatt blew him a kiss. "That's not it. As far as I know, Holden's still horny." He grinned at Cherry's blood-red cheeks. "Payback." He blew her a kiss too. "The real news is that Holden and Cherry were eavesdropping and heard me propose to Pattycakes. We're getting married."

Most everyone was genuinely happy for the news. Most. Missy's jaw fell. She stared at Pattycakes, disbelieving. Pattycakes dropped her gaze to the floor.

Wyatt stiffened. "You got a problem with it, Missy?"

"You're a dick, Wyatt."

"Do you have a point, or just a bunch of attitude?"

Missy ignored him, focusing instead on Pattycakes. "What are you thinking?"

"I love him. I want to be his wife."

"This is because of what he did with YOUR cousin. He doesn't care about you."

"Missy, shut the hell up." Wyatt raised his voice. "You don't know nothing."

"I know she wanted to cut your balls off this morning. So you used your ace. Do you have a ring? Is this something you were planning? Or did you realize how bad you screwed up and pulled out the big guns? How long are you going to drag out the engagement? Ten years? Fifteen? Until you can't get out of trouble again?"

Eric was close enough to see Pattycakes's eyes film over. "Why don't you knock it off, Missy. Don't begrudge her happiness because you want an ally."

That was it. The realization knocked the fight out of her. Eric had reached in and yanked her pain out so everyone could see it. She flicked the moisture out of her eye.

Amy, Cherry and Pattycakes reached her in a one, two, three succession. They crowded and hugged her.

"You still have allies." Cherry ran a soothing hand along Missy's arm.

"We're always going to be on your side," Amy said. "No matter how stupid you are."

"Yeah," Pattycakes added. "I haven't forgiven Wyatt. I'm not disregarding what he did. But, I do love him. I'm aligning myself more with you. I'm putting myself in the same impossible, stupid position."

Missy brushed the dampness off her cheek "Are you going to let the jerk get you pregnant?"

"I'll get right on that as soon as Cherry relinquishes the tree house."

"Is that where he had you? Eww." Amy made a yuk face.

"That's how you know nothing happened. Two sodas and a sleeping bag will not be the background memory for my first time."

"I don't know." Pattycakes sighed. "I've got some good tree house memories."

"Should I remind you that you're in love with a jerk?" Amy said.

"That's true." Pattycakes nodded. "If I was strong like you, Cherry, I wouldn't have to put up with so much."

"Me either," Missy agreed.

"You're both strong enough." Cherry gave them a double hug. "It's not your fault they're scum."

"And, don't put up with it anymore." Amy joined the ring.

Cory looked from Wyatt to Eric to Holden. Each brother's face reflected his own confusion. Giving up, Cory returned his attention to the tabletop football game.

The elder brothers were all thinking the same thing: this was not exactly wedding announcement conversation. However, they were smart enough to keep quiet.

·  ·  ·  ·  ·

Having come through the surgery successfully didn't make CW as happy as it should have. In the days to follow, he became overwhelmingly concerned about his mortality. The hospital Chaplain and the Priest from St. James the Greater Catholic Church, became frequent visitors.

# CHAPTER 22

"D-day!" Amy's voice echoed down the hall as she came in carrying the mail. "Where is everybody?"

Missy bounced down the stairs with Brucey on her hip. "Mom is at the hospital. Eric and Eli are riding fences. Holden is in the barley field. Bruce is fixing the green paddy harvester and Wyatt is doing the Mill run. Who do you need?"

"All of them." She held up five envelopes. "They're from Hydrochem Lab. Will the real procreator please stand up?"

Missy pulled two from Amy's hand. "Oooh. I don't know if I can wait."

"Me either. I think I'm going to accidently open them."

"No. Don't do that. They'll be up for lunch. Pattycakes and Cherry are still in class. If we wait, they'll have time to get here."

"I'm texting them right now." Amy reached for her cell. "Class is over for the day."

. . . . .

"Hey, Babe." Holden leaned down to get a kiss.

"Nice try." Cherry backed away. "Do you want a sandwich?"

"I do. Nice try for what?" He washed his hands at the kitchen sink. "What do you have against kissing me today?"

Cherry went to the refrigerator. "I have something against kissing you every day."

Amy collected a plate and a knife for Cherry. "If I were Holden, I would beat you silly, Eric, every time you stole my name."

"What'd I steal? Holden is my name. So is Eric. So is Latche. Don't blame that on me. It was Mom's idea."

"What was she thinking?" Amy crinkled her brow as if they were discussing a serious matter. "Anyway, pertinent business~"

When Cherry sat his plate down, he grabbed her by the waist and forced her to sit on his lap. "About that kiss? I'll take it if I have to."

He held her possessively, comfortably familiar with her body. It registered immediately. *Not Eric.* Cherry didn't struggle. Her eyes quickly accepted what her soul already knew. "Holden."

"Eric had better not be trying to kiss you." That said, he pulled her close. She came eagerly and let him take what he wanted.

"Aww, gross," Amy whined. "People have to eat in here, you know."

Once satisfied, Holden released Cherry so he could turn his attention to his other need. Lunch. He bit into his sandwich and had a swig of his drink before he was ready to be social. "Did English get cancelled?"

"Yes. By Amy." She pointed to the culprit.

He arched his left eyebrow.

"Been trying to tell you since you walked in. You got mail." Amy offered him his envelope.

He looked at the label. "Hmmm. Where's Eric?"

"No. No. No. You can't do this to me, Holden," Amy whined some more. "Open it now."

"Where's Eric?"

She sighed. "Since you're not him, I guess he'll be here in a minute."

"Where's Wyatt?"

"Celebrating with Pattycakes." Cherry showed him the two opened letters. "So are Bruce and Missy, presumably."

Holden glanced at the results. "I guess that's two down."

"If you'd open yours we'd find out about number three." Amy waved his unopened mail.

He took it from her and set it aside. "I'll open it when Eric gets here."

"Why?"

"They're his results."

"Then open his."

"They're his results too."

The argument was halted when Eric walked in, Eli a step behind. "Hey. Is somebody going to be nice enough to make me a sandwich?"

"Me too." Eli put out his cigarette.

"Yeah, yeah, yeah. We'll get your lunch." Amy grabbed the bread. "Open your mail."

For a minute and a half, the only sounds to be heard were the scraping of the mayonnaise jar and the tearing of envelopes. Eli's yelp of delight was easy to interpret. "Apparently, that Y-thing ain't everything." He dug into his sandwich with gusto.

Neither Holden nor Eric said anything.

"Well?" Amy slammed Eric's plate down.

"Mean anything to you?" One twin asked.

"You got me," said the other.

"Well?" Amy said again.

Holden gave his results to Cherry. "One test says yes. The other says no."

Eric offered his to Amy. "Mine is just the opposite. One no, one yes."

"How can that be?" Amy looked back and forth between the paper she held and the one in Cherry's hand. The stats were identical, right down to the probability.

Cherry pointed to a line of explanation. "He's definitely a relative; i.e., one of them is an uncle." She pointed to a different line. "But, they don't have a paternal match."

"But see here." Amy flipped to a second page. "Isaiah's Y chromosome is an exact match. He got his peepee from one of them."

"One of these tests has to be wrong." Cherry studied the pages.

"Or confused. The way they mix up their information. It's no wonder. They're probably going to have to retest."

"Probably," Holden agreed.

"This time make sure you get the eye-color right," Eric said.

Cherry was still thinking. "Even switched, the test shouldn't con...tra...dict...Hey, wait a minute." She took both tests results, gathered Eli, Wyatt and Bruce's, and retreated to the counter where she laid them out side by side.

Amy poured lemonade and opened a bag of waffle chips. The guys ate and talked about the farm, seemingly unconcerned with Cherry's study until she gasped.

"What?" Holden was on his feet as if he had been waiting for a reason to get up.

"Nothing. Sorry." Her wide eyes said there was definitely something.

"You lie like shit." Amy pulled out a chair, indicating that Cherry should sit.

Holden grabbed the test results and led her back to the table.

"It really isn't anything."

"You do lie like shit," Eric said. "Out with it."

*I do not lie like shit.* She took a deep breath. "Isaiah is your son, Holden." She chewed on her fingernail.

"Is he?" Holden didn't believe her. Nobody believed her. "How do you figure that, Miss Brookfield?"

She ignored the warning in his use of her last name. "This proves it." She held up his test. "It's a little confusing, but it's all there." *See. I know how to lie.*

"You figured that out from the tests?" Eric imitated Holden's left eyebrow arch.

"Yes, Eric. I did. Isaiah is Holden's son."

"You mean my son."

"Holden's son."

"Did you forget Holden's name is on my blood work?"

*Damn it.* She did forget. "It doesn't matter. Your tests are the same. If you want, he can belong to both of you. But he's Holden's baby. Mia knows it and so do I."

"Is there something you want to talk to me about?" Holden leveled his blue-green gaze at Cherry.

At that moment, the back door opened. Claire walked into the kitchen.

147

"Oh good. You girls took care of lunch. I was afraid I wasn't going to get back in time. There are some cookies in the pantry. Top shelf."

The Hellos and hey Moms rang around the room. Eli found the cookies.

"How's Dad?"

"He looks pretty good today. What are you all up to?" She busied herself with the beginnings of dinner.

"Paternity tests came back," Amy said.

Cherry, ambivalently watching Claire, noticed her stiffen.

Amy went on, unaware. "Apparently, Holden's a daddy."

"Oh. OH." At first relieved then excited, she turned to Holden. "I'm a grandma."

"You've been a grandma and that's not a fact."

"Why not?"

"The tests aren't conclusive but Cherry seems to think they are."

"She was going to explain it to us when you came in." Eric shot Cherry an assured glance.

Instead of answering, Cherry handed the paternity tests to Claire.

Claire looked at the papers and visibly blanched. She sank down into the nearest chair.

"Mom?"

"Mom? Are you okay?"

Now, everyone was paying close attention to her.

"I'm...I'm fine. I'm not sure exactly what I'm reading." She locked frightened eyes on Holden's girlfriend.

Cherry cleared her throat. "It seems pretty clear to me. Holden should accept responsibility and we should not put...Isaiah through anymore. He's a Latche and that's all that matters."

"What about you?"

"I'm ready for it." Cherry smiled her encouragement. "I think I would make a good stepmother." She sighed dramatically. "*If*, I can convince your son to marry me."

Claire returned the smile. "He better marry you."

That they were sharing a secret communication was clear to Holden.

"I'm still waiting to hear why you're so certain I'm Isaiah's father."

"Especially since you gleaned your information from my blood work," Eric said.

*She wasn't going there. She wasn't going there. She wasn't.* "Look, call it an instinct. The numbers add up to me. We all know it's one of you. Mia named you, Holden. She would know best. We need to drop it and move on." She got up from the table. "I have to get back to school. I have a paper due. I'll call you later." Then she kissed Holden like he was the most important man in the world. "See ya." She slipped out the door before his brain slid back into place.

· · · · ·

The phone call that came forty minutes later did not surprise Cherry. "Hi, Claire. How are you holding up?"

"Cherry. I don't know what to say. What must you be thinking?"

"I'm not thinking anything. Honestly."

"I know you're busy. But I was wondering if we could meet for a cup of coffee. I'd like a chance to explain."

"You don't owe me any explanations, Claire. Trust me, I'm no judge."

"Thank you, Sweetie. Still, I'd like to explain anyway. You deserve an explanation."

"All right. I'm not going to lie. I so want to know. Where do you want to meet?"

"I'd feel better coming up there."

"The Blue Moon Café is open."

"I'll be there in about fifteen minutes."

"I'll get us a table."

· · · · ·

The dank little college hangout was crowded but not overly so. It was a comfort. Life was still going on. The world hadn't come to an end.

"Let me start by saying this." Claire added creamer to her cup. "I'm amazed at how fast you pieced it all together."

Cherry hunched her shoulders. "It was probably because I was staring at all the tests together."

"However you did it. I can't thank you enough for you discretion. This is a mess."

"I feel like I should apologize to you. Technically, it's not my business."

"I think it is."

"If I wouldn't have noticed...And CW. His condition has to be taken into consideration."

Claire frowned into her cup. "He can't get enough of the clergy these days. He must have had his own suspicions." She gave herself a mental shake. "But this isn't about him, at least not yet. Let me tell you about me." Claire sat her coffee aside. "CW is a good man. A good father. A good provider. But my boys get it honestly. He could never be faithful. He tried. He loves me. But, he could never do it. He wasn't faithful before we got married. Just like Bruce. Worse than Wyatt." She glanced away then back at Cherry. "Holden and Eric are better men, trust me. Anyway, I foolishly thought marriage would change things. I guess that's where Missy got it from. We hadn't been married two years. I was devastated." Her eyes moved around the room, not actually seeing it. "I wasn't planning revenge, I wasn't planning anything. I just wanted to feel better. I drove for hours that night and ended up in a diner in Pennsylvania." She didn't say anything for a while.

Cherry sipped her coffee, not daring to interfere.

"His name was David. He was a soldier. Said he was on leave. He said I was pretty. He made me feel special. For those few hours, I mattered." She paused. Her green eyes held Cherry's attention. "I'd like to say I regret it, but I don't. I did at first. But I don't regret Wyatt. And, I don't regret knowing that I mattered. It may have only been one or two hours, but I was the one who was wanted."

"So, you already knew...about Wyatt."

"I was never positive. I have never been in contact with David since. When CW found out I was pregnant, it changed him...temporarily. He was a family man. He was going to have a son. He never left me alone for a minute. He loved me. I decided my infidelity was only as important as his was. It didn't matter anyway. CW was his daddy. When he got his first son, it was everything. My life was everything I had dreamed of. It stayed that way for a while. He didn't stray again until after the twins were born. I never strayed again, period."

"Were you concerned when all of this came up? The paternity tests?"

"You know, that's the odd part. I didn't think about it until much later. It hadn't occurred to me at first and then with CW's heart attack." She hunched her shoulders. "I knew it was possible, but I wasn't expecting those results. Wyatt is so much like his father. But the proof. He doesn't have any connection to Isaiah at all, while the twins are overwhelmingly connected. Even Eli. It shocked me that you noticed, but it surprised me more that you seemed to be the only one."

"What are you going to do about it?"

"I'm not certain. It's going to kill Wyatt if he finds out."

"How are they not going to figure it out? The tests are right there."

"People have a way of seeing only what they want to see. Wyatt is not Isaiah's father. I bet he'll never look at those tests results again."

Cherry wasn't reassured but choose not to comment.

"The bigger issue, for you anyway, is Holden...and Eric."

"What do you mean?"

"What are you going to tell him?"

"What should I tell him?"

"When it comes to someone you love, the best way to avoid messes like my life, is to stick with the truth. I will treasure what you tried to do for me, but you can't make him be a father when he's not."

"He'd do it for you."

"He shouldn't have to."

# CHAPTER 23

Cherry took her time walking through the barley. She needed time to think of what she was going to say. So far, she had no idea. Sooner than she wanted to be, she reached the clearing. Eric was there. *Of course. Holden probably called him the second I hung up.*

They were working the field together. They saw her and stopped the tractors almost at the same time. There wasn't a thing different about them except their t-shirts. She remembered the first day she saw them: the Sun and the Sun. She walked toward the brown-shirt Sun.

Brown-shirt remained seated. Red-shirt climbed down and moved toward his brother's tractor. It was a good indication she picked the correct twin. "Hi," she said when she was close enough.

"We'll see." Eric picked her up and handed her to Holden.

Holden had her seated on his lap before she could react.

Eric followed her up and perched himself on the large red hood.

"Now." Holden wrapped an arm around her waist. "What the hell is going on?"

Cherry couldn't help but laugh. "You are all about getting to the point, aren't you?"

"You don't have any idea how bizarre you were today, do you?" Eric plopped his hat down on her head.

"You don't have any idea how bizarre this is. I'm keeping your hat, just so you know." She adjusted it to her comfort.

"I don't care. It's Holden's hat. Why do you think Isaiah is our kid?"

The way Eric said 'our' went through Cherry. Of course, he would be here. Holden's problems were his problems and vice-versa. "I don't think Isaiah belongs to either one of you. But he's got to belong to someone. And you can't get retested. We've got to put these blood issues to rest."

"Hold on," Holden said. "Don't get worked up. Tell us what you saw in our results."

"And," Eric added. "Why you didn't tell us to begin with."

Following Holden's orders, Cherry took a deep breath. "I saw a couple of things. I couldn't tell you to begin with. All I had were suspicions. I wasn't going to make accusations without confirming anything."

"Did you get your confirmation?" Holden asked.

"I did. I wish I didn't know this. I wish I didn't have to tell you. But you have a right to know."

Neither brother spoke. They waited for her to get to where she could say.

"It's Wyatt." She didn't realize she was whispering. "He's not CW's son."

"What?" They sounded so much alike, it could have been one voice.

"Your mom had a small affair. He's got a different dad." She studied her feet.

For a while, nobody said anything.

When he could form a thought, Holden asked, "Are you sure?"

"Yes."

"What the hell is a small affair?" Eric pulled his hands through his hair.

Cherry made herself look up. "Your dad messed around on her first. He's done that a lot." When they didn't show signs of surprise, she went on. "They hadn't been married long. She was hurt and looking for comfort, retaliating. It was only the one time. CW kept doing it."

"So that means she's excused? She had a baby by another man."

"I don't know if she's excused or not, Eric, but you can reel in that double standard. If you want to judge somebody, start with your father. He started it."

"My father didn't get a married woman pregnant."

"No. He got a teenager pregnant, instead." She glared at one shocked face and then the other. "Isaiah didn't get his Y chromosome from either of you. He got it from the same place you got yours. CW stressed himself into a heart attack. He was worried about getting caught this time."

Holden had been quiet. He remained that way, unsure of what to say, unknowing of what to think, no idea of what to do. Eric slid off the tractor and paced. He didn't know what to say, think, or do either, and he couldn't sit still long enough to figure it out.

"I'm sorry." Cherry went back to whispering to her feet. "I didn't want to know this stuff. When I realized it, I tried to make it go away. I thought if we could take care of Isaiah, no one would need to know. I'm so sorry."

In that instant, Holden knew one thing. Cherry was his sine qua non, the essential element of his existence. Slowly, reverently, he guided her face to his. He kissed her, needing to show her what she made him feel. "I love you," he whispered into her mouth, but it wasn't enough. He deepened the kiss, wanting her to know the fullness of his emotion. He couldn't contain it. He had to give it to her.

Cherry felt the heaviness leave her. She was forgiven and clean and cherished. Holden understood and he loved her. She had no doubt about that. She could feel it washing over her. It was strong and pure and loyal and true. It was all that he was. It was all that she wanted.

Thump!

"Ugghhh..."

They were startled apart by a clump of dirt. Eric nailed Holden in the back. "Go find a haystack." He returned to his perch on the hood. "So this is what I'm thinking. We let them decide. Pop can deal with his kid and Mom can deal with hers. If he wants us to take his fall, so be it. If she wants Wyatt ignorant, so be it. But, they have to make the decision. I'm not."

"That's the best thing I've heard all day." Holden nodded. "I can live with that."

Eric found his cell phone. "Amy. Do you have a way to get in touch with Mia? ...Good. Will you call her and find out when she can bring me my son? ...My son, Holden's son, same difference. Ask her if he can stay for a few days... Thanks." He hung up.

"A few days?" Holden asked.

"I want to take him to the hospital to officially meet his...err...grandfather." He took his hat back.

.  .  .  .  .

Cherry rode behind Holden as he and Eric finished the barley. The three were the last to make it back to the house.

Claire watched with trepidation as the trio ascended the steps. Cherry stopped in front of her. The boys walked by pausing only to plant a kiss on her left and right cheeks before going into the house. Claire filled up with tears and struggled to blink them back. She cleared her throat and said, "I was thinking about the summer. Things tend to get crazy busy around here. I don't know what your plans are but it would be nice if you wanted to stay here when school is out. After you've had a good visit at home, of course. It would help us a lot and truthfully, I can't bear the thought of not having you around for three whole months."

"I hadn't thought about it," Cherry said with fluffy falseness. "Today."

Claire grinned.

"If it's not too much trouble, I can't bear the thought of leaving either."

Claire pulled Cherry into a tight embrace, sagging with relief and so much gratitude.

Cherry returned the hug full of affection for her wounded, wounding, hurt, healing, soon-to-be (she hoped) mother-in-law.

.  .  .  .  .

Inside, instead of preparing for dinner, Holden collected things from the pantry.

"What are you doing?" Missy was attempting to set the table and had to keep moving to get out of his way.

"I'm making dinner for Cherry tonight. The bunkhouse isn't stocked."

"Oh. Special occasion?"

"I'm in love. Is that special enough for you?"

"It's nice to know that romance isn't totally dead in this house. The last dinner I got from Bruce was Subway."

"At least it was healthy."

"Not really. It was a meatball marina."

"You can't win can you?"

"No."

The sound was lost behind the flushing of the downstairs toilet. "What did I do now?" Bruce came out without having touched the sink. His question went unanswered.

"Stay away from the bunkhouse." Holden found a bag for his supplies. "Pass that on to Eli and Wyatt. You too, Eric." Holden recognized his twin's footfall.

"Why?" Eric came down the hall with Tabby on his back.

Claire and Cherry came in the back door. Holden pierced her with blue-green heat. "Cherry and I are going to be there for the rest of the night."

"What's that mean?" Bruce tried to stick his finger into Missy's Alfredo sauce.

Missy slapped his hand.

Eric said, "It means, find somewhere else to go."

"It means stay the hell away from the bunkhouse."

"Watch your mouth, Uncle Eric." Tabby imitated her grandmother.

"It means stay the heck away from the bunkhouse," Holden corrected.

"Good boy."

. . . . .

Holden had Cherry slice vegetables while he showered. They had drinks – rum and coke for him, amaretto sour for her- while she watched him cook. Crab stuffed haddock, steamed corn fresh off the cob and zucchini, roasted baby portabella mushrooms, homemade rolls (a frozen batch from Claire's deep freezer), raspberry shortcake with whip cream and a chilled chardonnay. His intention was to impress and romance her. He exceeded his goal.

Later, on the bunkhouse balcony, she lay in the circle of his arms as they reclined in the hammock and watched the stars, one by one, fill the night sky. For the first time in Holden's memory, time alone with a girl wasn't shadowed by thoughts of undressing her. The sex was there, in his head- it was always there, but tonight, it wasn't important. What mattered to him were her thoughts, her voice, the feel of her cuddled against him. She was his sine qua non, the essential element of his existence.

He played with her hair, never tiring of the color. Slight waves and a few bouncy curls today – always exotic. "Did you have a lot of racial stuff to deal with growing up?"

Her laughter was rich, half muffled by his chest. "All the time. From all sides. But I wouldn't change a thing. As kids, we learned the greatest racial lesson in the world."

"Which was?"

"When it comes to race, everybody is full of it."

The unexpected comment made him chuckle. "I bet you're right."

"I am. Bi-racial children get to see the junk on both sides. I'm quartered. I saw four times as much crap. Oh, the poor babies. They're all misunderstood. They all think they know what everyone is thinking about them. And, they all have it wrong." Warming to her subject, Cherry continued. "Take the black/white thing. That one is easy because it's always in your face."

He nodded his agreement, noting her animation. This was a topic she favored.

"For a white person, racial usually implies the pre-civil rights definition: Oh, look. There's a black person. Let's beat it, rape it, lynch it, whatever, because it's black. That's all the reason you need." She hunched a shoulder. "Nowadays, you probably won't find too many white people who think like that. It's beyond ridiculous. Most of them don't have anything against black people. They'll tell you about their black friends, all that generic crap."

"It's not generic," Holden said. "It's the truth. For me, anyway. I don't think of my black friends differently than I do my white friends. They're just people. And black women, well..." He patted her thigh. "You've got that going on."

157

She rocked into him, enjoying the contact. "That's the problem. When black people say racial, they're not talking about any of those things." She sensed his puzzlement. "Black people are primarily talking about negative stereotypes and first impressions: There's a black guy walking down the street. Is he up to no good? There's a black woman with three kids. Is she on welfare? Do they have different fathers? When something bad happens because someone is trying to answer a stereotype question; that's racial for a black person."

"That sounds like two separate conversations."

"It is."

"Hmm. I've got to process that for a minute."

"Add this to your processing. According to the white, pre-civil rights definition of racial, black people come across as more prejudice than whites. They don't think any of you know jack because you don't understand what they're talking about when *they* say racial."

"Who gave you the harder time?"

"Depends on what I'm wearing and who I'm talking to when I'm wearing it. Black people have trust issues. White people have judgment issues. Koreans have identity issues~"

"Identity issues? Aren't Koreans supposed to be smart?" he teased.

She nudged him. "Judgmental white boy. They get sick of being called Chinese or Japanese or Vietnamese. Even if they were born and raised here, people assume they're outsiders. Once, when she was in high school, Peaches got accused of taking jobs from Americans. The funny thing was the girl who said it was talking to Beany. You should have seen her face when she found out they were related."

"Were you and your siblings close growing up?"

"We were. Had to be. The mutt club is sparse."

"Elite."

. . . . .

Cherry was asleep when Holden heard the door slam. He peered over the side of the balcony. Claire's bedroom light was on and Wyatt was stomping across the yard. He didn't get into his truck, but turned toward the orchard. Holden took it for a good sign. With the least amount of movement possible, he swung out of the hammock and covered Cherry with a blanket thick enough to replace his body heat. He grabbed a six-pack of Budweiser from the refrigerator on his way out.

Eric was in the yard by the time he got there, toting a six-pack of Budweiser from the house. "I thought to give him a five-minute head start."

"He's in the orchard."

"Let's go."

· · · · ·

Cherry was still asleep when they ran out of beer and had to come back to the bunkhouse for more. They kept the party relatively quiet, alternating between serious and nonsense topics. They were doing the only thing they could: joking and philosophizing, breathing through the pain in their masculine way. Taking the blow together, side by side by side with beer for a band-aid.

Victory came with the first darts of daylight. Getting to the morning meant they could get to another one. That was all they had to do -get to another day by any means possible. They celebrated with more beer until Eric passed out on the sofa and Wyatt stumbled back to the main house. Holden slid back into the hammock grateful that Cherry hadn't been disturbed. Grateful, also that it wasn't his day to feed the animals. He was tired. The corn could wait.

· · · · ·

Nine thirty a.m. It was late by farming standards when Amy came to the bunk house. Holden and Cherry were having breakfast –Holden's to die for western omelets, Italian sweet sausage, fresh slices of cantaloupe and watermelon, rye toast and French roast coffee – when she came in. Eric was somewhat awake, but not inclined to move.

"I got tired of waiting for you to come up to the house. Ohhh that smells so good. Holden, please feed your baby sister."

"Is Elizabeth hungry?" Holden took his plate over to the stove so he could eat while he worked.

"I said baby sister, not baby alien. Anyway, these are yours." She handed Cherry several bags. "I need somebody to look at my car. Yesterday, it was making a funny noise."

"Your car makes a funny noise about once a month," Holden talked over the sizzling pan. "It's just like you on your period."

"Instead of looking at your car, you should get somebody to teach you how to drive." Eric called out from the couch.

Amy ignored them, focusing instead on Cherry.

"What is all this?"

"It's what you are wearing today. And...some other stuff I caught on sale." Ignoring Holden's incredulous look, she said, "Now, you'll have some stuff already here should you stay over unexpectedly. Or for the summer." She smiled.

So did he.

"You heard?" Cherry watched for Holden's reaction.

Eric said, "We all heard."

"It wasn't news." Holden winked at her.

Cherry felt warm.

"Back to me." Amy pinched a bite from Cherry's plate.

"Thank you, Amy. I was just getting ready to leave. I guess now I don't have to go."

"Thank Holden. He sent me shopping."

"Holden!" Cherry gasped. "You shouldn't have."

"As long as I didn't have to pick it out." He shrugged. "I'm not ready for you to leave yet." He was never going to be ready for her to leave, but that was beside the point.

Amy waved Holden away. "He hates shopping. Are you going to look at your stuff?" She ruffled a bag. "I want to hear about what great taste I have."

"I can tell you what a big mouth you have," Eric said. "I hope you're cooking double, Holden. If not, I'm taking Amy's. Thanks to her, I'm awake."

"I don't think so." Amy helped herself to Cherry's orange juice.

"Did you get her some apple bottoms?"

"Because you would know what they are." Cherry and Amy responded to Eric at the same time with the same comment.

"I know the song."

"Don't sing it. Please." Amy rolled her eyes.

Cherry sifted through the bags. Amy didn't forget anything, right down to the toiletries. "You thought of everything, didn't you?" She pulled out a lacy top. "This is pretty."

"I know. That's why you got it. You should see the one I got for me. And, of course, I thought of everything. That's why he sent me."

Holden had cooked double. "Eric. Food." He sat one plate down in front of Amy and another before a vacant chair. "You used my truck last night. You didn't even drive your car."

"Because it was making a funny noise."

"Do I want to know how much you spent?"

"Dude. When you see her all dressed up, you'll be thanking me."

# CHAPTER 24

Holden did thank Amy. Cherry was always beautiful to him. Always. But there was something about knowing that she was wearing what she was wearing because of him. His satisfaction was the objective. It worked. He saw her through possessive vision and she was gorgeous. Unless Eric was feeling generous, the corn wasn't going to get done today.

Cherry helped him clean up breakfast and they hung out in the bunkhouse with no particular plans beyond him holding her while they watched the silly movie she had on. He silently contemplated the joy of stroking her hair and breathing her in. He toyed with her new dangly earrings and tickled her neck until his game of distraction became a distraction. Her neck didn't need to be tickled, it needed to be licked. So he licked it. She murmured her pleasure and he licked it again. This time he kept going, nibbling her jaw, her cheek and finally her mouth.

Her mouth was eager. She was eager. She wanted his attention as much as he wanted to give it to her. Cherry was soft and alluring, winding her arms around his neck, pulling him closer, tempting him beyond endurance. They slid down into the sofa cushions, everything about the moment felt one hundred percent right.

Eric walked in. "I bet that's fun."

Holden and Cherry broke apart. She was embarrassed, he was annoyed. "I'd say I'm sorry for interrupting, but I don't really care."

"What do you want, Eric?"

"Your baby's here. His momma is coming this way."

"So?"

"Your little display might make her jealous."

"So?"

Two minutes later, Mia let herself in. She held Isaiah in one arm, diaper bag and a small suitcase in the other. "Here's Daddy. Which one of you is Daddy?" she singsonged.

"Don't you knock?"

"Why are you always so rude to me, Eric?"

"I'm not Eric."

"Do you always walk into people's homes uninvited?"

"Your behavior invites rudeness."

"Come on, Holden. I've been in here a hundred times."

"I'm not Holden."

"How many times have you been in here, invited?"

"This is petty and pointless." Cherry stood up. "Hello Isaiah, you sweet little man. May I hold you?" She went for the child with open arms.

"Dadadada..." Isaiah cooed and stretched.

Mia stiffened. She drew the baby close and half turned away.

Having been so recently lavished with adoration, Cherry was emboldened. "Mia, I've been as nice to you as I can be. Now, I'm done. Holden is not available. I'm a part of this picture whether you like it or not. I'm sure you'll find that I am welcomed to play with the Latche children. There's not much you can do about it, unless no one here has any paternal rights to him."

"There's something I can do about it. As long as he's my baby, you better believe there is something I can do about it."

Both brothers came forward. "You can find him a father on another farm," Eric suggested.

"You can raise him yourself," Holden said. He slid Isaiah out of Mia's arms. "But you can't have it both ways. If he's a Latche, he's subject to Latche privilege."

He gave Cherry the baby.

"Privilege?" Mia fumed.

"I consider it a tremendous privilege to be in Cherry's arms."

Cherry muttered through her smirk, "This is about as productive as the last conversation."

"You started it."

She flashed his favorite dimple.

Mia handed Eric the suitcase. "I packed enough stuff for a week. He's a good baby, you shouldn't have to call me, but I'll probably be around."

There were a few seconds of silence, broken only by Isaiah's gurgles. Mia looked from one brother to the other, expectantly.

Holden arched his left eyebrow.

Eric cocked his head to the side. "What?"

"When are you going to tell me who's who and which one of you is Isaiah's daddy?"

Their identical grins were pure evil.

"Don't you know?"

"Didn't you get the test results?"

Mia shifted uncomfortably. "Yeah, umm. I wasn't too sure about what they meant. But, I know one of you is Isaiah's daddy. I know you know which one."

"Actually, I'm Isaiah's father."

All four people looked up, startled. Wyatt had come in. No one seemed to know what to say.

Isaiah did. "DADADADADADADADA..." He bounced up and down, reaching for Wyatt.

Wyatt strode forward to retrieve the waddler.

"DADADADADADADA..."

"That's right." Wyatt gave him a little bounce. "The fact of the matter, Mia, is you might want a twin, but Eric and Holden's tests are no more conclusive than anybody else's. They're his uncles, not his father."

"You're his father?" Mia was surprised but not altogether unhappy. Wyatt was a well-off, handsome Latche brother too.

"Do you see anybody else volunteering?"

"Umm...no...I...umm...I...thought Holden...or Eric...you have Roslyn. I heard you were getting married."

"We are. You should be grateful. His stepmother is already related to him. Pattycakes loves Isaiah. There won't be any conflict."

Mia sighed. It was the best she was going to get without telling the truth. And Wyatt wasn't married, yet.

"We're changing his name to Latche," Wyatt decided.

"DADADADADADA..."

Once Mia had given instructions she didn't linger. She'd been a mother for almost ten months. A week off was nice.

Wyatt had one small exchange with his brothers.

"Are you sure you want to do this?" Eric asked.

"It's the one thing I am sure about." Wyatt rocked his son. "Isaiah and I are the bookends of this shit. We have to stick together."

Holden said, "I guess having the same history will give you two some sort of special bond."

"I'm counting on it. Somebody has to teach him that as screwed up as we are, family is about more than just blood."

# THE END

# CHAPTER 25

Holden wasn't Jealous. He would not allow himself to become jealous. This was Eric. He and Eric were one and the same. They would always be one and the same. Eric would die before he would intentionally hurt Holden. Holden was more certain of that than he was of himself. Besides, if he did...Holden wouldn't think about that. THAT would never happen. Cherry was his girl. Eric knew Cherry belonged to him. There was no reason to be jealous. So Holden fought back the emotion every time it surfaced. Every. Single. Day.

· · · · ·

Coming out of the storage shed, he adjusted his baseball cap. His earring – a diamond stud – caught the sunlight and glittered. He stepped around Claire's flowerbed, keeping his eyes averted while he waited for Cherry's attack.

"Boo!" She jumped on his back, having snuck up on him from behind.

"I knew you were coming. Your brake pads are getting thin." He spun around fast.

"Ericccc!" She squealed, holding tight until he released her. "Now, I can't walk straight. Brake pads, huh? Is that what that noise is? You need to get right on that."

"You've been hanging out with Amy too much."

"Learning from the master. Where's Holden and what are you up to?"

"I'm right here."

She pursed her lips.

He held up his hands in mock surrender. "It's not my fault you thought I was Eric."

"Holden?"

His wicked laugh gave him away.

She punched him.

"Holden's riding fences. He asked if somebody would take you out." Looking left and right, he said, "I suppose it will have to be me."

"I suppose so, unless you want to be held accountable for me getting lost."

"It's not my fault you have no sense of direction."

"It will be." She punched him again, because it was fun. "I'll see to that."

"Definitely too much Amy-influence."

"And Missy. And Pattycakes. And Elizabeth. And Tabby. They've all got your number." She did an Amy imitation. "Dude."

"Do you want to ride with me to the mill first? I'll get you to him eventually."

"Sure. Let me go pee." She sprinted off into the house.

"Can she tell you and Holden apart?" Bruce walked around the side of the house. "Or are you two interchangeable as far as she's concerned?"

He readjusted his cap. "What are you whining about today?"

Bruce scratched his head. "Touchy. I must have hit a nerve. All I did was ask a question. I see Cherry pouring herself all over you like you were her man. I don't know. It makes me wonder if sometimes she thinks she got the wrong twin."

"Calling you an ass would be a compliment. Do you know why?" He didn't wait for an answer. "Because *you* got the wrong twin."

Bruce stopped short. He assumed it was Eric because he heard Cherry asking about Holden. But the fact was, he had no idea. He knew Eric was going to do the mill run, but that didn't mean anything. The twins switched something almost daily.

They also lied, all the time, when it came to their identity.

"Doesn't matter who you are," Bruce said. "She thinks she's with Eric. And that's making her real happy. So my question is still valid. Does she want to be with you or your brother?"

"And the answer is still valid. Calling you an ass would be a compliment." He went to the Ram with Bruce's comment creating an unnatural echo in his ears.

. . . . .

They fought over the radio all the way through town, more interested in arguing than the music. At the Mill, he dared her to carry some of the feed he was loading. After one fifty-pound bag, she ignored him. She made him buy her a root beer, and then she decided she wanted a float, so he had to stop again to buy her a vanilla milkshake to put her root beer in.

They were in a little bubble of magic. Clearly, she was enjoying his company. Every look she gave him, he interpreted as warm. Everything she said sounded seductive to him. After all of his months of wondering, finally, here was an opportunity to see if he had been reading her right. What was she really thinking? As they got closer to the farm, his focus became internal. For once, letting his imagination run free.

Cherry noted the quiet. "What are you thinking about?"

"I'm not sure you want to hear it."

"Of course I want to hear it."

He pulled onto the shoulder, cutting the engine. "I'm thinking about you."

"Me? What'd I do now?"

"The list is long, but I'm not worried about your activities at the moment."

"Enlightenment, *Dude*. You used to be great. Now, you're weird. What's going on?" She sucked the last of her drink down, making a loud slurping noise.

He breathed in, deciding to go with it. "Can I ask you a question?"

"Shoot."

"What was the difference? That first night. You didn't know us. Didn't know a thing about our personalities. You saw us at the same time."

Cherry thought about it. If the truth were known, she had often wondered herself. "Technically, I saw you first but he was the one who came after me."

"I wanted to meet you when I saw you, but you were on the phone."

She didn't know what to say so she tried to drink some more. The cup was completely empty. She gave a lot of attention to setting it down.

"I've thought about it, you know. Pretending to be him."

That one, she could respond to. "You pretend to be him all the time."

"I don't mean as a joke."

"I know the difference, Eric."

"Do you?"

"Yes. I do... Mostly."

"Not if we didn't want you to. Mom can't tell us apart when we don't want her to."

"The whole of your mother's existence isn't centered on one of you."

He cleared his throat. "You didn't know who you were with today, Babe."

Cherry's jaw dropped. Holden was sitting beside her, wearing his half smile, caressing her with his voice.

"Eric thinks if you had the opportunity, you'd go for him. I had to prove him wrong."

"You're doing a great job, ERIC, but I am not convinced." *Only partially.*

He arched his left eyebrow.

"Stop it. You're freaking me out."

"How do you want me to prove it? Kiss you? You should be able to tell the difference. Provided you haven't already kissed us both."

"Okay, now I know you're Eric. Holden would never suggest something so asinine."

The left eyebrow went up again. "Wouldn't I?"

"You, yes. Holden, no."

"Do you remember the first morning when I took you to breakfast? That was Eric."

170

*Absolutely not.* "Eric. I'm in love with Holden. I'm always going to be in love with Holden. I don't want anyone but Holden. I'm not even willing to settle for his devastatingly handsome, bad as hell brother, who would stoop to impersonation if he thought it would get him some attention. Holden is the one. Deal with it." To take the sting out of her rejection, Cherry leaned in to peck his cheek.

Faster than she could react and he could think, his cheek was turned and his lips were brushing against hers.

It wasn't altogether unpleasant.

Eric increased the pressure and gave in to his fantasy.

Cherry allowed it. Later, she would rationalize that she allowed it to call his bluff. To show him that only Holden could stir her. She allowed it because he was incorrigible. Much, much later, she would admit- to no one but herself- it wasn't altogether unpleasant. No, he wasn't Holden, but he was...Eric.

Eric was euphoric. The kiss had started out chaste. He meant it to be quick. But without realizing it, Cherry closed her eyes. She parted her lips. A silent acknowledgment that he too had some control over her will and...wants.

But Holden was too important, to both of them. Eric would only take so much advantage and he would never, ever, intentionally, with his thinking mind, hurt Holden. He pulled back, smiling this time, not with Holden's half-smile, but with his own full-blown, devilish smirk. "You're right, there's no way you could confuse him with me. I'm much better at it."

"You wish." She waved him off.

"You love him?"

"With my whole heart."

"Do you think it will it always be that way?"

"For my part, yes."

"Not even the perfect substitute will do?"

"He's irreplaceable."

"He's damned lucky, that's what he is."

Eric started the truck, half-wondering what had come over him, half-relieved to have the matter settled in his mind, in his heart. Cherry was

Holden's girl. He made a mental note to flatten Bruce's tires tonight.

. . . . .

Holden's cell blared from the front seat of his Silverado. It wasn't Cherry's ring. That was annoying. She should have been here by now. It was getting close to lunchtime. He planned to spend it with her. He had packed them a picnic, intending to surprise her. It was time. For the tenth or twelfth time today, he pulled out the engagement ring. Things had been feeling the slightest bit off-kilter. He concluded it was because it was time for them to move on to the next phase. The -to have and to hold- phase. He wanted to hold her more than anything. He wanted to wake up beside her. He wanted to have her with him every day, not just for lunch. *If* she would ever show up. He would give her a call when he was done with whoever was texting him.

It was Eli: `Ur grl. erics truk. whos lip actN? cn I git som? rofl.`

# CHAPTER 26

Holden's truck was in the yard when Eric and Cherry turned into the drive. Eric didn't stop, but pulled around to the barn.

"Aunt Cherry! Aunt Cherry!" Tabby ran toward them. "Come see! Come see!"

Cherry hopped out of the cab. "Come see what, Tabby-cat?" She caught the four-year-old and hoisted her onto her hip.

"The new horsey, Grandpa made. He pulled it out of his mommy's tummy. Like Brucey. He's got brown hair and I want to call him Sally because he's going to be a girl."

"Is that so?" Cherry laughed. "Let's go see." With Tabby in her arms, she went into the barn.

Eric didn't follow. He wanted Holden. Luck was with him, Holden was in the first place he looked- the bunkhouse.

Holden turned off the shower. He toweled himself vigorously, needing to put his energy somewhere. He opened the door unprepared to see Eric leaning against the wall waiting. The sight of his twin made him want to punch something.

"You look mad."

"What do you want, Eric?"

"I need to talk to you."

"Could there have been another reason you were hanging around outside the bathroom. What do you want?"

"To apologize."

Of all the things Holden was expecting, that wasn't it. He blinked several times, waiting for more. Finally, he said, "About?" He already knew, about.

"First, for not bringing Cherry to you. I thought you'd be out all day."

That wasn't the about Holden was most interested in. "So why didn't you bring her out?"

"Because I was busy taking advantage of her."

Now, they were getting to the right about. Holden crossed his arms, leaning against the opposite wall. "How did you do that and why?"

"I got riled up. No. Correction. Bruce got me riled up." He shook the thought off. "Still my fault. I got caught in a dark thought." He paused, thinking through his admission. "A reoccurring dark thought." He sighed. "Sometimes, I wonder why you. We were both there, side by side. It bugged me that I didn't know what the difference was. Sometimes, I wanted it to be a matter of enee menee minee mo. Whatever, I just needed something I could understand."

Holden wasn't prepared to sympathize, but he did. If Cherry had picked Eric, he, Holden, would be tearing himself apart wondering why.

"You have an answer now?"

"I do. My life would be a lot easier if I'd went with the obvious."

Holden arched his left eyebrow.

"She wouldn't have picked me if I'd been the only other person in Applebee's."

Holden arched both eyebrows.

"It's you. She's that one special, unique person made especially for you."

Holden felt a tightening and release in his chest.

"She couldn't not love you if she tried. Not even an exact duplicate will do."

Now it was Holden's turn to pause, to think through his musings. "Because you tried to see if she would accept an exact duplicate?"

"I asked her. More to put the matter to rest than because I wanted her to."

"What if she would have said yes?"

"Then she wouldn't be good enough for you."

It took a lot for Eric to be forthright. Holden knew that. Holden felt that. But they didn't have secrets. They never had any secrets. Now, the peace would come. It was already descending. "How do you feel about this?"

"Better. Now that I can get over myself, I'll have time to be happy for you. I can stop wasting my efforts pretending she means something other than what she means. I don't have to worry anymore that my girl got us confused."

Holden smiled. He'd had that thought before too.

Eric smiled too. An identical smile. "Hey, Mom can't keep us straight. It is a concern."

Holden moved then, heading toward his bedroom to get dressed.

"One other thing." Eric followed him in. "I did kiss her. But it wasn't anything and it was my fault. She was too busy rejecting me to notice I was about to pounce."

Relief washed over Holden. Pure. Clean. "I know."

It was Eric's turn to raise an eyebrow.

"While you were attacking, I got a text. That's why I'm not riding fences." He locked his blue-green stare onto Eric's green-blue one. "I was getting ready to go hunting."

"Damn." Eric was clearly impressed. "This town isn't small. Technology has made it microscopic."

. . . . .

Claire and Amy reorganized the bookshelf while Elizabeth watched from a safe distance.

"How does this thing get messed up?" Amy asked.

"The boys throw all of their junk on it." Claire dropped a stack of horse magazines on the floor.

"I didn't know any of the boys could read," Elizabeth said. "Can I hold your phone, Amy?"

Amy tossed her cell across the room. It nearly hit Cherry as she came in.

175

"Whoa!" She ducked just in time.

"Opps. Sorry."

Elizabeth caught it with one hand. "That was close. You okay?"

"You missed," Cherry replied. "Claire, help me out. Scar? Birthmark? There's got to be something different about them."

Claire added to her pile. "What did Eric do now?" Before anyone could comment, she said, "Ninety percent of the trouble the twins get into is because of Eric. Unfortunately, it usually doesn't matter who thought of it."

"So Eric was pretending to be Holden and got you to do what?" Amy asked. "You didn't sleep with him did you?"

"No." Cherry scoffed at the ridiculous thought. "But it was worse than just pretending to be Holden. He pretended to be Holden pretending to be Eric."

Everyone stopped what they were doing. Her comment required some thought. Amy articulated for the group. "Do what?"

"Honestly, I'm still not one hundred percent sure of which one I was with. One of them was seriously messing with my head and needs to have a body part removed so I can tell them apart."

"That bad?" Claire asked.

"It was like being with a schizophrenic." She imitated someone talking to himself. "I'm Eric. No, I'm Holden. Now, I'm Eric again."

"Maybe one of them has developed a multiple personality disorder," Elizabeth said. "Maybe he didn't know who he was either." She laughed at her own joke.

"They both have a personality disorder," Amy said. "It's called having an identical twin."

"Which is why I'm here." Cherry spread her hands out. "I want to figure out how to make them un-identical."

"I wouldn't worry about it." Claire went back to organizing. "You do a pretty good job most of the time."

"Yeah," Amy agreed. "They get us all. Even me. Most likely, it was Holden being insecure or something. Or just shutting Eric up~"

"He said that." Cherry remembered. "He said he had to prove Eric wrong about something."

"See."

Elizabeth got off the sofa. "If it wasn't, he'll kill Eric and nobody will have to guess anymore." She left the room.

"There is that. Hey! Bring me back my phone!" Amy called after her.

A moment later, they heard Elizabeth yell, "Hey! I wasn't done with that!"

Holden walked in carrying Amy's phone. He gave it to his sister but spoke to his girlfriend. "Are you riding fences with me or what?"

"I don't know. Who are you?"

Her response made him smile. It appeared that Eric's trick had made her a little leery. Good. He came over to stand beside her. Leaning down, he whispered something that made her giggle and left her no doubt about his identity.

"They are so cute," Claire said when Holden and Cherry walked out.

"I know." Amy nodded. "Eric better not mess it up."

"Do you think he's jealous?"

"No. I think he's Eric."

. . . . .

It wasn't until later, after he and Cherry spent the afternoon riding fences; after dinner; after she fell asleep in his arms on the porch swing and he led her up to his room; after he was back at the bunkhouse having a beer and making plans with Pop and Wyatt; after Bruce joined them, wanting to know what was going on -pointedly mentioning he talked to Eli, did Holden's relief evaporate. It was replaced by a heaviness he could barely maneuver under. Thanks to Eli and of course, Bruce, everybody knew about the kiss. Yet, Cherry hadn't said anything to him. She didn't mention it. Holden wasn't sure if that were a good or bad thing. Maybe it was insignificant... or... was she keeping it secret? He didn't know.

The heaviness lifted slightly when, after having his night spoiled, he went for a walk and came across Eric, flattening Bruce's tires. The twins exchanged a silent communication and Holden went to help his brother.

• • • • •

Eventually, CW drifted off to bed. Bruce and Wyatt went down to close up the barn. "We've got to do something."

"Do something about what?" Wyatt asked.

"Holden."

"What about him?"

"That boy has lost all semblance of being a man."

"According to you?" Wyatt slid the back door closed.

"According to anybody with eyes. Cherry was kissing Eric today." He hit the lights on that side of the building. Together they moved forward.

"It wasn't her fault. Eric tricked her."

"I saw her. She knew exactly who she left with. And that's another thing, didn't nobody force her to go with him either."

"We don't know what happened. Eric and Holden are okay."

"That's my point. That girl has got him by the balls. On one hand, she won't let him be a man and on the other, she's whoring around. With his brother. Eventually, she's going to come between them."

Wyatt didn't have a response. Watching Eric get sillier every day did make him wonder. Could Cherry be the thing that came between the twins?

Bruce cut out the second set of lights. He waited while Wyatt closed the front of the barn. "I love your brother. Both of them. And that's why something has to be done."

Wyatt didn't care for the conversation. It was making too much sense. "You don't like Cherry."

"I like Cherry fine. I think she should quit minding other people's business. I won't like her if Holden gets hurt."

Wyatt didn't argue. He loved Cherry. Nevertheless, if Holden got hurt, he wouldn't like her much either.

"And, I'll tell you another thing. I won't like myself at all if I don't do something to help him get his manhood back. I think Eli would agree with that. Hell, even Eric would agree."

# CHAPTER 27

Cherry glanced heavenward, soaking in the sunshine. One errand. That was all she was going to do today. One errand...for Holden. It was a strain being at the farm lately. The girls were normal, but the guys were inconsistent and moody, in her opinion. Except Eric. Eric was always Eric. But Wyatt and Bruce and Eli all had their moments. Sometimes Holden too. He could go from attentive to reserved to happy to annoyed in a heartbeat. The only time he seemed truly content was when they were alone. Cherry had the distinct impression something had gotten under his skin.

She wanted him to know they were a team, she was on his side, and she wasn't going anywhere. She hoped this little gesture would help.

· · · · ·

Holden turned into the parking lot at KOHL'S. He hated shopping. He hated it when he wasn't in a bad mood. He hated it on principle. He hated it because it was there to be hated. Today, it was the best thing- the only thing –for his black mood, because he needed jeans and lately, he hated his family more than he hated shopping. He hated the looks he got, at first covertly, now open and continuously. He hated the pity. Damn, he hated the pity. Bruce, feeling sorry for him? How is that right? He's not having sex. So what? Lots of people in the world are not having sex. It's a choice, not a problem. Why don't they get that? Why do they care? Eric should understand. They were twins, damn it. How could he not understand? If not for the automatic doors, Holden would have walked through the glass for all the attention he was paying.

Twenty minutes later, he had a pair of Lee's over his arm but he still wasn't paying attention – he wanted Levi's. The musical voice had to summon him twice before he looked up.

"I was hoping it was you. It is you, isn't it?"

"Lilly." For the first time today, Holden was something other than angry. "It's me."

"How do I know for sure?" The sassy brunette stepped in close, offering him an unimpeded view of her cleavage.

Holden hadn't seen her since the last time he screwed her. *When was that? Two days before I met Cherry. The last time I screwed anybody.* "Given the things you were saying the last time I saw you, I wouldn't think you'd have a problem identifying me." His eyes lit up. It was a good memory.

"It's been too long. Why is that, do you suppose?" She pulled her fingers through her hair.

His eyes followed the movement. "I've been involved."

"I heard something about that. Since when did your girlfriends have anything to do with us?" She smirked.

So did he. "This one is different."

"Come on." Lilly touched his chest. "This is me, Holden. You can't improve on perfection. That's us and you know it. See. I'm not even jealous. If I recall correctly, I worked hard the last time—"

He had to grin. It was true.

"—you owe me. You have to pay up."

"Lilly." An unhappy man called her.

Lilly turned to acknowledge the speaker then turned back. "See ya later, Holden. Tell Missy I said hi." She mouthed, "Call me."

Holden watched her walk all the way away.

"What exactly do you owe her?"

Startled, Holden swung around to face Cherry. "What are you doing here?"

"Asking you a question. One, I'd like answered."

Every iota of anger came back tenfold. "I don't owe her anything. Were you listening to my conversation?"

"Yes, I was. I came over when I heard her call you. You were too preoccupied to notice." Cherry had more than enough of her own anger.

"So what, are you following me around? Spying on me?"

She made a face. "Are you doing something that I need to spy on? What are you doing here?"

"I thought I asked you that same question."

"KOHL'S is having a sale. I like to shop. I thought I would do something nice for you." She held up three pairs of Levi's.

"I can shop for myself." He was being a jerk. He knew it. He just couldn't help himself.

"I never said you couldn't."

He stared at her.

"I was trying to be nice to you. That's what's supposed to happen in relationships."

"A lot of things are supposed to happen in relationships that don't happen in ours." As soon as he said it, he regretted it. He knew he hurt her. He wanted to stop being a jerk but he didn't know how.

Cherry blinked the tears out of her eyes. She furiously flung one away with the back of her hand.

"Cherry, I~"

"You're right, Holden. Shop for yourself. Do everything for yourself." She threw the Levis at him and stomped off.

Holden watched her walk all the way away too. Before she reached the door, a couple of gothic teenagers -one with orange hair- stopped her. Holden moved then. The freak had his hand on Cherry's arm. That made him the ideal place for Holden to put his anger...and maybe a fist.

Cherry pulled away and hurried out. Four steps later, Holden was within hearing range. The orange-head Goth said to his friend, "I went out with her once."

Holden stopped short. He had been with Cherry since she came to West Virginia. The guy was lying, he was certain. But, that didn't make him any less angry ...At Cherry.

. . . . .

Three days. How could she stay away for three days? It was a stupid fight. Everybody has fights. Missy and Bruce had at least one a day. How could she stay away for three days because of a fight? It wasn't his fault they hadn't spoken, it was hers. He called her. She turned off her stupid cell phone. If she wanted to make up, she had to call him. He wanted her to call him. Why didn't she call him?

If he weren't so miserable, the first day would have been great. He wallowed. Wyatt, Bruce, Eli and Eric wallowed with him. They wallowed at the casino. He won twelve hundred dollars. They made him buy the drinks.

He didn't want to go out the second night so they left Eric to wallow with him. He learned that while he was wallowing, Amy and Cherry went out (Amy refused to tell him where). After that, no one came near him, much less participated in his pity-party. He liked it that way, preferring to wallow alone.

. . . . .

Holden pressed the speed dial and hung up a second later. Someone was at the bunkhouse door.

"We need to talk."

"Not now, Eric. I'm busy."

"Yeah. You look busy. Moping around like Elizabeth. It's time for you to get it together. You and Cherry need to get it together."

"This is your business, because?"

"Because you are moping around here like Elizabeth. Because you and Cherry are screwing up a good thing. Because if I intended to see you hurt, I would hurt you myself." Neither man blinked. "I'd break you up myself, if you weren't supposed to be together. But you *are* supposed to be together. Cherry is a part of this family. She's a part of you. That's not going to change just because you're pissed off.—"

Eric wasn't saying anything Holden didn't already know. It was still good for Holden to hear it. It was nice to listen to someone who wasn't shooting negativity at him. But still...

"—It's one misunderstanding. One. That's all it is. You need to move past it."

"It's more than one."

"Whatever. You still need to work it out." Eric debated. He wanted to say more, but didn't.

"And?"

"You have to stop listening to~"

"Does anybody know what Bruce is up to?" Wyatt came in. He picked up and pointedly ignored the tension.

"Bruce is an idiot," Holden said. "What else is there to know?"

The door opened again. It was Eli. "Is Bruce in here? He told me to meet him."

Eric sighed. He and Holden would have to do this later. "He sent that message to all of us."

"What does he want?"

"Is my name Bruce?"

"Somebody call me?" Bruce stuck his head in, grinning pure evil. "Everybody here? Good. Let's party." He held the door open and two underdressed women with overdone makeup switched to the center of the room, one behind the other. The first was long and blond. Her full breasts spilled out of her narrow halter-top. The other was smaller, spiked red/orange hair, more curvy. Her bottom peeked out from beneath her cut off shorts.

"This is Angela." Bruce gave the blond a squeeze. "And this little wildfire is Darla." He hugged the red-head. "She's the newbie over at Vixen's. Angela saw us at the casino the other night. I have an idea for a way to celebrate your upcoming nuptial's Wyatt."

Angela looked at Wyatt and licked her lips.

Wyatt boldly studied her rack. "That so."

"Yep," Bruce said. "She and Darla have a new act. I thought they could practice for us. Kind of an early bachelor party. There's some fringe benefits being offered, Holden. If you're man enough."

"If his pecker don't work, mine will." Eli passed closed to Darla.

"Don't worry." Angela thrust her breasts forward. "We'll get it to work. We'll get them all working."

"Where can we get ready?" Darla asked. She had been eying the twins. She wanted one.

"Right this way, ladies. "Bruce draped an arm over each of their shoulders and led them to an empty bedroom. "Grab some beers," he called over his shoulder.

"Yeah!" Eli was already going toward the refrigerator. "Good thing your parents are gone. I guess we're knocking off work early."

"And Missy. That's why he doing this today, moron." Wyatt reached for a beer and sat in the recliner, smug as a king.

Bruce came back, twirling a CD on his pinky. "The mood music, they called it." He threw it into the CD player.

"Holden, you have to get out of here." Eric took a step toward the door, expecting his twin to follow.

Holden took a step but Bruce's comment stopped him.

"Why does he have to leave?"

Eric looked from Holden to Bruce to Wyatt to Eli and back to Holden. It was a showdown. "Holden," he begged.

Holden knew Eric like he knew himself. "This is about Cherry?"

"She's on her way over here."

"Oh. Come on," Bruce whined. "This don't have nothing to do with Cherry. She hasn't been here in three days. Shit. Holden, you're not married to her. Damn. She does have you by the balls. You can't get nothing from her and you can't get nothing from anybody else either."

"Shut up Bruce," Wyatt said without any real conviction.

"All I'm saying is here we are, guys being guys. This is a little bachelor party for you. Nothing we haven't done before. Ain't nobody hurting nobody. I ain't running from Missy." He pointed to himself first and then Wyatt. "You ain't running from Pattycakes. Eric mentions Cherry and there goes Holden. No balls at all. W.T.F?"

Holden studied the faces of his family and something in him died.

Wyatt was looking at the floor. Eli was struggling not to laugh. And, Eric was pathetic, pitiful in his transparency. He was angry on Holden's behalf, sharing in Holden's judgment, fighting Holden's battles.

"Holden." Eric felt the death in his brother and something in him died with it. "Don't do this to her."

It was hard to talk when you knew you had died. Eric understood as well as Holden did that if Holden left, he would be leaving without his pride. He would be a man those remaining would not respect. The true question that lay between them was: Did it matter? Holden didn't know. "Why is she coming here?"

"You left her a message. You asked her to come over so you could apologize."

Exactly the message Holden would have left.

"So actually," Wyatt guessed. "Eric, you sent for her."

"They need to talk."

"At some point, she should start trying to tell them apart." Eli spoke to no one but was heard by everyone.

"Why?" Bruce asked. "It don't make a difference. This way, she can have them both."

What was left of Holden crumbled. "She's coming in response to a message from your phone." Everything in him that could hate focused on Eric.

Eric responded in kind. Wounded, betrayed that anything, anybody, Bruce, of all people, could drive a wedge between them. He folded his arms. "Don't be stupid, Holden. You don't have time for this."

Holden didn't move. He couldn't move.

"You're going to hurt her. You're going to screw it all up. Permanently."

"She'll still have Eric." Bruce was facing Eli, but they knew who his intended audience was.

Angela stuck her head out of the bedroom door. "We're ready, if you gentlemen are."

Holden slashed his eyes at Eric. The decision had been made for him. "You called her. You deal with her."

185

# CHAPTER 28

Cherry pulled into the Latche drive, angrier than she had a right to be. Bruce was a bastard and she had half a mind to put him out of his misery. Missy was his wife; the mother of his kids. This was her family's farm. Bruce was a dog and if Holden and Wyatt and Eric didn't bury his sorry ass in the orchard, she would do it herself and bury them right alongside of him.

Amy was on the back porch, talking to someone on the phone. "She's here. Come on back." She clicked the cell phone off. "That was fast. I didn't know what to do."

"Where's Holden?" Cherry stood on the steps.

"I haven't seen him. Wyatt either. Eric came out of the bunkhouse. He was hostile. I don't know what's going on. But I know what I saw."

"What exactly did you see? I mean, are we making something out of nothing?"

"I was in my room when I saw Bruce drive past the house. That's what made me look out. He parked behind the barn like he's not here." She pointed to the driveway. "I saw him and a giggling bitch in hoochie-shorts walk down to the bunkhouse. There was somebody else, but they were on Bruce's far side. Probably another girl but I never got a good look. I threw on some clothes so I could go beat them silly. By the time I got halfway down there, Eric was tearing up the walk. He was pissed. I think he was trying to call you~"

"I wonder why?"

"I don't know. He nearly broke my arm dragging me back up to house.

He told me to stay out of it. I'm telling you, Cherry, he scared me. He said he'd be back and he threatened to put his foot in my butt if I didn't listen. Then, he took Holden's truck and drove off. I haven't seen him or Bruce or the giggling bitch since. That's why I was so glad you called the house."

"Earlier, I got a call from the house. The message was from Eric pretending to be Holden. I wanted to know what he thought he was doing. I called his cell, but he didn't answer."

"That's because when he couldn't reach you, he hurled his phone across the yard. It took me almost fifteen minutes to find it." She held Eric's phone up. "Right after he threw it, the idiot snatched mine."

"Wow. He must have been extremely pissed."

"I know."

"Bruce is a dick."

"I know."

Cherry searched for Missy's car. "Where's Missy?"

"She's on a field trip with Tabby's class. She won't be back until about seven or eight tonight."

"I guess that's good. Or not. Probably why Bruce did this today."

"That's exactly why he did this today. Mom and Dad are with Elizabeth at Nationals all week. Pattycakes is babysitting Brucey at her mom's house. You're at the dorm annoyed with Holden and I'm at work. No women around."

"This is going to tear Missy up."

"I know."

"Bruce is a dick."

"I know."

Cherry thought about it. "Are you sure it was Eric? Why did he take Holden's truck?"

"No idea. You said he was pretending to be Holden."

"You're sure he wasn't Holden?"

"This is Eric's cell phone." Amy held up the device. "He behaved like Eric. He yelled like Eric."

"I've had enough of these games. When this is over, I'm going to beat the crap out of him."

"I'll help you."

"All right, let's get this over with."

"Eric said~"

"Eric told you to stay away from the bunkhouse, not me." Cherry turned to go down the steps with Amy on her heels.

Screeching tires and a storm of dust announced Eric's arrival. The Silverado hadn't fully stopped before he was out of it. He charged them, eyes bulging, face contorted. "What the hell are you doing here?"

"What are you yelling at me for?" Cherry snapped. "Suddenly, I'm not allowed to be here?"

"That's not what I mean. You were supposed to be at the dorm. I was on my way up there."

"Now, I'm here. Why were you pretending to be Holden, again? And what's Bruce doing with a woman in the bunkhouse?"

"I am Holden," he shot back. To Amy he said, "I told you not to go down there."

"When you start having labor pains, you can be my mother. And anyway, I didn't. I already knew Bruce took a girl down there."

"Why did you have to tell her?"

"Why not?"

"Because...this is shit and she doesn't need to be here~"

"Why wouldn't you want~" Cherry stopped in mid-sentence, several things clicking into place at once. "Where's Holden?" She started toward the bunkhouse.

Eric's arm snaked out to capture Cherry around the waist. "I am Holden. Come on, Cherry. Let's go somewhere and talk."

"Get off me." She pulled free. "Why don't you want me here, Eric? You called me, remember? Where is Holden? "

He grabbed her again. "Why don't you believe me, honey? I'm sorry I snapped at you, but this is shit and you don't need to be here. I don't want you involved. That's all."

Cherry paused. "Holden?"

"Holden?" Amy said into the cell phone. She locked her gaze on Eric. "Thought so. Your brother is trying to confuse Cherry. Is that his idea or

188

yours?"

"You don't want me involved," Cherry repeated. "Apparently, I'm not the one currently involved." Acid dripped from her tone. "Amy, let him know I'm on my way to the bunkhouse."

"NO." Amy shook her head, horrified. "I thought Eric was the one screwing up here. You are not in the bunkhouse. Holden, tell me you are not in the bunkhouse."

"Holden." Cherry frowned at Eric. "Are you in the bunkhouse?" She stepped out of his grasp. "Is that why Eric is running around pretending to be you?"

Eric let her go. His hand dropped. He was tired, defeated. "I'm sorry, Cherry. It's not what you think. It's not anything. I promise you~"

"I'm done with you!" Cherry waved him off and stomped down the path.

Amy tried to follow, but Eric pulled her back. "She's on her way." Amy hung up and leaned into Eric. "I messed up, didn't I?"

"Looks like we all did." He pulled her into his muscled embrace, giving her his shoulder.

· · · · ·

Cherry was three-quarters of the way down the path when Holden met her. He strode forward with purpose. They stopped within a foot of one another, staring. Him angry, her wounded.

"What are you doing here?"

"Until today, I was always welcomed."

He didn't comment.

"Holden, what's going on?"

"I could ask the same of you but I don't give a shit."

"Excuse me?"

"I tried to talk to you yesterday, and the day before, Cherry, but you didn't feel the need to communicate."

"Because you were being stupid and I didn't want to hear it."

"You wanted to hear it from Eric."

"What?"

He blew off her confusion. "I'm feeling the same way. Whatever you came here for, I don't want to hear it."

"Holden, what is your problem?"

"At the moment, you."

"Me?"

"You. You should probably go now. I have things to do and there's nothing more we need to say."

Cherry was stunned. This wasn't Holden. She didn't know who this person was, but he wasn't Holden. "Are we not going to discuss this?"

"Discuss what?"

"Discuss the fact that we were supposed to be in love, yet you've got a girl in there. I think that's something we should talk about."

He was silent for a long moment. Thinking. Deciding.

Her mind would not let her believe what was happening. It wouldn't accept, so she waited for him to make it make sense. When it seemed he was never going to comment, she asked, "Are we breaking up? Is this what this is?"

"If you think I've been unfaithful to you, then yes, we're breaking up."

"What am I supposed to think, Holden? I know you have a girl in there." She pointed behind him to the bunkhouse. "You're acting like a jerk and you don't want me here. Tell me exactly what I am supposed to think?"

"I don't know what you're supposed to think. I can tell you what I know. I know our relationship isn't what it should be. I know I don't feel like I used to about you. About us. I want some time...off. Some time to figure out what we're doing and if it's worth it."

"Translation: You want me to go away so you can screw around. If that's the case, let me know and I am out of here. You won't ever have to deal with me again."

"I'm a man, Cherry. I'm sick and tired of being your doormat. What I want right now is for you to go back to school. Give me some space. Just back the hell off and let me breathe."

Cherry searched his face, looking for any resemblance to the man she loved. He wasn't there. In his place was this cold stranger. A stranger who was intentionally and successfully trying to wound her. They were in love four days ago. Day before yesterday they had a fight. Today, he was gone. She couldn't comprehend it.

For one second, his mask slipped. She could see the emotion in his countenance. There was rage, pain and retaliation. Before she could make anything of it, his eyes clouded over into a blue-green mystery.

"Are we done?"

She knew a dismissal when she heard one. "I guess so. Good-bye, Holden." She turned and walked away.

# CHAPTER 29

Holden stood statue-still watching Cherry leave. He held himself in tight check against the slightest thought, the slightest breeze that would send him flying up the path behind her, stopping her from getting into her car, begging her to want him. But, she did not want him. She didn't try, she didn't fight. She simply said, all right. It's her way or nothing. Her idea of life or they couldn't have a life. And then he was angry. *She accused ME of cheating.* The accusation was more than he could bear. Maybe because of its proximity to the truth. Maybe because he didn't like pots and kettles and things that made his heart black.

Holden chose to stop thinking, to stop feeling, to stop caring. They were over. Problem solved.

. . . . .

The atmosphere had changed in the bunkhouse, progressed. The lights were dim, the music was on. The entertainment had begun. Angela and Darla stood in the center of the room, embracing. Wyatt, Bruce and Eli sat in the shadows, nursing beers in a loose circle around the women.

Holden watched, half mesmerized, half blinded, as they swayed and kissed and undressed one another. He heard a zipper, possibly two. The breathing around the darkened room got heavier as the girls got nastier, doing things to each other that all the men wanted to do to them. Things they would do if they weren't married, if they weren't attached, if they weren't afraid they would get caught.

Holden wasn't married. Holden wasn't attached. Holden had already been caught.

Not willing to let hurtful thoughts intrude, he focused on the undulating backside of the girl nearest to him. He didn't know which one she was. He didn't care which one she was.

Holden wasn't aroused. The girls weren't getting him aroused. He could get hard for Cherry in a flash, but he'd never been with her. She didn't want him like that. Hell, she didn't want him. He didn't want to think about Cherry. So he thought about sex. He hadn't had sex since he'd met Cherry. He wanted sex. He wanted sex with Cherry. He fantasized about how she would feel, how she would taste.

Holden had to shake his head to clear it. In the confines of his jeans, he was starting to hurt.

The girls separated, Darla backing off to allow Angela the spotlight. Dipping, bending, twisting, Angela commanded their attention. While everyone watched her, she watched Wyatt, mesmerizing him with her movements. She danced for him. She became his fantasy, his addiction...his secret shame.

Holden felt a trickle of disgust. He wasn't enjoying himself. He wasn't going to enjoy himself. He couldn't stay focused on the lust. Cherry had ruined everything for him. Even sin. Especially sin.

A smooth hand slid across his crotch and gently squeezed. Holden stiffened. His mind stepped back an inch. His body, however, had other plans. Darla's too-red lips smiled up at him invitingly.

They stood quiet while she rubbed lazy circles across the front of his jeans. Accepting his silence as assent, Darla unzipped his pants and slid her hand inside.

Holden gasped, springing to life beneath her talented fingers. He didn't want Darla near him. He didn't want her touching him. But he wanted, needed the release. Cherry never touched him- not there. He wanted

Cherry to touch him. He wanted Cherry. He wanted...

. . . . .

Eric looked from Wyatt to Bruce and back again. "Did he or didn't he?"

"I don't know." Wyatt hunched his shoulders.

Bruce shook his head, clueless.

"What do you mean, you don't know? You were here."

"Nobody was watching him. We were all busy."

"Yeah, busy being a damn dog."

"It's not like you wouldn't have been doing the same thing," Bruce said. "You left on your own accord."

"One, I'm not attached to anybody, jackass. And two, yes, I left. I didn't want any part of your shit. You set Holden up. That's all there is to it. You won't shut up about how he ain't getting it. How she's working him and what he should do about it. Then you bring in a couple of whores when you know he and Cherry are having trouble. That's low, Bruce, even for you."

"At least I've never tried to dick his girl. The only trouble they had is you. Holden don't need Cherry. I'm the only one trying to help him get his pride back. What'd you do? Run off to tattle."

Eric lunged at Bruce but Wyatt caught him. "That's enough. Both of you. We're supposed to be dealing with Holden. Not either one of your sorry ass attitudes. Can we get to that now? Please."

Eric straightened up and Bruce backed away.

Eric looked to his brother. "What are we going to do?"

"It's been long enough. Time for us to straighten him out. Make his ass come back to life."

. . . . .

"Holden." Amy let herself in and sat on the edge of his bed.

He didn't acknowledge her.

"I know you don't feel like talking, so I'm just going to assume your self-inflicted coma doesn't affect your hearing. Finals are almost over."

He didn't acknowledge her.

"Cherry's almost done. She's supposed to be moving into your room in the next day or so.~"

That got his attention. He sat up intending to see if she was there yet.

Amy shook her head. "She hasn't been here. She hasn't dropped off anything. If she's not going to stay here, where is she going to go?"

"She'll be here." His voice was dry, having gone unused for days. He got up. "I'll go get her."

Amy watched him leave. She believed he would do exactly what he said.

. . . . .

Holden drove around the empty campus. It didn't make sense. Where the hell was everybody? School shouldn't be out yet, but most of the students were already gone.

Yesterday, when he arrived at Cherry's dorm, Candice, Cherry's roommate, was packing. Cherry's side of the dorm room was empty.

"Sorry, Holden. I'm really busy and I can't help you anyway."

"You can tell me where Cherry is and I'll get out of your way."

She left him standing in the doorway and returned to her bed where she was in process of sorting books. He followed her in and silently glared at her back until she turned around.

"What?"

"Where is she?"

"She's gone. She took her last test early and...flew off somewhere."

"She didn't tell you where?"

"No. She did not tell. Me. Where."

"Candice, I don't have time for this bullshit. Where is she?"

Candice shrugged. "Gone. I really have to get these to the bookstore." She pointed to a small box of used textbooks. "Today is the last day for buyback."

Holden made a mental note to have Eric charm the information out of her. He'd do it himself, but his immediate inclination was to backhand her.

That didn't seem like a very good tactic.

The next day, Candice was gone. She had taken all of her information with her.

His desperation rose as he searched one unlikely place after another. Cherry hadn't checked into any hotels. He never spotted her car at any establishment they frequented. She wasn't with Pattycakes, who wasn't with Wyatt. Both Missy and Amy claimed ignorance. It was as if she had vanished.

Cherry was supposed to be staying on the farm for the summer. His words- go back to school, give him space- pounded in his head to the rhythm of an offbeat drum. He meant a few hours- long enough for him to cool off. Obviously, she thought he meant for her not to come back. Why would she think that? She had to come back. She belonged on the farm. She belonged with him. Where was she? Where were her things?

It did not take long for him to run out of options. Where else would she be? It was a testimony to the seriousness of the situation, as if he needed proof.

Holden drove to the Eastern Shore, not certain if he was going to stop when he ran out of land.

# CHAPTER 30

Holden swallowed his nervousness. He didn't have a reason to be nervous. He pushed the doorbell.

"Who is it?" The thin, raspy voice of an elderly woman on the other side responded with expectancy, as if she had been waiting for someone to ring the bell.

"It's Holden Latche," he said to the still closed door.

"Who's Holden Latche?"

He stopped feeling nervous and went straight to feeling stupid. "I'm Cherry's... boyfriend." The last word spoken a little weaker. *What did Cherry call him?*

"Holden?"

He cleared his throat. "Yes Ma'am."

"Do I know you?"

*Oh, come on.* "Yes, Ma'am. I came here last Thanksgiving with Cherry."

"Yes. Yes. I remember you. Come on in. It's open."

*Of course.* "Thank you." Holden pushed the door, slowly stepping into Sidney's living room. It was smaller than the bedroom Holden shared with Eric before the boys took over the bunkhouse. Or, at least it felt that way with the amount of furniture she had packed in there. Couch, loveseat, coffee table, two end tables, armchair, ottoman, rocking chair, floor model television, stereo system, desk, hutch, three bookcases, a curio cabinet and barely enough floor space to turn around in. No wonder the door was unlocked. If you stood at the door, there wouldn't be room for anyone to walk in. "Hello, Aunt Sid."

"Well, hi. I do remember you. Come on in here, child." She beckoned him forward. Sidney was fast approaching eighty with twice the energy and only half the aches and pains that came with the age. Holden remembered her sweet, if somewhat chatty, disposition. He also remembered she had barred him from this house while they were visiting. "Did you have trouble finding the house?"

"No Ma'am." She sounded as if she had been expecting him. *That was encouraging.*

"Well, then, what are you doing all the way down here?"

*...Or not.* "I haven't been able to get in touch to Cherry. I was hoping she would be here."

"Boy, you're late. She's been here and gone. Left yesterday morning right after breakfast. Did you eat? Let me make you some tea." Sid got up. "Do you want butter or jelly with your toast?"

"Oh, no Ma'am." He tried to sound upbeat about not wanting breakfast. He wanted to drown himself. "I'm not hungry."

"Nonsense. Come on in the back." She led the way into the kitchen. In addition to the appliances, that room had a table, six chairs, a desk, a utility cart, a deep freezer, a microwave stand, and another hutch. Apparently, overcrowding was a decorating technique. "I got sausage. How do you like your eggs?" She put water in the teapot.

*Doesn't listen is always coupled with talks-a-lot.* "However you make yours will be fine."

"I think we're going to fry them up today. I tell you, that rain was something last night. Did you get caught in the storm..." Sidney talked the whole time she worked.

Having nothing to say but 'yes ma'am' and nothing to do, he fried the sausage while she set the table.

They were halfway through breakfast- Sidney was halfway through Irma's hip replacement- when the phone rang. "Wait a minute, let me get that." She moved almost as fast as Elizabeth. "Hello. Ruth. Yes, this is Sidney...Yes. That's Holden's truck in the drive...Holden is Cherry's beau...Yes. Yes. He came all the way down from West Virginia...Well, I'll tell you. He's a cowboy. You don't hear too much about them anymore, but I think they make good money—"

If he didn't have more pressing issues, Holden would have found the situation amusing.

"—I agree. I do. She ought to settle down... I've got some cranberry muffins the bread-man dropped off on Tuesday. If you can get Merle to help you, come on by and get a look at him. He's easy on the eyes. That's for sure...No. She left before he came. She don't know what he tried to do for her...Well, of course I blame her, but I blame him too...I told him not to let her go because I knew she was going to run...It's church. She don't go so she don't know...That's right...No, he don't go either, so he don't know what to do about her...I tried to tell him, I've been trying to tell him all day. Children nowadays don't listen. They think just because we're old, we're stupid...We don't know nothing—"

Holden disagreed. He drove three hours this morning to find out what she knew. Not that she had supplied him with a tenth of the information she was giving Ruth.

"—I'll tell you this. I've been around the block a time or two. I know what's what...If you've got extra, go ahead and bring it. He's going to be here for a little while. I want him to go up on the roof...That storm was terrible. I saw some shingles in the side yard...No, it won't take him too long. He's strong...Yes. Yes. Certainly easy on the eyes, that's for sure...I didn't think of that...I'm going to send him to the hardware store...all you need is oil for those hinges? Wait. Let me a get a piece of paper..."

Yes, he would definitely laugh. It didn't matter that she was in the process of filling up his day. Cherry wasn't here. His other option was drowning himself.

Holden waited only until she hung up. "What did she tell you about us?"

"Who? Cherry?" Sidney added hot water to her cup. "She didn't have to tell me anything. She showed up here three nights ago all bleary and teary-eyed. I knew you had a pretty big fight. Now here you are, with your tail between your legs like the sorry dog you are. I've been around the block a time or two. I don't need no instructions. I know what happened. Did she catch you with another woman?"

"No." He shook his head. "It's not like that." What it was like, he wasn't exactly sure.

"She caught you with another woman." Sid nodded in rhythm to her bobbing teabag. "Why did you do it? Start from the beginning."

Oh, yeah. *Now,* she wanted to be quiet. He had half a mind not to tell her anything. Unfortunately, half a mind was all he had. And, he needed help. "What happened? Hmmm." Holden sighed and suddenly he had more to say than he would have thought possible.

He fixed her shingles. He replaced the lock on her basement door. They went to the hardware store and Wal-Mart. They had lunch at Bob Evans and were driving back to her house before he was done telling her what happened.

"She didn't give you any warning did she? Well, she did, but you didn't know it was a warning, did you?"

"What warning?"

"Let me tell you. I'm going to tell you because I know you love her. So you got to do what you can to make this work out."

He nodded. That was why he was there.

"Cherry is a runner. That's what she does. That's all she knows how to do. That and meddle. That's your Cherry."

He wasn't following. She could tell.

"Let me tell you about her life. My baby is all broken and she won't do what she needs to do to get fixed. She spends all her time waiting for people to make mistakes. That way she don't have to think about her own. It didn't start out her fault, but she's old enough to do better now."

"What happened to her?"

"I'll tell you. All little girls want to be Cinderella. Cherry still wants to be Cinderella. You're supposed to be the prince who makes all her troubles go away without any help from her. She never learned any better and she don't want to learn any better. Her mother's death was too hard on her. She wasn't emotionally developed enough for it. After her momma went away, her daddy did the same thing. That's how Cherry thinks problems get solved. If something hurts you, you go away. "

It was making sense.

"What's more, after their parents died, Beany, I don't think you ever met him. He's Cherry's brother. Anyway, Beany got into trouble. He's in jail. So, he left her too. Her sister, Peaches, well, Peach dropped out of high school and moved to New York. Cherry went to college up there for one semester. That was it. One. She thought she was going to help Peach with her girls. Pretty little things, both of them. It wasn't until they took Peach's kids away from her, that Cherry found out Peach was a prostitute. From what I hear, a good one too. Pays her bills. She just didn't pay enough attention to her babies. Did I offend you?"

"No, Ma'am." Holden wasn't offended, but he was surprised. He and Cherry had been together for almost a year and he hadn't heard anything about her siblings except her brother lived in Jessup and her sister lived in New York. At least that illuminated the mystery surrounding Beany's phone calls.

"Everybody in the family solved their problems by leaving. Cherry don't know no better. She's so scared she'll start having nightmares if she stays near the pain too long. But, she has to stay near it if she ever wants it to go away. I told her, she's got to go to church so she can learn that everybody is messed up. Even you. You can't fix it. You need Jesus. But, she won't listen. Instead, she goes around trying to fix other people so they won't see that she needs fixing too. And when somebody does something she can't fix, she runs. I'll tell you for a fact, my baby loves you. I'm guessing she done ran all the way to the moon by now."

. . . . .

Driving into the ocean was still and option but, sitting on the beach gave Holden the time to reflect. He watched the waves for a day and decided against it- driving in. Instead, he drove to church. He drove home. After that, he didn't do much of anything.

. . . . .

In the days that followed, it became a little easier to tell Holden and Eric apart. Holden was the devastated twin and Eric was the confused, guilty, angry one. The Latche brothers shouldered one another's burdens. This was no exception. Holden was wounded. Eric held himself accountable for not protecting him. Not that he could have, really. But, when he should have had Holden's back, he was preoccupied with his fantasies. He had been keen to impersonate Holden, less interested in reasoning with him until it was too late. All he could do now was share the weight, and share the wait. She was coming back.

. . . . .

"Cherry. Where are you? I've been worried to death about you child."

"I'm at the airport, Aunt Sidney. I was calling to say I love you."

"You are not still going on that trip, are you?"

"My flight leaves in two hours."

"You can't go, baby. Don't do it."

"I told you, it's an educational trip for school. I'll be home in a few weeks."

"You need to cancel that trip and come home. Today."

"Why? Is something wrong? Are you sick?"

"Yes, I'm sick. My heart is all broken up for you~"

"Aunt Sid. No more of that. I'm fine. I broke up with my boyfriend. It happens all of the time. I'll get over it."

"But you love him."

"I'll get over it," Cherry said louder.

"By then it might be too late."

"What soap opera have you been watching?"

"The Cherry-Holden hour. And I know what you don't know."

It had been two weeks since Cherry last saw Holden. The mention of his name made her eyes film over. It took two gulps of air before she could comment. "What would you know," she paused, then qualified, "that you haven't already said."

"I was with Holden all day long, yesterday."

Two more gulps of air. "Pardon me?" *Yes, Aunt Sid still drove. No, Aunt Sid did not drive to the farm.*

"I prayed you would call home yesterday. You never did. I was waiting, because the Lord told me to wait. He told me you would call me today."

If Cherry had been able to function, she would have reminded Sid that she promised to call before she left. But, it had been two weeks since Cherry had lost her ability to function. "Holden." A tear slid between her cheek and her cell phone.

"That boy loves you, Cherry. He drove all the way down here to find you and tell you that. You've got no right to walk away from somebody who loves you like that."

Movement cut across Cherry's blurred vision. A flight had been called. "Holden?"

"Go see him, baby. Go talk to him."

"He doesn't want to see me, Aunt Sid."

"He didn't drive all the way down here to see me. I tried to keep him here. I put him to work, but you weren't here so he didn't stay."

Cherry took a deep confused breath. "We broke up. He broke us up. I can't help that. I can't do anything but go away and heal."

"If you don't help it, who will?"

"Nobody. It can't be helped."

"It could if you wanted to. But, I guess you don't."

"I can't make him love me, Aunt Sid."

"You don't have to. He already loves you."

Instead of weakening Cherry's resolve, hearing of Holden's love had the opposite effect. "That's not love. Whatever Holden is feeling isn't love. That much I know."

"You know so much. I'm going to get off of the phone. You call him. See if he loves you."

"Aunt Sid~"

"I mean it. Call him. Call him before you get on that plane. Before it's too late."

For long minutes after Aunt Sid hung up, Cherry stared off into space. She didn't wonder. She didn't dare wonder. Instead, she thought of things like Aunt Sidney hanging up. Aunt Sid never said good-bye first. Normally, Cherry had to wheedle or trick her way off of the phone. Why would Aunt Sid hang up first? She didn't fret once about the plane or the distance or the time Cherry would be away. It was almost as if Sidney didn't expect her to leave. Why?

She thought of Sidney putting Holden to work. What would he have done? Why would he do things for her Aunt? Aunt Sid had help. Where was her help?

She thought about the number of phone calls she had ignored in the last two weeks. Amy. Eric. Holden. Holden had called her. But, it wasn't until days later. After he had all of his fun. After he was done being horny. After he had time to miss her. Well, it was too late, now. Maybe if he would have wanted her, wanted to fix this the day he threw her away or the next day, maybe. But he didn't. He may want to pick up the pieces now, but he didn't want to keep them from falling.

She thought about Amy worrying, not understanding. She would certainly blame herself. But Cherry couldn't talk to her. It hurt too much. Being rejected. Pitied.

She thought about Eric. Wanting to fix everything- wanting to be Holden. Why didn't she fall in love with Eric? Eric wouldn't have thrown her away. Would he? She couldn't think about Eric. Thinking of Eric was the same as thinking of Holden.

Holden was everything painful.

If she thought about calling Holden, she would do it. She would call him and beg him and cry. And he would laugh at her. He would tell her to leave him alone. He would say he did not love her. And she would die.

She didn't think about it, because if she thought about it, she would die.

Cherry turned off her phone and put it in her suitcase. Then, she checked her bags. She wanted to put it all away from her. Reason. Emotion. Temptation.

Forty-five minutes later, without the help of temptation or emotion or reason, Cherry boarded her plane. When it taxied down the runway she felt safe enough to break down. It was a daily ritual, fourteen days running. She was new to the group she was traveling with, so no one intruded on her grief. She was glad they didn't.

Six hours later, the plane landed and she began to do what she had been trying to do for fourteen days running. She let her heart get cool, then cold. One broken piece at a time. With effort, the shattered fragments would be frozen before she returned home.

# THE BEGINNING

# CHAPTER 31

"Shit." Cherry only had seconds to decide. She slowed her G5 down, already regretting her decision.

Amy looked up from her raised trunk, relieved someone had pulled over to help her. Shock came the instant recognition did. She would not have been able to close her mouth even if she had realized it was open.

Cherry turned off the ignition, pasted a plastic smile in place and stepped out of the car. "What is it with you and car trouble?"

"It's just a flat. But I don't know where the jack is. Plus, my cell phone isn't charged. I'm going to be so late for work."

"I can do something about the work part. Get in." Cherry took a few calming breaths as she sunk back down into her driver's seat.

"Thanks." Amy followed her over.

"Are you still working at IHOP?"

"Yep."

The clicking of seatbelts seemed loud. Cherry's engine seemed loud. The tires pulling off the gravel shoulder seemed loud. But, nothing seemed louder than the silence.

"I was on my way to the gas station. Will you be very late if I stop? I'm on fumes."

"That's fine. They'll be happy I showed up at all."

More silence. Finally, after weighing her options, Amy shifted in her seat. "Where the hell have you been?" Her happy, angry, blue-green eyes bore into Cherry; blue-green, like her brother's.

"Nowhere. I'm not here now. You don't see me. You will not tell anyone you saw me~"

"Oh yeah. That's going to work."

"Amy please~"

"Don't please me. Give me some information."

"I don't have any information."

"You happen to be driving down a road, less than six miles from the house, yet no one has seen or heard from you in over a year. You better have some information."

"I don't."

"Cherry, you and Holden broke up. As far as I know, the rest of us didn't have anything to do with it. We love you."

"I love you too, but you're Holden's family. You all belong to Holden."

"We're your family too."

For this Cherry had no answer.

"We didn't get to find out what happened. No good-bye. Nothing."

"I sent a Christmas card. And I sent Tabby a birthday present."

"You sent the tea set?" Amy arched her eyebrows surprised.

"Yes."

"You didn't sign any cards or leave a return address."

"I was trying not to intrude."

"Did you ever think we might miss you?"

"Don't miss me. As you can see, I'm fine and I know you are too." Cherry pulled into the gas station. She went inside to pay before she pumped. She needed the time to compose herself.

Apparently, Amy did likewise. She was calm, almost serene when Cherry returned. "So what have you been up to for the last ummm... year or so?"

"Nothing much."

"Cherry. A little help here would be nice."

Cherry sighed. It wasn't Amy's fault. "I moved on. That's all."

"Obviously, you didn't move far."

"I don't live around here, Amy. In all honesty, I'm passing through, that's it. I had a meeting with a college acquaintance. I would have bypassed Charles Town altogether but I needed gas."

"Where do you live?"

"Oakland."

"Which?"

"Uhh...California."

"Umm hmm."

"I do. I know you don't believe me, but I do."

Amy went on as if they were having a different conversation. "We're all fine. Do you want to know how Holden's doing?"

Cherry willed herself still. A tear had better not escape. "I hope Holden is great." That part was true at least. "I don't want any details."

"Why not?"

*Too hard to hear.* "It's not pertinent. I have a new life. No sense in complicating it."

"New life?"

"Yes." Cherry cleared her throat. "I got married. We're trying to have a baby. So you see, I'm all happily ever after and if you tell anybody you saw me, it will make a big, unnecessary, complicated mess."

"You don't have a ring."

"Oh. Uhh...It's getting resized."

"I bet. Married to whom? For how long?"

"His name is Henry. We've been married for about... six months. Yep. Six happy months."

"Congratulations."

"Thank you." Cherry was sadly relieved when she turned into the IHOP parking lot.

Amy fished through her purse. "Since you haven't gotten around to calling anybody, what's your number?" She pulled out a notepad. "Give me a second. I need to find a pen. I'd put it straight in my phone but lucky me, it's not charged."

"I don't think that's a good idea. Please, Amy, don't tell anybody you saw me."

"Dudette, I've seen you. Do you want me to pretend I don't care? That I don't miss you?"

"I don't want you to care. I don't want you to miss me."

"Cherry, I don't know what game you're playing, but I'm not having it. I have to go to work. Are you going to give me your number or not?"

"How about if I call you?"

"Because you've been so good about keeping up with that."

"No, no, I will. I promise. I'll have to get it together, though. Hol~Henry doesn't know about my life here. If you call the house, he should at least know about what."

"Umm hmm." Amy reached over to hug Cherry. "You lie like shit. Always have." She kissed her cheek. "Don't make me hunt you down." Then she was out of the car. "You're not getting away this time, Cherry." With that, she slammed the door and bounced into the restaurant.

Cherry was shaking when she pulled out of the parking lot. "Shit."

. . . . .

Amy didn't bother clocking in. Instead, she went straight to the phone. "Missy," she barked when her sister answered on the second ring.

"What's up?"

"Two things. One, I got a flat~"

"Where are you? I'll come~"

"No. No. Listen. I'm all right. I got a ride to work. My car is on old 9 before the light. See if somebody will get it for me."

"Sure."

"Good. Can you pick me up tonight?"

"Yeah, somebody~"

"No. Not somebody. You."

"Me?"

"Yes. It has to be you. Leave the kids. You can bring Eric if you want. But it has to be you."

"What's going on?"

"I'll tell you about it tonight. Trust me. It's a big ass deal."

"Tell me now."

"I don't have time. You just need to be here. Oh, and Missy?"

"Yes."

"Other than picking me up from work, don't mention this conversation to anyone. Don't tell anybody I've gone off the deep end."

"What about Eric?"

"Only if you bring him. I have to go. Bye."

"Bye." Missy hung up the phone. She jumped when Claire opened the refrigerator, beside her.

"Jittery much? Who was on the phone?"

"Amy. She got a flat or something. She wanted to make sure she had a way home tonight."

"Where's her car? I'm going down to the barn in a minute. I'll see who's around and send somebody out to fix it."

"I told her we would." Missy left it at that.

· · · · ·

Amy walked out of IHOP and ran to Eric's truck. She slid into the back seat behind Missy. "Hey. Thanks. We're going to 127 Wilgate drive. It's on the other side of Shepherdstown."

Eric started the engine. "What's at 127 Wilgate drive?"

Missy turned around in her seat. "All right, Amy. I'm out of patience. What's going on?"

Amy took a deep breath. "Cherry gave me a ride to work."

"What?" Missy's eyes bugged.

Eric hit the gas.

· · · · ·

Twelve minutes later, they pulled into the driveway at 127 Wilgate, behind a silver G5.

Amy read the license plate. "This is it."

"Are you sure?" Missy asked.

"Positive."

"Is it unlocked?" Eric wasn't following. Instead, he searched the neighborhood.

Missy checked. "Yeah. What are you up to?"

"Pop the hood."

At the end of the drive, an impressive colonial with a brick porch sat on a manicured lawn. The house was quiet. Upstairs, a light was on. Amy's finger shook when she pressed the doorbell. Nobody spoke as they listened for movement inside.

Cherry opened the door and froze with guilty surprise. One breath. Two. Then a heart-wrenching smile split her face. "How did you find me?" She opened the door wide.

Amy grinned and led the way inside. "While you were at the gas station, your registration accidentally fell into my pocket." She held up the offensive piece of paper. "We came all this way to return it. I had no idea Oakland was so close. All this time, I thought California was on the west coast. You've been living here for at least four months. That might be something you'd want to tell your husband, Mr. Fiction."

Cherry shut the door and followed them into her living room. "They have a name for people like you."

"Yes," Amy said. "Smarter than you." She plopped down on the loveseat. "I told you, you lie like shit."

"Cherry." Missy couldn't stop her tears. She gripped Cherry as if she thought the other girl would disappear if she let go. "Cherry."

"Missy. You've have no idea how much I've missed you. All of you."

Eric pulled his hands through his hair. And then he couldn't wait any longer. Applying only a little of his bear-like strength, he separated Cherry and Missy and enfolded Cherry in his own embrace. "Damn you, girl. Damn you to hell." He kissed her forehead.

"I know. I know." Cherry nuzzled his chest, breathed in his scent...and remembered.

Finally, they composed themselves. Missy folded herself into an overstuffed chair. Eric hauled Cherry over to the sofa, locking her to his side with one arm. Using his other hand, he grabbed a box of Kleenex from the coffee table. Yanking a handful, he tossed the box to Amy. "Give Missy the box. You." He put the pile of tissues in Cherry's lap. "Start from the beginning."

Amy grabbed a handful and threw the box to Missy.

Cherry studied her pile of tissues. "I...I don't know where to start."

"Why did you leave us?"

Slowly, Cherry raised her eyes. They were already starting to sting. She focused on each face. Amy was nervous. Missy was scared. Eric was...mad and something else. Something tender, something dear. They were all dear. They loved her. "Why did I leave? Hmmm." She took a deep breath. She needed a deep breath. "Holden and I broke up."

"Really?" Amy said. "We weren't able to figure that out."

Cherry snickered. "I wasn't sure. You can be slow on the uptake."

"All right, Amy." Missy angled her head. "Don't make a habit of interrupting."

Suddenly, Cherry was eager to share her tale. "Holden and I broke up because he was with somebody else. But you knew that part." She frowned at Eric.

He didn't flinch. "That's not why you broke up."

"He didn't feel the same way about me, about us, anymore. He wanted some time to rethink our relationship. That translates into he wanted to sleep around guilt free. He told me he didn't want me to come to the farm. He wanted me to...to give him some space. So I gave him space. I moped around the dorm for a few days and then I made plans. I got lucky. My roommate knew about a class trip that still had room. Fifteen days after we broke up, I was in Senegal, West Africa."

"Africa?" Missy's jaw dropped.

"You went to Africa?" Amy sat forward in her seat. "Wow."

"You left the country to get away from him?" Eric's tone hovered between exasperation and awe.

"I know me well enough to know, it would have been only a matter of time before I started making a fool of myself. Senegal was good. It was hot. The tears dried faster than I could shed them."

"How long were you there?"

"Thirty-two days."

"Okay, you've been gone for thirteen months," Amy said. "That still leaves eleven plus months unaccounted for. Where else have you been?"

"For the most part, here."

"What?"

"Excuse me?"

"I came to the college," Eric said. "Several times."

"We all did," Missy added.

"I never moved back into the dorm. I boarded here with a Lady named Doris. I took care of her during the day and finished my last semester at night. When I graduated, I *did* move to Oakland...Maryland. A little while ago, Doris sent for me. I was the only family she had. She died two months ago. As soon as I can get all of the legal stuff wrapped up, I promise, I will disappear and never set foot in West Virginia again."

"All this time, you've been here. Fifteen minutes from the farm." Eric was mad again. He was mad on Holden's behalf. He was mad at Holden for letting her go. He was mad at Cherry for leaving. Leaving Holden. Leaving him. Eric was mad.

For a long while, no one said anything.

Amy finally dared to break the silence. "He's still in love with you."

"Shut up, Amy." Eric's eyes, more green than blue, blazed. "Holden made his choice."

"Holden made a mistake and Holden knows it."

"Holden doesn't know shit."

Missy said, "Eric, Cherry has a right to know."

"No," Cherry said. "I don't have a right to know. I don't want to know. I've honored his request. I've been honoring it. My heart can't take knowing anything about Holden. And, please, please, don't tell him about me."

"We have to."

"No, Missy. You don't. You can't."

"You don't understand. Holden has suffered. He hasn't been the same~"

"STOP IT!" Cherry jumped up. "Stop it. You don't understand. I can't hear this. I've done nothing but try to get over him. Don't take that away from me."

"It doesn't have to be like this." Amy stood up with her. "You and

Holden had the real thing. You still do. It's not right that you're not together. We want to make it right."

"You may want to. But that's not your decision. It's not your choice. Just because you want us together, doesn't mean we have to agree to it."

"Holden would agree." Missy's voice was quieter than the others.

"I don't agree. None of you have a right to force your desires on me. This is between Holden and me." She pointed to herself. "He asked for this. I gave it to him, willingly. You don't have to like it, but you do have to respect it. This life belongs to me."

"Calm down, Cherry." Eric was beside her, embracing her, soothing her. "Nobody is doing anything right now. Holden is a subject for another time. For right now, let's be happy that we've got you back."

Cherry studied each of their faces, innately knowing no matter what they said, none of them would leave it alone for very long. "Okay," she said, inwardly planning.

# CHAPTER 32

Amy, Missy and Eric walked into the kitchen and stopped in a one, two, three sequence. The room was full for that time of night. Claire rocked Brucey while he drank from his sippy-cup. Holden sat across from Wyatt. He was in the room, but Holden was never fully anywhere. Pattycakes fed Isaiah a jar of apple sauce. Tabby combed her Aunt Elizabeth's hair. Only Hunter and Cory were missing.

"Mommy!" Tabby ran to Missy.

"Hi, Baby. What are you doing still awake?"

"Waiting for you. Everybody is, 'cept Cory and Hunter. It's wartime online."

"What's up?" Amy ignored the obvious tension.

Eric glared at Holden.

"Where have you been?" CW leaned back in his chair at the head of the table.

"Picking Amy up from work." Missy tossed her wavy hair behind her shoulder.

"She works ten minutes from here. You've been gone a long time."

Missy pointed to Amy. "No, Dad. We didn't pick Amy up. She's walking home as we speak."

"Don't be rude Missy," Claire said.

"Does this have something to do with Austin?"

"NO." Missy's eyes flared. Everybody knew Austin was forbidden territory.

"Calm down, Daddy," Amy said. "I got there late, so I had to stay late. Missy and Eric hung out and waited. Sor-ry."

"Funny, nobody saw you after four-thirty, when your shift ended." Wyatt reached down to pick up Brucey's cup. The waddler had hurled it just to see how far it would go. "Any of you."

"It was busy. Whoever you talked to probably didn't look." Amy weaved her way through the room.

"Where have you been and what are you lying about?" Holden asked. He pierced Eric with a flat uncaring stare. "What are you looking at?"

Amy nudged Eric. "Knock it off."

Bringing the subject back to where she didn't want it, Missy folded her arms, preparing for a fight. "Why do we have to be lying about anything? Is it some sort of crime for sisters and brothers to hang out? I confess. We're selling arms to the Russians."

"You're lying." Wyatt picked up Brucey's cup again. "Because I fixed Amy's tire and later, I drove it to IHOP. I got there in time to see Eric flying across the parking lot. You're lying, because when you didn't come home, I stopped by IHOP on my way to get Pattycakes, just to be sure. Amy wasn't working late and you and Eric weren't there waiting for her. In fact, this town ain't that big. None of you were anywhere to be found."

Elizabeth stood up. "Amy got off at four-thirty. It's after eight. I couldn't call Nikki all evening because nobody will buy me a real cell phone and I'm out of minutes. Mom wouldn't let me use the stupid house phone because they thought one of you might be courteous enough to call and let us know you were alive since, big coincidence, all three of your phones were turned off. Now, seeing as how you're back and safe and unappreciative of our concern, I guess I don't get a room to myself after all." She made a face at Amy. "I'm going to call Nikki." That said, Elizabeth left.

"Missy, you were acting strange, all jittery when Amy called." Claire returned them to the conversation. "You may not have wanted to share, but we know something is going on."

Missy looked at Amy who looked at Eric who looked at Missy who looked at Eric who looked at Amy who looked at Missy who knew she had to make a decision. "Okay. Let me put the kids to bed and then we'll..." She didn't want to say talk- talking implied answers. "We'll figure out something." Before any more could be said, she carried Tabby out of the room.

Claire followed with her son.

·　·　·　·　·

While waiting, Eric and Amy busied themselves with the leftovers from dinner. Amy was careful to avoid eye contact with everyone but Eric. Eric alternated between staring at Holden, glaring at Holden, and finding reasons to bump against Holden as he moved around the kitchen. He wasn't hiding his annoyance with his brother. That was the oddest part of the evening so far. Holden hadn't done anything to anybody. Holden hadn't done anything.

As if sensing the importance of the occasion, nobody pressed. Nobody spoke. Everybody waited.

·　·　·　·　·

Of all the nights for Tabby and Brucey to co-operate and fall asleep almost immediately, this would not have been the night Amy, Eric or Missy would have chosen. For the others, it took long enough.

When they returned to the kitchen, Claire was pale and silent, brushing a loving hand through Holden's hair. Amy and Eric were eating. Except for the brief time it took for Pattycakes to put Isaiah down, everyone seemed frozen, exactly the way they had been when Missy and Claire left.

Pattycakes started right away, looking from Missy to Amy. "Eric knows, but I don't. I feel left out."

"Don't." Missy shook her head. "You are better off. Trust me."

"Is this really such a big deal?" Pattycakes asked. "Were you doing something to warrant all of this?" She waved her hand around the room.

"That's what we want to find out," CW said.

Amy shook her head. "I swear. If this had been any other night, who would care where we were?"

"Obviously, you weren't doing what you would have been doing on any other night," Wyatt said. "Come on. Out with it so we can all go back to our lives."

"Maybe it isn't any of your business." Missy crossed her arms.

"If you thought that, you would have said so instead of lying the second you came in."

"I'm saying it now."

"Too late for that, Missy. It's our business now."

CW looked back and forth between the most hotheaded of his children. They were starting to get riled up. "That's enough, you two. It's everybody's business now. Not telling is only going to make matters worse."

Somebody sighed, defeated.

"Amy?" Missy focused on her sister.

"No." Eric stood up. "We can't do this."

"It's Amy's decision, Eric."

"My decision?"

"It's another betrayal."

"It's Amy's decision."

"Why is it my decision? You were there too."

"Because you called me. You decided to involve Eric and me. Wait," she said when Amy would have interrupted. "It was a good decision. I'm glad you called. But, you made the decision that we should know. You have to decide if..." Her eyes swept around the room. "...anyone else should know."

Amy swallowed.

Eric hit the refrigerator.

"Look." Missy addressed the room. "Here's the thing. We've got an issue. It's a big one. No matter what we do or don't do, somebody we love is going to get hurt. We don't know how to reconcile that. There is no right choice here. We don't want to keep secrets. We don't want to lie. But we're damned if we do, damned if we don't. We're just damned. So cut us some slack. This is hard."

Eric hit the refrigerator again. "Holden, you're a bastard!"

"Eric!" Amy yelled.

"Eric, calm down." Missy was in slightly more control, slightly.

Holden studied Eric. It was obvious his twin was spoiling for a fight. Odd. He and Eric hardly ever fought, except over...Holden caught and held Eric's eyes, searched them and found the truth. He stood up. "Where is she?" Fire and ice in shades of blue and green shot between them. They were both hot and cold in the same moment.

In a short flurry of steps, Amy was beside Holden, unsuccessfully trying to push him back into his chair. Missy put a restraining arm on Eric. She stepped in front of him, preparing to use her whole body if necessary.

Neither man flicked an eyelash. Icy-fire and fiery-ice. Before the last of the oxygen could be sucked out of the atmosphere, Holden repeated, "Where is she, Eric?"

"Ask Amy. It's her decision." Eric sneered. "Apparently, Cherry's life is in her hands."

· · · · ·

"Jeanie, this is Cherry. I'm sorry to call you so late, but I have kind of a situation. I think."

"You think? What's that mean?" Jeanie, Cherry's boss and friend, twirled a lock of newly permed hair around her finger.

"That means, there is a better than good chance I won't be in to work tomorrow. Or ever."

"What in the name of sanity is going on?"

"Nothing in the name of sanity. I'm about ninety-six percent sure I have to leave town."

"Did you murder someone?"

"I wish it were that easy."

"You saw Holden."

"No. His sister. That's why I'm only ninety-six percent sure I have to leave."

"Ohh baby. Does she know where you live?"

"Oh yeah."

"Does she know where you work?"

"Not to my knowledge. But I didn't give her my address and that didn't stop her."

"I bet she doesn't know where I live. Come on over. Hide here until we figure something out."

"I can think of at least forty-nine better states to hide in."

"Cherry, I'm not letting you leave town."

"Are you sure?"

"Positive. Don't make me come and get you."

"I'll be there in an hour."

. . . . .

Holden was as still as a stone, listening to the retelling. Cherry was here. She had been here the whole time except when she was hiding in Africa. Here. Right here. His heart, his life was fifteen minutes away.

If their perceptions were accurate, she wasn't going to stay.

"The thing is, Holden," Missy pushed her hair out of her way, "you can't go see her. Not yet, anyway."

"He has to," Pattycakes said. "He's got to stop her from taking off again."

"If he shows up at her house, do you think she will ever trust any of us again?"

"Come on, Missy, do you think Cherry believes you weren't going to tell Holden?" Wyatt shook his head.

Amy said, "The problem is she thinks he is going to be mad that she's so close. She's going to run because she thinks he doesn't want her here."

"And, she's going to think we betrayed her if we don't give her some time to adjust," Missy added. "You heard her. Regardless of what any of us want, she doesn't think we have the right to interfere. We've got to give her some respect, somewhere."

"No, we don't." Wyatt turned to Holden. "If we respect her wishes, she'll be gone in the morning."

"Probably not." Eric said his first words since the debate began. All of his energy had gone into silently probing Holden, trying to read his mind.

Eric seemed to have resolved some internal struggle. He was less hostile, more determined when he said to his twin, "I pulled her starter relay. Nevertheless, if it were me, I wouldn't test the theory."

"No!"

"No!"

Missy and Amy spoke in unison. One look at Eric and they could tell his personal storm had passed. He switched his loyalty.

"We are not giving him the address." Amy had a hand on each hip.

"Think of Cherry." Missy tried the more devious tactic.

Eric cocked his head to the side. "127 Wilgate Drive. On the other side of Shepherdstown."

Through the course of the conversation, Holden hadn't moved, hadn't spoken, hadn't dared to function. Now, he was gone.

Eric had barely uttered the piece of information he had been waiting for- the only thing he cared about knowing- before he was acting on it. From the moment he was assured Cherry was within reach, he had barely restrained himself. He wanted to rip his siblings apart and pull the information out of them- it didn't matter which one. But he had to bide his time, wait while they discussed things that didn't make a damned bit of difference. Ponder Cherry's wishes and wonder if he should see her. If he would have cared, he would have been angry that they made him wait this long, furious with Amy for not calling him right away. But, he didn't care. He didn't have the time or space or inclination to care. All he had was his need for Cherry.

127 Wilgate Drive. In one motion, Holden started his truck and gunned it.

The Latche clan was silent in his wake. Wyatt was the first to shake it. "I think that's the most life I've seen in him since she left."

"Because she is his life." Claire shut the back door. "You might want to remember that in the future." She glanced at her boys with a touch of chastisement in her gaze.

"I feel like crying." Pattycakes dabbed the corner of her eye. "I hope they can get it worked out."

"You know," CW said to Eric. "For all the fooling around you two do, here's the one scenario where switching might have helped and neither one of you even thought of it."

"No, Pop." Eric shook his head. "Holden has to do this. Switching is fun, but it never actually helps anything."

. . . . .

"Jeanie, it's Cherry. I don't know if I will be in tomorrow, but I won't be over tonight."

"What now." Jeanie blew on the shimmering gold nail she had just polished.

"My car won't start."

"This is so not your day. I'll come and get you."

"No, don't do that. I'm too tired to care at this point. I'm going to bed."

"Are you sure?"

"Yeah. He hasn't shown up yet. That means either they've put off telling him or they've told him and he doesn't care. Either way, I'm safe enough tonight."

"All right. Call me if you need me and don't worry about work."

"Thanks, Jeanie. You're the best."

"Don't you know it."

Cherry hung up the phone and started crying again. That had been her pattern all day. Do something. Cry. Try to get it together. Fail. Cry. Pretend she was all right. Do something. Cry. "Damn you, Holden. Why did Amy's car break down? And why do I love you? And ..." She paused to find a Kleenex. "Why did you do this to us? Why am I not over you? And..." She paused again, hovering over her current heartache. "Why didn't you come?"

Cherry lay curled in the fetal position, rocking herself, staring blankly at the mountain of tissues she'd gone through. This latest bout of 'cry' would not end. It was late and she had nothing else to do. Nothing to make herself focus on. Only time, her open wound, and a mountain of Kleenex.

A car door slammed. Why it registered was beyond Cherry's

comprehension, but it sounded close. There was nothing, and yet there was something. Something she couldn't explain. It was just something. The echo of the car door and the pile of tissues. The only thoughts she had that didn't hurt. So, she thought of them: The pile of tissues and somebody's car door. The door closed hard. The tissues were white, mostly. Some were blue, from the other box. The door had a vibrating, echoic sound. She needed a Kleenex...

# CHAPTER 33

Cherry opened her eyes and tried to remember when she closed them. It was early. Too early for pain and way too early for thinking. She moved around her room in a robotic trance, oblivious to the rich, dark wood of her four-poster bed and dresser or the Celtic metal-work framing her mirror. She didn't luxuriate in the feel of the plush beige carpet cushioning her steps. She felt claustrophobic and tight. She needed to get out, to get air. It was close to three a.m., too early to go anywhere, too hard to stay in her room. She'd go see if her car would start. If it did, she would take a drive. Go wake up Jeanie or see if Amy was somewhere out of gas or something. If her car didn't start, she would kick her tires until *she* got a flat. Anything was better than being in her room.

Finding her shoes was easy. She hadn't bothered to take them off when she fell across her bed some five hours earlier. She trudged down the steps lacking grace or poise. It was difficult to hold her head up. She fumbled with the lock, stumbled through the door and stopped.

Holden looked up from the rocker on her front porch. He was unreactive to the suddenness of her appearing in the doorway, as if he had been expecting her -as if he had been waiting for that moment.

Cherry couldn't process it. Holden was there...on her porch...in her chair...staring at her...not saying anything... just...staring...What did it mean? Why was he here...staring? If you are going to be on somebody's porch, you ought to say something...anything.

Like a deer caught in headlights, Cherry stared back, wide-eyed, afraid.

Afraid she was dreaming, more afraid that she may not be.

Holden didn't move, didn't blink, didn't look away. Time stopped, capturing them in that moment, holding them in place.

He had always been more stubborn than her. Cherry caved under the pressure. Her instinct took charge- her survival instinct. She stepped back and slammed the door. She turned the lock and slid the deadbolt home, innately knowing that if Holden wanted to come in, a door, a lock, and a measly deadbolt would not stop him.

Cherry went back to bed, again not bothering to remove her shoes. She buried herself beneath her blankets, pulled the covers up over her head and returned to her cry.

· · · · ·

By the time she could think, more than an hour had gone by. Nothing had changed except the increase in light. The stillness made her edgy. The need to move, escape was on her heavily. She had to do something.

This time when she moved around it was with a purpose, although she did not yet know what that purpose was. She showered and dressed for an occasion -whatever the occasion may be.

No amount of makeup was going to help her tear-swollen eyes (especially since she was still crying) but, checking her reflection, she thought she looked pretty good. The short skirt helped.

With determination she did not own, Cherry marched down the steps. She yanked the door open like she was bad. She held her breath and strode across the porch.

Holden was still sitting there, in the same position, with the same expression.

She was caught in his gaze as if she had never left.

Cherry's determination evaporated. She could barely lift her feet. Her steps were heavy. She felt clumsy walking past him, pretending he did not exist when they both knew perfectly well he was sitting right there, watching her. Her hands shook opening the car door. She jammed the key in the ignition. "Please Lord. Please Lord. Please Lord. Let it start."

Nothing.

"Damn it!" It was too much. Just too much. "Damn it!" She hit the steering wheel. That didn't help. She got out, humiliated and angry about it. "Damn it!" She kicked the tire. Again. And again. And again.

"Here."

Cherry jumped, startled into silence.

Holden was there beside her, quiet except for the one word. His earring caught the moonlight as he held out the keys to his truck.

Inside her, prideful rejection and her need to run were fighting. So far, they had taken out a lung. She couldn't exhale. Fear and embarrassment were instigating, drowning out all sense of logic.

Holden stared at her, intently.

Running won. She snatched the keys out of his hand. "Thank you." She slid past him. "I don't know why you're here, but I'm going to find out. The door's not locked. Feel free to use the bathroom or eat or whatever. But, I want you gone by the time I get back." She got into his pickup. "If you're still here, I'll call the police."

He snorted. It was a small sound, an odd sound coming from him.

"I mean it." She slammed the door.

Holden stood back out of her way, not bothering to mention that she was taking his truck. He wasn't leaving without his truck. He wasn't leaving without her. Hell, he wasn't leaving.

· · · · ·

Cherry skidded to a halt in the dusty Latche drive. It wasn't too early for activity, but it was still a small surprise for her to see Wyatt crossing the porch with Eric following on his heels. Amy's hair was everywhere and she was still in her pajamas. Clearly, she had been awakened.

Cherry jumped out of the truck and stormed across the yard, her earlier fire returning with each step. "Why is Holden at my house?"

Amy pointed to Eric.

Cherry made a beeline toward him. Up the steps, she shoved past Wyatt and put all of her frustration into her swing as she punched Eric in the stomach.

It would have been nice if he would have doubled over, or groaned, or winced, or something. Anything. He didn't seem to notice she was trying to kill him. She hit him again.

"Stop." He said it like he was disciplining Tabby. "Holden loves you, Cherry. He's never going to stop. You need to accept that. He made a mistake~"

She hit him again.

This time, he grabbed her hands to keep her from hurting herself. "He made a mistake, that's all. He's not going to stop loving you."

That wasn't what she came to hear. She tried to pull away, but he held her fast.

Wyatt stepped in close beside her. "He hasn't left the farm since he found out you were gone. Except to go to church. Did you hear me? Church. He goes to church. He doesn't live well without you, Cherry. He told us you were coming. He followed you here. You can't outrun him this time. He's not going to let you get away again."

Definitely not what she came to hear. She turned her head away.

"Please, Cherry," Amy begged. "Can't you listen to him, just this once?" She smacked Eric's hands away. "He's been at your house all night. Why don't you see what he has to say?"

It was easier to discuss it with Amy. Amy didn't ignore the fact that her brother was a dog. "See what he has to say? He hasn't said a word to me. He's expecting something from me, but I don't owe him anything."

"No, you don't. This isn't your work, it's his."

"You're damned right it's his."

"Still, it's not right if he's trying to do the right thing and you won't let him."

"I'm not stopping him. I'm not doing anything to him. I'm trying to get on with my life."

"He's got to get through this so he can get on with his."

For this, Cherry had no comment.

"Can I say something?" Wyatt's eyes were the bluest of the blue-green bunch.

Cherry huffed.

Wyatt took it for a yes. "This is Holden's fuck-up, we know that. But, he had help. You know he had help. None of us are proud of what we did to him, to you. It never would have happened without us riding his ass. You should know Holden doesn't make the same mistake twice."

"You know, Wyatt, that is so Latche-man-like. One for all and all that crap. Don't worry. If you want, I can blame you too."

"I do worry. Because you should, but I don't think you get that. You've put Holden in the same category as the rest of us assholes, but he doesn't belong there. He's better than that. He got sucked into it. We pulled him down where we were because we didn't understand. We didn't know any better. He didn't fit there before you came along. Nobody thought about that. All we could see was this different kind of man. We didn't recognize it as better, just different. But he is better." He weighed his admission. "We shrunk in comparison. It was hard, uncomfortable. I guess the twisted logic was, all men should act the same way, should be thinking and doing the same things. If somebody was different, they weren't being a man. We were all pulling him down, trying to get him to be more like us. If he lost some of his luster, didn't shine so bright, maybe we wouldn't look so dull."

There was something true in what he said. Cherry didn't like it. She didn't want any Latche-male saying anything true, anything believable. Because believing any one of them meant believing Holden. There was no way in hell she was doing that. "Let me see if I have this right." She pushed her anger to the forefront of her thoughts. "You and Eric and Eli and Bruce and whoever else, forced Holden to be unfaithful."

"Not forced. More like manipulated. We pushed him." Wyatt threw his arms out. "Cherry, we're men. Men screw around. Men fuck-up. That's what we do." He smacked his hands against his thighs, frustrated. "It's all we know."

Cherry wasn't aware her mouth was hanging open until she had to swallow the bitter bile that was threatening to spew forth.

They all waited, watching while her mind worked to absorb the information. Cherry closed her eyes against the tears. They came anyway. She took a few breaths so she could talk around them. "You're right. I should blame you, and I do. All of you. You have the nerve to stand there telling me screwing up is a man-thing. You are an imbecile. Apparently, you don't realize you have a penis, Wyatt, because you are a man. Not the other way around."

Wyatt didn't miss a beat. "Exactly. We don't realize. And who, besides you, ever tried to teach us? You expected Holden to know the difference. None of us knew the difference."

"And you know it now?"

"Yes. We know it now," Eric said. "You better believe Holden knows it. Even Bruce knows it now. What I don't know is how you can come into our lives, change everything and then run away when we don't get it right. We didn't get it right because we didn't know what we were doing, Cherry. We didn't know. "

"Our? We? This is somehow about you?"

"Yes." All three siblings voiced together.

Wyatt said, "This isn't just about you and Holden and some...lovers... whatever. We are a family. You don't get to run out on us anytime you want."

"That's exactly what I get to do. I'm not in your family."

"The hell you ain't."

Cherry didn't have an argument. Nobody was listening to her anyway. "So...so what am I supposed to do?" She eyed them one by one. "Hang around having my heart broke on a daily basis because you've decided it should be this way? Did it ever occur to any of you, Holden might be better off without me? Or without you meddling, at least?"

"No." Again, the siblings spoke in unison.

"I told you," Amy said. "You don't have to do anything. It's not your work. But you do have to let him do his. Please, let him do his."

There was a time of quiet. Everyone was waiting for something. No one knew what.

"You know what?" Cherry could only take thinking for so long. "I can't do this." She turned and went down the steps. "I'm tired. I have to go home," she muttered, retracing her steps to Holden's truck. "See ya later."

Eric pushed forward, following her down. "He loves you, Cherry. You love him. Neither one of you ever stopped."

She rolled her eyes and pulled off.

# CHAPTER 34

Cherry did not notice she was crying again when she pulled out of the Latche drive. She had been doing it so much since yesterday it was starting to feel like a habit. There was a car on the side of the road. She glanced at it as she passed. It was her car. Her ex-boyfriend had followed her to his house. *That wasn't comprehendible.*

The engine surged to life as she went by.

She wanted to run over him, but seeing as he was in her car (her car that wouldn't start!) she reined in the temptation. However, she refused to look into her rearview mirror the whole way home.

Holden pulled into the drive behind his truck. It heartened him to see the anger radiating from Cherry as she stomped over.

"Get out of my car." The statement wasn't necessary since he was in process of doing that when she got there. "Why are you in my car?"

"You were driving my truck."

"You told me to."

"I wasn't complaining."

"Did you do something to my car?" The obvious became apparent when he opened her hood. "Did you make it not run?"

"No." He touched something she couldn't see then quickly closed the hood. "Not at first."

"Why wouldn't it drive for me?"

"Eric disabled it."

"Ohhhhh." She kicked the air.

"Do you want to go in the house?"

"No. I want you to go away and leave me and my car alone. Why are you here? Why did you follow me?" She started walking toward the house without her awareness.

"I don't mean to upset you, Cherry. I'm not trying to do anything other than breathe." He stopped at her door. "I'm just breathing. I haven't had a deep breath since you left. All I'm doing is breathing. I'm learning how to breathe again."

Her hands trembled as she opened the door and held it. "Holden, don't do this to me. I can't go through this again."

He didn't answer. He stepped back and sank into the rocker.

"Holden."

"I'm not leaving. I understand you don't want to see me. I'm sorry it hurts you to have me here. Try to pretend I don't exist. I won't bother you, I promise. But, please, don't ask me to leave, because I can't." He looked down at his massive hands. "Don't you leave either. If you do, I'll follow you. It's the only way I can breathe."

"Holden." Her voice cracked. "Don't do this to me."

"I'm sorry, Cherry. I don't have a choice." He buried his face in his hands. "I have to breathe."

Cherry went inside, closing the door softly. She took three more steps and broke down at the foot of the stairs. Weeping and thinking and feeling, all over herself. Only she was thinking and feeling things she hadn't counted on. She didn't want to miss him. She didn't want her fingers to tingle with the need to touch his hair, his face. She hadn't counted on absorbing Holden's confession. And Eric's. And Wyatt's. It was too much. The minutes were slow and her thoughts were way too fast. She should have left Amy to fend for herself. Her life would still be right-side-up if she had. But she hadn't. Now, she was being forced *not* to ignore Holden. It was too much.

Her legs were unsteady and she felt anxious, making herself go back to the door. She wouldn't look, trusting he was still there. "If you want to come in, I'll try to talk to you."

He was there, right beside her, having moved the exact moment she spoke. "Thank you," he said, reverently accepting her gift.

It felt awkward, having Holden in her foyer. She had never envisioned him in her house. "Umm. Sit down." She led the way to the living room. "Do you want a drink or something?"

Holden did as he was bidden. "A drink would be good."

"Juice, water, soda? There is a bar in the dining room." She pointed. "But, you'll have to get it yourself. I'm still a total novice with alcohol."

He remembered. Of course, he remembered. "Thanks." He headed toward her bar, already impressed. "This is a beautiful house."

"Thank you," she said. "How long are we going to be stiff and formal?" She muttered, not intending for him to hear.

He heard her anyway. "I'm just grateful you let me come in." He returned with two drinks, handing one to her. "Do you still like amaretto sours?"

The memory hurt. Her first taste of an amaretto sour and her first taste of him. "Yes." She reached for the glass, unable to meet his gaze. "It's delicious," she said after a sip. "I don't know how to make them."

"I'll teach you."

By now, they were back in the living room. Holden sat in the same chair Missy sat in the night before. *Was that only a day ago?* Cherry sat on the sofa- the opposite end from where she curled up in Eric's arms.

"What are we doing, Holden? Why are we here, like this?"

"We have unfinished business, you and I."

"Our relationship is over." It shouldn't hurt this much to voice it.

"For you maybe. It's not over for me. It's never going to be over for me."

Attitude. All attitude. "Excuse me? If I remember correctly, and I can assure you I do, you were the one to end it. You didn't want what we had anymore."

"That doesn't make it over." He took a drink.

"It does in the real world." So did she.

"I don't give a shit about the real world, just us."

"You didn't give a shit about us. That's the reason we're here."

"Cherry, I love you. I have always loved you. I always will."

"Stop. Holden." She couldn't hear that. She didn't want to hear that. "Please, stop." She moved her hair out of her face and sucked in all the air she could. "What I remember, what I know, is that you had a problem with us. You wanted to be involved with other women. You asked me to kindly go away so you could screw-up in peace. I've honored your request. I've left you alone. What else do you want from me?"

"A chance to explain."

"Did you not make yourself clear when you told me to go away? You had a life and plans that did *not* include me and it would be better for me *not* to hang around to see it? It all seemed clear to me. Did you leave something out?"

"Actually, I did. But, that wasn't what I meant. I'd like a chance to explain how it got to that point and what I've learned since."

She sat her glass down with more force than necessary. "It doesn't matter how it got there and nothing that came after has anything to do with me."

"You're wrong. It has everything to do with you. It's always been about you."

"What's that mean?"

"It means my life is about you. You don't have to accept it, but it is."

"Perhaps you should work on getting over this and getting a new life."

"If I could, I would have. Cherry, I fucked up, royally. That changed your feelings, not mine. You've been gone and all I've done is wait. I know it's too late, but I waited anyway. The fact is, there is no getting over you. The fact is, I've hurt myself almost as much as I've hurt you. The fact is, I'm as angry with you as you are with me. Everything is all about you."

Of all the things she'd expected to feel, she was surprised to be so annoyed. "You're angry with me? For....what? Doing what you said? Leaving the man who told me to go?"

"Yes, I'm angry about it. But not for the reasons you think."

She raised her hands, palms up. A pose indicating she wanted him to elaborate.

"Why didn't you tell me about Peaches?"

Her hands plopped down. "Pardon me?"

"You know what I'm talking about. You didn't tell me about your brother either."

"What's that got to do with anything?"

"Everything." He slammed the rest of his drink back.

"I don't see how."

"It does."

"Tell you what? What do you want to know?"

"Tell me what?" he heaved, annoyed all over again. "What did you think? I was going to stop loving you because of their mistakes?"

The sad surprise in her gray eyes confirmed his suspicion.

"Everybody makes mistakes. Everybody has life happen to them in some form or another. Hiding it doesn't change it. And hiding it from me is just wrong. Cherry, it's just wrong."

"What was I supposed to tell you about it?" She didn't believe she had done anything wrong, but the slight burning in her chest made her nervous. It wasn't the amaretto. "That's them. What Beany and Peach do is their business. Their lives, not mine. That's not me. I didn't bring any of that here with me~"

He leveled his gaze at her. "You did. That's where all of this comes from. They are a part of you and you take how you feel about it wherever you go."

She had been leaning forward, interested. Now, she understood. She could relax. This was a fight she was familiar with. "I know what this is. Thank you, Aunt Sid." She couldn't or didn't want to help the sarcasm in her tone. "I know. I don't address my problems. I'm a runner. I've heard it a million times, Holden."

"Did it ever occur to you that maybe she's right?"

Cherry's brow crinkled. No. Aunt Sid was not right. She never allowed herself to believe Aunt Sid could be right. It was too difficult a thought.

"Africa, Cherry. You went to Africa." He said it as if that explained everything. It did explain everything.

Going to Senegal to get away from him didn't make her a runner. Except, she did go to Senegal to get away from him. She was a runner. But what else was she supposed to do? She felt herself go stiff again, tight. "What should I have done?" She didn't know. She wanted to get up and bolt out of the door, but given the conversation- and the fact that she couldn't remember where she laid his keys- she didn't think that idea was going to work.

"Instead of being evasive, you should have told me Beany was in jail. And I would have gone with you to visit him."

Her pupils dilated. The thought had never occurred to her.

"I'd have taken you to see your nieces. We could have brought them down for a visit. Teach them to ride. Something. Anything. I know you, honey. As kind and giving as you are with Missy and Amy and Pattycakes. As much as you love Tabby and Brucey and Isaiah. I don't have a doubt that you would move heaven to help your own blood. I know what it must have cost you to know you couldn't fix it. You couldn't save them."

Cherry was completely stunned. This time, beyond tears. She could feel the tremors. The shell woven around her soul was cracking, breaking off in painful little bits. Everything she held in for so long threatened to come out. She was a volcano, about to erupt.

He switched seats, coming closer to her on the sofa. "That burden made you run...here. Someplace where you could sleep at night and not have to think about it. You wouldn't have to feel like a failure because you couldn't fix it."

It was too difficult to form words. She nodded. Admitting it. Owning it. For the first time, unable to keep her inadequateness from being exposed.

"You should have shared that with me. That's why I have shoulders, Cherry." He tapped the broad expanse of muscle. "I would have taken that burden from you. I wouldn't have judged them. Or you. But I would have taken that burden. If our relationship would have worked like it was supposed to, I would have taken your burdens and given you some of mine. But that's not what happened, is it?

"I knew I was making a mistake as you were walking away. I just didn't know what to do about it. I was fighting you, me, the world. I did it wrong, but I was fighting. You, on the other hand, you just rolled over and died. You quit, for no other reason than somebody told you to. It pisses me the hell off that after all your talk of love and forever, you dropped us on a whim. My whim, but still just a whim. All I'm left with is knowing you had your expectations for your perfect life with your perfect man and your perfect happiness. Everything was fine as long as your expectations were met. I messed up once." He held up a finger. "Once. I stopped being perfect and you were done. Actually, you didn't stay long enough for me to mess up. You didn't pray or hope I wouldn't. Once you realized how flawed I am, you cut me and everything associated with me right out of your perfect picture. So much for forever. So much for love. It obviously only counts when it's perfect...for you."

"No. No. No..." Cherry shook her head against the pain, against the truth. "This is not about me or what I think or feel or said or did~"

"Why not? It's about me and what I thought and felt and said and did. Why is it only about me and my lack of loyalty to our relationship? Why is your lack of loyalty excusable? Mine isn't."

"You want to make this a fight about my responses. It's not about my responses. It's about what I was responding to. It's about what you did to cause me to respond."

"Yes. You're right. It is about what I did. What I did was respond! I was responding to a situation I had no business being in. I responded poorly. But what I thought and felt and said and did didn't come out of thin air, Cherry. You're okay with excusing your actions and behavior. I'm wondering if you could extend to me some understanding. And maybe, in time, some forgiveness."

Cherry slumped back into the sofa. *This is wrong. It's not about anything but what he did to me, to us.* While she was still thinking it, she felt selfish. That was wrong too. "This is wrong. You have no right to try to make me feel bad because I had the nerve to get hurt."

"I'm not trying to make you feel bad. I'm not trying to justify my behavior. I'm trying to get you to see me as something other than a villain."

"I don't see you as a villain, Holden."

"What do you see me as?"

She didn't answer. She didn't want to.

He waited.

When the silence got heavy, she repeated, "I don't see you as the villain."

"If not a villain, who?"

"I see the man who stopped loving me. Who chose to hurt me. Who's angry because I couldn't take it."

"I'm angry because I needed you. I can't fix this without you. I thought you would love me even when I wasn't loveable."

"You can't fix this, Holden. Just like..." She had to make herself complete the sentence. "I couldn't fix them."

"You see, that's the difference. You can't fix Peaches or Beany any more than you can fix Pattycakes and Wyatt. You can help them when they want it, but you can't fix them. We can't fix the outside world. We're not supposed to. But we can, we must, we can fix what's inside. We can fix us."

"How?" She looked up at the ceiling, ignoring the tiny fluttering of hope. She knew better than to hope. "How does that work?"

"We start with this~"

"We nothing. I'm not doing anything~"

"You don't have to. We start with this. You get used to the idea that I'm not letting you go~"

"You don't have me. You can't hold me."

"I'm not letting you go again. Eventually, we'll get to understanding everything that happened and why. Finally, we begin to heal. When all that's done, if you can get back to being in love with me, I'd appreciate it. If not, I'll understand. And, I'll still be here because I'm not letting you go. That's the basic plan."

Cherry got up. She couldn't take anymore. She was close to having a meltdown and she wasn't about to have it in front of him. Without another word, she went to her room, grabbing a new box of Kleenex in route. She threw herself across her bed and gave in to the biggest fit of hysterics she could muster.

# CHAPTER 35

*Something smelled delicious.* Cherry blinked, for a moment wondering where she was. She blinked again and her bedroom came into focus. Her head hurt. Something was making her mouth water. She sniffed but couldn't identify the aroma. How long had she been asleep? She gasped when she looked at the clock on her nightstand. Five thirty-seven! With all that was on her mind, how could she have fallen asleep? For the entire day? Was Holden still here? She didn't want to focus on the spike of panic she felt at the thought that he wasn't.

Stiffly, she got up and spent some time in the bathroom. First, searching out some Advil, then washing the tear streaks and swelling from her eyes. After a few pointless minutes, she settled for brushing her hair and teeth. Anything was an improvement. She smoothed the wrinkles from the front of her skirt. Ten hours ago, the outfit was on point. "Time for round two," she told her reflection.

He was in her kitchen, at her stove. Why else would her house smell so yummy? Her stomach growled in agreement.

"Hi." He gave her a soft half-smile and returned his attention to the pan in front of him.

He left while she was sleeping. He was showered and shaved and in fresh jeans. His shirt was unbuttoned, revealing a snow-white beater and the imprint of his chiseled pecs.

*Damn the man. He had no right to be so appealing.* "Hi." She tore her eyes away. *You have no right to be looking, either.*

"I made dinner. I hope you don't mind."

For the first time, she noticed the table was set for two. "Uhh...No. Can I do something?" Asking if she could help in her own kitchen, how weird was that?

"You can grab the appetizer, it's on the counter." He pointed to his right. "Oh, and the wine. I'm almost done here."

"It smells great. What did you make?" When she got to the counter, her stomach growled again. She hoped he didn't hear it.

"Smoked duck a l'orange, sea salt and lavender fingerling potatoes, sweet peppers and onions, a few portabellas." He worked from a mental list. "You're holding lump crab on baguettes with melted Monterey Jack."

The boy knew how to charm. She couldn't deny that. Wordlessly, she sat down while he prepared their plates.

. . . . .

Holden poured the wine and served them. They finished the crab in companionable silence. It was too good to talk through.

"I can't believe I slept so long." Cherry bit into her duck and moaned with pleasure.

"You were up very early this morning. It was bound to catch up with you."

"I guess. What did you do today? Besides all of this." She waved her fork over her plate then stabbed a pepper.

"I took a nap myself, on your sofa. I went home for a while. I went to the store, came back and started dinner."

Inwardly, it amused Cherry. They sounded so normal.

"Everybody said hello and Pattycakes was wondering if you would consider going with her to the gym again."

His easy comments made her wistful. She missed the Latches. "This is so good." Cherry savored the potatoes. She hadn't forgotten what a good cook he was, but the proof was overwhelming.

"Thank you. I haven't done it in a while. It was fun." He studied her across the table, his gaze softly intense.

"So what have you been doing with yourself since...you know?" It had been pleasant. She hadn't planned to go there.

"Since you've been gone? I haven't done anything. I couldn't function without you."

"Holden, let's not do this. Your dinner is wonderful, but it doesn't change anything."

"What?" he scoffed. "Do you think I'm trying to seduce you or something?"

"Aren't you?" It stung a little that he didn't seem interested, but she wasn't going to dwell on that.

"What would that earn me?" His gaze was thick with knowledge. "I cooked because I was hungry and I thought you would be too. There's no secret meaning behind it." He picked up a portabella with his fingers and offered the tasty morsel to her with a wink.

She accepted his offering before she realized what she was doing. She squeezed her eyes shut against her unguarded behavior. The man was lethal.

"You might as well relax. This is going to be a bumpy ride, but we're already on it. There's no point in making things any harder than they need to be for either of us. Let's just get through it."

"You seem... I don't know, relaxed."

"I am. At least a little more relaxed. We've already survived seeing each other for the first time. Those first moments. I confess, I hadn't meant to fall asleep. I was terrified when I woke up, but you hadn't disappeared. I made myself go home. You were still here when I got back. It was a relief."

"I live here."

"With your track record, that didn't give me any confidence." He refilled their wine glasses. "Being able to breathe for an entire day has been great."

"Why do you keep saying that?"

"Because that's what it felt like, not seeing you. Like I couldn't breathe. I couldn't. Not when I didn't know if you were okay."

"Y-you can't say things like that to me." Before he could ask why, the phone rang. "I'm sorry. I have to get this," she said when she heard the ring tone. "My friend's worried. I should have called her." She reached for her cordless. "I know. You were worried. Sorry, Jeanie. I should have called."

"Pppfffhhh. I know you're all right. I didn't call for you. Where is that yummy hunk of man of yours?"

"W-what?"

"Holden. He's still there, isn't he? Tell me you did not send him away. If you did, please tell me you sent him to my house."

"How did you~"

"Chica, please. I've talked to him three times already. I was going to have him for dinner, but he's an awful lot to eat."

Cherry closed her mouth, held out the phone and said, "It's for you. Although I've no idea why you would be getting calls from my so-called friends."

Holden gave her a shameless grin as he accepted the device. "Jeanie."

Cherry's nostrils flared. "Of course." She remembered when he was on the phone with her, he always sounded like he was in between licks of something he thought was delicious.

"I'm putting you on speaker, Jeanie." He pushed the button. "We don't want to give Cherry the wrong idea."

"Pppfffhhh. Cherry knows me well enough to already have the wrong idea. Did you use the candles?"

"No. I told you, I'm not going for romance." He shot Cherry a smoldering glance. "Not tonight, anyway."

"What a waste. Mister, you were made for romance."

"What are you calling me for?" He didn't sound at all disturbed.

"'Cause you're yummy. And because I couldn't remember what you said to do with the potatoes."

"Mash them like you normally do but instead of milk, add about a cup of ranch dressing."

"Gotcha. And the pumpkin cheesecake?"

"Drizzle the caramel. If you put on too much, it will overwhelm it. You want to be the sweetest thing in front of him."

"Ohh baby. Can I keep you?"

"My dinner is getting cold."

"Set it on your lap. That will heat it right up. That would heat me right up."

"Have fun tonight, Jeanie."

"I will. Especially later tonight. You are going to star in my dreams as a pirate."

"Arrgghhh."

His pirate impersonation was dead on. Jeanie hung up giggling. He set the phone aside. "You have an interesting friend."

"Jeanie is...uniquely...Jeanie. As you just pointed out, she's my friend. What was that?"

"She came over while you were asleep. She said she had called a couple of times, got worried when she didn't get an answer. Anyway, we hung out and shopped and swapped recipes." He rolled his eyes heavenward. "We didn't swap recipes. She can't cook. I know she can't cook. That's it. Are you ready for dessert?"

"Umm. Yeah." She wondered if it had caramel drizzled over it.

It didn't. He went to the refrigerator and pulled out a plate of white-chocolate sin.

"Wow. When did you have time to do all of this?"

"You did sleep all day."

He poured more wine and they quietly enjoyed the last of their meal. It was too easy to imagine this as perfect. Cherry searched her mind for some imperfection. "So... err... What did you and Jeanie talk about? Exactly?"

"When she wasn't being suggestive, us."

"Us?" Cherry choked. "As in you and her?"

"Don't be absurd. Us as in, you and I."

"What about us?"

"I gave her my side of the story and we debated tactics. She thinks I should romance you first. I know better."

"Tactics? What am I, a country to be conquered?"

"Something like that."

He was using that voice again and he wasn't even on the phone. "Candles or no candles, I'm not about to be conquered."

"I said, I know better."

She was going to emphasize her point, but she remembered something else he said. "Your side of the story? What's that mean?"

"I think we know your perspective. However, I doubt you have any idea of my side of the story. That's a problem. You know everything you've been through since we broke up. You're prepared to do whatever you have to, to save yourself from being hurt again, but you don't know anything about what I've been through."

"Should I care?"

"Yes. You should and you do."

She stared at him.

"Say whatever you think will work, but you care, Cherry. We both know you do."

Suddenly, she felt defeated. There was no way she was getting out of this untouched. She was tired of trying. "All right, Holden." She had her last fork-full of the dessert and chased it down with several gulps of wine. "Rip out my heart again. Tell me your side of the story. Don't spare the details. Make sure I remember how good we were and how much I loved you and all that I've lost." She finished her wine. "It's important for me to remember how much I've lost. I should probably have something else to drink. Something strong. Loving you and not loving you takes large quantities of alcohol." She scraped her finger across her plate, sucking the mound of cream she collected. "Another slice of pie too, because fat and depressed work well together."

Holden came around the table and caught her by the hand. He pulled her to her feet. "Calm down, honey. It happened a year ago, not last Tuesday. We'll get through it. I've got something stronger than wine planned for this conversation." He picked up the pie plate with his free hand. "Let's go into the living room."

Cherry followed, mutely. Stunned, shocked. Holden was holding her hand. She couldn't believe how right it felt.

# CHAPTER 36

They sat on the sofa, her at one end, him at the other. On the coffee table, between them, the pie, fresh plates and forks, a chilled bottle of Vilmart Grand Cellier and two flutes. Also, a fifth of Jack Daniels and two shot glasses.

Cherry watched him pour the champagne and fill the shot glasses. "That's different."

"The conversation will dictate which drink we need."

"The conversation has already dictated which drink I need." She threw back a shot, making a face while she waited for the burning to subside.

He refilled her glass. "Careful. If you miss this talk, we'll have to do it again."

She sat the glass down and picked up her plate. "I'm positive one time will be more than enough."

"Let's hope." He started with a shot too.

"Okay. Let's have at it. This is the best pie I've ever eaten, by the way."

"Thank you. It has alcohol in it too, but not a lot."

They both found that amusing. Then the atmosphere stilled. Holden stared off into space, trying to pick a beginning. Cherry stared at Holden, tense, waiting.

"Do you mind if we examine your sins first." He cut her a rueful glance. "They're not as bad as mine."

She braced herself. "Have at it."

"Why didn't you tell me about you and Eric?" There was no accusation in his tone, just sadness.

"Tell you what?"

"You were intimate with my brother. That's something we should have discussed."

"It wasn't like that. We weren't intimate. You're making it sound like we were having an affair."

"I'm not going to do wordplay. He kissed you. You didn't tell me about it and I was left to burn."

She wanted to argue, but didn't see any point in the endeavor. "I never knew what I was supposed to say about it. I didn't want you to be mad at Eric."

"That wasn't a decision you needed to make for me."

Maybe not. It wasn't something she was willing to debate. "When did you find out?"

"The same day it happened. Eric told me. Don't worry, he told me the truth. He could have kept it to himself, but he wasn't willing to let anything come between us. Him and me or you and me."

She was glad she didn't argue. She didn't have a case.

"I spent every day watching you be close to him, knowing you were entertaining thoughts~"

"No, I wasn~"

"Yes, you were. I could see that too. You let it come between us~"

"I didn't let that come between us. If you were holding on to something that was nothing, you let it come between us."

"I wasn't the one kissing another man. Want to know what I was doing while you were with Eric."

"Riding fences." She remembered.

"Waiting to propose."

There was an explosion of silence. There was nothing to be said. That was all her fault. She covered her mouth, physically trying to hold the scream in. One kiss. It hurt him, hurt her, hurt them. She squeezed her eyes shut, needing to rein herself in.

He allowed her the time to compose herself or to burn. Whichever.

When he felt she was in as much control as she was likely to be, he said,

"There's more."

She nodded.

"That was your habit. I was a part of your life, but not an interactive part."

"Holden, you were my life."

"Only in as much as I fit the perfect picture and stayed out of your way."

She shook her head and reached for the Jack Daniels. "I don't know what you mean."

"I didn't matter enough for you to tell me about Eric." He held up his hand to halt her interruption. "I didn't matter when you decided to help Missy or Pattycakes. I didn't matter when you decided I should be Isaiah's father. You just made your choices, you chose for me to follow your lead. Information came on a need to know basis and how I felt was never in your calculations." He reached for the Jack Daniels, the bottle. "Here's the thing," he said after a big swig. "When you were helping Missy, I would have said don't do it and I would have been wrong. I would have been wrong with Pattycakes. Hell, I probably would have been wrong with Isaiah. But, I would not have been wrong with Eric. If I had been a part of your decision to go with him, I would have said no and I would not have been wrong." Another swig. "That's how relationships work. Both people participate. I was a prop, not a participant. I had gotten pretty damned angry. Explosive angry. Everybody could see it, but you." He slammed the bottle down, focusing all of his anger on Cherry. "Eric was trying to be there, to pick up the pieces, because he saw us falling apart. I didn't have your respect and Wyatt and Eric and Bruce and every other man in town could see it. They were working hard to help me gain some self-respect. They'd have laid off if I had any, but I didn't. I had to wear it, your disrespect. I had to live with it because I loved you and it was supposed to be worth it. It was supposed to work out in the end. I was supposed to mean something to you. Only, I didn't. When the explosion came, you ran off and made other plans for your life. Plans that once again, didn't include me." That last sentence hung in the air between them. He went back to staring into space.

Long minutes ticked by while Cherry processed his perspective. She could see it. She could understand it. It made her hurt to have hurt him.

"I'm sorry," she said at last. "It was never my intention to hurt you." They were sitting closer now, leaning toward one another. Tentatively, she touched his hand.

He wrapped his fingers around hers, desperate for the contact.

"I never thought of it that way. I never considered what I might have been doing to you. It was always so easy to be with you. You made me feel free. Like I could do anything. And, I did." She shrugged. "I did whatever I wanted, all the time. Because you loved me. I thought I had that right. I thought that's what being free was about. You were Mr. Wonderful, making it possible for all my dreams to come true, so I chased my dreams. I never stopped to see if you were following. I always thought you were."

"Those were your mistakes." He handed her one glass of champagne and touched the tip with the other before taking a sip. "The one being, your freedom. While you were being free, you didn't realize that you aren't free if you are in a relationship. You can't be tied to someone and be free to do whatever you choose at the same time." He leaned over to brush a tear from her cheek.

"I was living a double-standard." She hadn't been aware she was crying until he touched her.

"The other was your expectation that I was following. I'm not a follower, Cherry. At best, I can do it fifty percent of the time, and that would only be for you. I don't belong on a pedestal. I don't belong on a trophy shelf and I don't belong on the sidelines. I'm either in the game or I don't play."

"I wished we could have talked about this."

"You didn't talk to me about anything."

"Why didn't you make me listen?"

"I didn't know what the problem was until it was too late. I didn't figure it out until I had months of nothing but time and my thoughts. After a while, even Bruce left me alone."

More minutes ticked past. He switched the Vilmart for the shots. It was time. It was coming. They both knew it. He waited, still, statue-like, while she gathered her strength, her nerve. It was coming. They both knew it.

She swished the amber liquid around the glass. "There was a girl in the

Bunkhouse."

"Yes."

"Did you bring her there?"

"No."

"Who did?"

"Bruce."

"Why was she there?"

"Mainly, for me."

She didn't want to ask, but she had to know. For sure. For certain. "Did you sleep with her?"

He thought about it for a long moment. "I won't lie to you Cherry."

She couldn't help the trembling. The truth didn't hurt any less just because she already knew it. "H-had you b-been...with her before I got there."

"No."

"But you slept with her after I left." It wasn't a question.

"I did." Holden wiped another tear from her cheek. She twisted her face away. In the heavy silence, he wiped a tear from his own cheek. "You had already accused me of doing it. I had already broken us up. I wanted you to fight for me, for us. But you walked away. I was angry and hurt. At the time, I thought, what the hell. My life was over anyway, why not put the nail in the coffin. Afterwards, I felt like shit and I've felt like shit ever since."

She hadn't taken her hand from his. If she withdrew it, she would be running. She willed herself to leave it there. "How long did you stay with her?"

"I haven't seen her since."

Cherry forced the words out, needing to engrave them in the air. "You cheated on me, Holden. You had an affair."

"I didn't cheat."

"I get my part in this. I took you for granted. I can see why you think I was dishonest. Maybe I was. I don't know. But, I never slept with anyone. I never would have cheated."

"I didn't cheat on you. We had broken up, Cherry."

"That's a technicality and you know it."

"I know it's a technicality to you. An insignificant one. Nevertheless, for me, it's the difference between life and death. It's the only hope I have. Given my family's history, what I've done. That one choice, that one step, was in the right direction. I'm at least facing the right way. I can be redeemed. In spite of everything, I can get it right. I know how to do right. If I don't hold on to that one little insignificant technicality, I may as well curl up and die. That difference is all I have." He sat his glass down. He was done drinking. He was done everything.

Inhale. Exhale. Cherry was still alive, still breathing. She didn't know how that was possible. "What did you do then?" Inhale. Exhale. Inhale...

"I turned over and waited to die. When that didn't happen, I tried to find you so we could figure this mess out and fix it. When I couldn't find you, I went back to waiting to die for a while. While I was waiting, I went to church. I went to work. I didn't do much else until yesterday."

"Why not?" Exhale. Inhale. Exhale...

"I was waiting for you to come home. I couldn't find you. You didn't return my messages. What else could I do but wait?"

Inhale. Exhale. "You went to church?"

"Yes."

"Why?"

"At first, it was because Aunt Sid said so. Then because it was a good idea. I felt low. Dirty. I wounded you. I used her. I failed at being a man. After all that time, fighting to be a man and then I failed. I wanted to get clean again. I wanted that stain off my soul. I wanted it gone."

"Is it gone?"

"Not all of it. I'm better, although I don't think it can go away completely until you let yourself forgive me."

Inhale. Exhale. Inhale. Forgive? Let herself? Her mind couldn't even touch that. "Why not?"

"Because I need your forgiveness, Cherry. I need you to erase it. I need you to heal me. To heal us."

"I...I c-can't...I don't...I...I..."

"Only you." He whispered his love, his pain, his desperation.

She was aware of the slightest tug on her hand. The tiniest pull of his fingers drawing hers, his heart drawing hers. Then they were kissing and she wasn't aware of anything. The alcohol, the honesty, the pain, the inhaling, the exhaling, the need, the love, the intensity swirled together. She couldn't think. She couldn't talk. She could only feel. Passion. His. Hers. Theirs. Passion.

She didn't know if he pulled her or if she moved on her own, but she slid across the cushions. She was on his lap straddling him, riding him. He held her to him, moving her body over his. He fisted her hair, caressed her face, her back, her butt. They had never made love, but they were making it now. He suckled her through her top while his erection pushed against her core. Hot. Hard. Fast. Even fully dressed and not penetrating, it was everything.

He licked his way up her neck as she kissed her way down his face until their lips fused. She moaned into his mouth, shoving her tongue as far down his throat as possible. He sucked her tongue as he had her breasts seconds before. She gripped his shoulders, melting over him.

Of their own volition, his hands searched beneath her skirt. Pushing it up out of his way, he massaged her, stroked her thighs. He increased the friction and she moaned again as her orgasm spilled over. And then his heart exploded. He bucked, gasping as his orgasm followed hers.

They kissed and cried and loved some more, not needing to understand or define the how's or why's of the plateau they had come to. Only reveling in it until all the emotions were spent. He cuddled her, not allowing her to move. She remained straddled across him, unwilling to move. More kisses. More touching. And the alcohol, the honesty, the pain, the inhaling, the exhaling, the need, the love, the intensity swirled together, knotting around them and in them and through them. Breathing heavily against his throat, stroking his chest as he rocked her, Cherry's eyelashes fluttered down and she fell asleep.

Holden breathed her in, the white chocolate, the champagne, the muskiness of sex. He would never again be with another woman. He'd wait forever for Cherry. For the moment, he was at peace. For the moment, he was without stain. He kissed the top of her head and closed his eyes, content.

# CHAPTER 37

Cherry tried to blink her bedroom into focus. It was impossible to see around the white t-shirt Holden was wearing. She couldn't begin to imagine how they came to be sleeping, entwined, in her bed. Except for her shoes, she was still fully dressed, as was he. That was a good sign. She heard stories of girls waking up, unsure if they had sex. She could never bring herself to believe someone could be that naive...or dumb. Yet, she did have a lot to drink and he was in her bed. If she'd lost her virginity, she hoped she wouldn't be the last to know.

"You look like you've been caught stealing something."

His morning voice was the sexiest thing she had ever heard. Her pulse quickened. Guiltily, she looked up and felt like she was falling into the blue-green mystery of his deep eyes. "Hi."

He lavished her with a smile that would have knocked her off her feet, had she been on them. "Good morning."

"Did we, did I, drink too much?"

"I don't think so. Do you have a hangover?"

She thought about it. Headache –none. Nausea –none. Dizzy –no. Upset stomach –nope. "No, I'm not hung over."

"Good." He kissed her forehead.

"Holden?"

"Yes."

"What happened? How did we get here?"

"Don't worry. I didn't ravish you, Cherry. I was afraid your legs were going to cramp so I put us to bed."

"Oh." She waited. When he didn't offer any more, she asked, "And, before? I don't understand. Did I attack you? Did I do this?"

"Actually, we kind of attacked each other. I've been thinking about it. A lot. My best guess is that we both got overwhelmed with emotion. Everything became too much. For me, it was impossible to contain myself. I had to hold you, touch you. I didn't have a choice."

"We've never done anything quite like that before."

"Maybe we should have."

She snickered and silently agreed. "What do we do now?"

Holden shifted, leaning over Cherry. Without warning, he claimed her mouth. Her ability to think evaporated. He pressed into her. Involuntarily, she wrapped her arms around him, dragging him closer. He kissed down her cheek, licked the underside of her jaw and nibbled his way up to her ear, swirling his tongue around the lobe before whispering, "I'd like to do more of that." The next moment, he released her, swinging himself around and coming to his feet.

Cherry was hot, cold and ashamed. She knew, without a doubt, if he wanted to continue, she would not have stopped him.

He held out his hand to help her up. "We don't have to do anything. It will happen, if you let it."

She shook her head slowly, partially because she didn't understand, mostly because she wasn't able to speak yet.

He dragged her up against his solid frame. "If you let yourself forgive me, it will happen." He freed her, moving about with sudden energy. "I was thinking, wondering if...you wanted to go to church with me."

Today was Sunday? How did that happen? She drank too much and spent the night with a man. Not any man, with Holden. Two minutes ago, she would have let him take her virginity. "Umm. Yeah. Church would probably be a good idea."

"I think so." He strolled out of the room.

A few seconds later, she heard him moving around in her guest room. His nerve mortified her, but as quickly as her ire flared up it died down. He had been in her bed all night. Being in her guest room was relatively mild by comparison. Besides, this was Holden, not a stranger. Also, if she told him to get out, he would. Of course, he wouldn't actually leave. He'd sleep in his truck or on her porch. He was fine in the guest room. Still, it might have been nice if he'd asked. However, after last night, formalities seemed a little awkward.

She closed her bedroom door and went about getting herself ready. She took an especially long shower, hoping the time away would help to clear her head. She hadn't seen Holden in over a year and within twenty-four hours he was in her bed. They were not a couple. The man cheated. *Not technically*, an annoying little voice reminded her. She wasn't completely innocent. She did kiss Eric. She had to admit- if only to herself- she enjoyed it. She kept it a secret from Holden. But still, he slept with someone. What was she supposed to do? She stared absently out of her window, wondering...

Caught in her musings, she did not hear him come in. Suddenly, he was behind her, wrapping her in his massive embrace. She jumped, startled, then relaxed in his arms. It was against her better judgment. Everything was against her better judgment.

He rubbed his nose along the side of her neck. "What are you thinking about?"

It didn't occur to her to lie. "About us."

"Mmmm. Good thoughts, I hope."

"Some. I don't know. I don't know what this is. I don't know what this means."

"We never fell out of love. You know that."

"I don't know anything. It's all too confusing."

"It will get clearer with time."

"Aren't you the least bit tangled? Insecure?"

"Uh-uh. I love you. That's the only thing that matters to me. If you let yourself forgive me, you'll get there too."

His declaration thrilled and scared her. "Suppose I don't get there?"

"That won't change how I feel."

"You changed how you felt before."

"My feelings never changed."

They were silent for a few seconds. It felt peaceful. It felt right.

"Let yourself forgive me, Cherry."

"I don't know how to do that."

"Keep doing what you're doing now."

"What am I doing?"

"You're letting me love you. You're not turning me away. That's all you have to do. Don't turn me away."

"I'm not letting you love me. I just don't know how to stop you...it...this...us..."

"Same difference."

She felt his smile and smiled herself. This was too easy to be right. It was certainly too soon.

"Do you remember when we first met?" He kissed her ear. He had to. "How easy it was."

"I remember."

"We didn't have to work at being together. We were a couple, we just were."

"Yes."

"That's how I know it's going to be all right. We're supposed to be together." He whispered into her hair, as if he didn't really want her to hear, "We have to be together."

"Why?" She closed her eyes against the yearning.

"Once you get struck by lightning you can't go back to being un-struck."

It was amazing, the things he made her feel.

"Can I show you something?"

There was a catch in his voice that made her turn. Seeing the uncertainty he claimed not to have somehow made her braver. She nodded once and let him lead her away from the window. They stopped at her dresser, both of them briefly studying the couple in the mirror. Holden switched his focus to the real Cherry. He pulled a small box from his pocket.

Cherry took a step back.

"Calm down. I just want you to see it." He opened the box to show her a sparkling antique diamond.

She couldn't breathe.

"I bought this almost a year and a half ago. If you like it, we'll sit it right here." He put it on her dresser. "When you're ready, let me know. I will get down on my knees." He demonstrated by going down on one knee.

"Holden~"

"I will place that ring on your finger." He kissed the third finger of her left hand. "And I will beg you to marry me." Slowly, he lifted her top out of his way. She gasped when he unbuttoned her dress-pants and rubbed his face against her abdomen. "I want to give you babies." He kissed her bellybutton several times. "Girls that look like you and boys that behave better than me." He brushed his chin along her panty line. "I want to love and protect you. I want to honor you and call you my wife."

Her hands were in his hair, too busy to stop her tears. Holden on his knees before her. Her diamond engagement ring glittering on the dresser behind him. The Celtic mirror enhancing every detail. The picture he painted with his words and actions, it was too beautiful. She couldn't speak.

"I won't force anything. Just know, when you are ready, that's what I'm going to do."

"Helllooooo," Jeanie called out. She peeked into the living room. "Champagne. Jack. Dessert." She stuck her finger into the remains of the pie. "Yummy dessert that tastes even better than mine. It looks like you had some night."

Holden stood up and refastened Cherry's pants with disconcerting efficiency.

"Jeanie," he called out.

"Stop using that voice on her," Cherry said through her teeth.

"What voice?"

"Where are you people?"

"Upstairs." Cherry chose to answer for them. "We're coming down now."

"Upstairs? Ohh baby. Definitely, some night."

Cherry followed Holden down.

"We're about to leave, do you want to come?"

"Anywhere with you." Jeanie slid her eyeglasses down so she could peer over the rims. "I bet you taste better than that pie."

Cherry giggled. "You want her to go to church?"

"Church?" Jeanie's face dropped.

Now, it was Holden's turn to laugh. "Can you think of anyone who needs it more?"

"Agreed."

"Church?"

"We should give her to Eric."

"Eric?" Jeanie perked up.

"I love my brother."

"Brother? You have a brother? Is he in church? Lead the way."

"He's not in church, but after service we have to stop past the farm. You can come with us if you like." Holden threw Cherry a crooked grin. "Everybody misses you. They want a real visit."

The thought of going to the farm gave her a thrill. A nervous thrill, but a thrill nonetheless.

"A real live farm-boy." Jeanie led the way out. "With a tractor and horses and muscles. Ohh baby."

•  •  •  •  •

Jeanie followed Cherry into the ladies' room. "You look a little peaked."

"Overwhelmed. That was some sermon. Redemption begins with forgiveness. I feel like Holden told the pastor what to preach on." She went into the first stall.

"He got lucky." Jeanie went into the one beside it. "Granted, he lined up everything else on the menu, but I don't think he has that kind of clout yet."

"What do you mean?"

"Come on, Cherry. I have on heels." Jeanie stuck her shiny red foot under the wall. "I didn't pop up at your house all dressed up, for no reason. Although, my acting was great, if I do say so myself." She imitated herself. "Church? Why ever would I go to Church?"

"Okay, I'm confused. This might be a good time for an explanation."

They met at the sink.

"Holden had already planned for me to come to church and hang out with you today."

"Why?"

"He thought, regardless of how the evening went, you would need me. Comfort, support, cheerleader, keep you from dwelling, getting depressed, all that jazz. Let me see. How did he say it? Oh, yeah. 'She needs somebody guaranteed to be on her side.' I'd like to be on his side and on his top and on his bottom too."

Cherry burst out laughing, strangely comforted. "Jeanie, we're in Church."

"We're in the bathroom. The place where crap happens."

"You're sick," Cherry said. She went serious. "Are you on my side?"

"Always. And I don't even know what your side is."

"Me either."

"That's a step in the right direction."

"That is? It doesn't feel like it."

"Anything is better than closing the door on him completely. He does love you."

Cherry's voice was tiny. "He does?"

"He does, Cherry. That happened a year ago. He's doing everything he can to fix this. Who fixes a year-old mistake? If he didn't love you, he'd move on...to me...but he won't because he can't. He loves you. You love him. When it's all said and done, that's all that matters." Jeanie led the way to the door.

Holden was waiting, watching.

"Sorry that took so long. I was trying to drown her so I could have you to myself, but she wouldn't quit breathing."

Holden appraised Cherry, his eyes smoldering with blue-green mystery. "Breathing is good."

# CHAPTER 38

"You look nervous." Holden caught hold of Cherry's hand across the cab.

"You think?" She pointed to the Latche drive, a few feet in front of them.

"You look green," Jeanie said from the back seat. "In which direction are you going to hurl?"

"I don't know if this is such a good idea, Holden. I think this might be a little soon for me."

"You were here yesterday."

"I was out of my mind yesterday."

"You're out of your mind every day." Jeanie leaned forward to pat Cherry on the shoulder. "But there is no way I'm getting this close to a farm without getting what I want."

"You want to ride a horse, Jeanie?" Holden glanced over his shoulder.

"No, a cowboy."

"You have no shame." Cherry shook her head.

"Based on the history of my ancestry, I am not required to have shame."

Holden parked the truck and Cherry shook her head again. This time, in denial.

"Breathe, Cherry." Holden got out and walked around to her side. He helped her down. "It's not that hard. Just breathe."

They weren't to the porch before the front door opened. Tabby flew down the steps. Squealing with delight, she leapt into Cherry's arms where they exchanged hugs and kisses. "Aunt Cherry! Aunt Amy said you were coming! You've been gone forever and ever! Mommy said you gave me the tea-set and I want a Barbie. And Uncle Holden gave me a little horsey. His name is Sally. And Uncle Eric is teaching me to ride him because he's a girl like I always wanted."

"Hi, Tabby-cat." Cherry kissed the happy little cheek again. "I missed you so much. You got so big."

Eric held the door open. His grin was broad. "Nice hunting."

"Jeanie this is my brother, Eric. Eric, Cherry's friend, Jeanie."

Eric put Cherry into a headlock and kissed the top of her head. He nodded at the other woman. "Jeanie. As in, I dream of?" His eyes lingered.

Jeanie didn't smile, but her eyes lit up appreciatively as she peered over her glasses. "Why don't you do that?" She walked past him poised and statuesque.

· · · · ·

Except for the smiles that wouldn't go away, it was as if Cherry had never left. Surprisingly enough, the only comment about her absence came at dinner, from CW, the patriarch himself. "Cherry," he said in the most authoritative voice Cherry had ever heard. "I hope you and Holden work out your differences, but I don't give a damn if you don't. You are not allowed to abandon the family. Period. And I will tell you another thing, young lady. If you ever think about walking out on us again, you better think again. Tabby is five and she knows better. You don't have an excuse."

Cherry sat up straight, taken aback and a tiny-bit frightened by his manner.

The thing was he meant it.

And, everyone agreed.

And she never thought she could feel so loved.

"Sorry." In a strange way, she was. "Where I come from, it was the thing to do."

"You come from here," Eric said. "Deal with it."

"Is anybody going to blame you?" She frowned at Holden.

He was unrepentant. "They do. That still doesn't give you permission to leave."

"Learn to deal with him," Missy said with a wink. "I'll show you how."

"Shut up, Missy." Holden, Eric, Wyatt and Eli spoke in forceful unity.

"Bluuhhhhh...." She happily motored her tongue at all of them.

Talking over the display, Jeanie said, "Permission to leave? A prisoner? Ohh baby. Bring on the chains." She held her hands up in mock surrender.

"I'll get right on that." Eric cut her a meaningful glance.

"You'll put up a good effort." Jeanie didn't look away. "And then you'll fail."

Eric cocked his head and grinned.

Amy rolled her eyes and huffed.

Cherry looked around the dinner table. It was missing a few faces. "Where are Pattycakes and Bruce?"

"Pattycakes is at her mother's," Wyatt said. "I'll bring her by to see you later."

"Oh." There was something in his tone that did not invite further inquiry. "And Bruce?" The only person Cherry hadn't missed.

"He's at his mother's too." Missy smirked. "Probably."

"I'll tell you about it later," Holden said.

"I'll tell you about it now."

"Shut up, Missy." Holden, Eric, Wyatt and Eli spoke in forceful unity.

Jeanie pointed to Missy. "You're my new hero."

Missy hi-fived her.

Amy huffed and rolled her eyes.

· · · · ·

Holden and Cherry walked along the back fence, sometimes holding hands, sometimes without contact. The mountains were beautiful, silent sentinels surrounding them in this peaceful valley of his existence. She hadn't realized how much she had come to love the land- Holden's land- until now, when she had the chance to regain her memories. The farm had been as much a part of her life as the family had been. It felt like home.

He helped her climb the wooden fence. Then he straddled it, facing her. "What are you thinking about?" He would never get tired of looking at her, breathing her in. He was never going to test the theory by letting her out of his sight.

"I like being here. No. I love being here. That scares me a little...a lot."

"It's all right to be afraid, Sweetheart." He toyed with a strand of her espresso hair. "That kind of fear is proof you're on the right track."

"How do you come to these conclusions?"

"No one says I'm too scared to hide. Or, I'm afraid of what I know. Only the coming out and moving forward." As he talked, he leaned closer. "You're afraid to love me, to let me in." He whispered in her ear, "You already love me. I'm already there. I belong there. Your heart is my home."

The enormity of his truth overwhelmed her. She had to give something back. "Holden."

"Yes?" He drew back a little, but only a little.

She took a deep breath. "My brother...Beany...Beany will be up for parole in a couple of months."

The change in topic was strange, but it was the catch in her voice that made him focus. "Good for him. I hope he makes it."

"I was...considering asking him if he wanted to come here, or wherever, with me. Maybe have a fresh start if he's interested." She hunched her shoulders, full of uncertainty.

The gift of sharing was a tiny, tiny thing, and yet, it carried the weight of gold. Holden felt like a rich man. "It won't hurt to ask as long as you realize he's not obligated. If he is interested, you could tell him there is farm work available. We'd be happy to have him."

With effort, Cherry relaxed her jaw and closed her mouth. "You would..." She could barely form the words. "But he's... We don't even know what's going on with us." The ease with which he offered. The possibilities. The hope.

Holden caressed her cheek. "Thank you for sharing that with me."

What she felt before was nothing compared to the emotions overwhelming her now.

They watched the others ride out, racing the last rays of the sun. Eric was taking Jeanie on a horseback tour of the farm. He waved his hat triumphantly as she was behind him in the saddle.

Jeanie waved too. Also, triumphantly.

Amy and Eli rode with them: Eli amused, Amy resigned. Jeanie wouldn't go with Eric unless they had company. Eric didn't give Amy a choice.

"I don't think Amy likes Jeanie much." Cherry waved them off.

"Jeanie's not Amy's problem, Eric is."

"What's that mean?"

"Those two are pretty much a tag team. And possessive. It takes them a little longer to adjust to either of them giving someone else attention. She'll be all right in a day or so. In fact, Amy will be the best indicator of how far gone Eric gets."

"How far gone he gets?"

"Eric has never been thwarted by a girl before. Never. He may want to marry Jeanie for that reason alone."

"She surprised me. The way she pours herself all over you, I thought she would die when she found out you had an identical twin. Honestly, I wondered if she was going to strip when he said hello."

"Don't let Jeanie fool you. That girl's a genius. She can be crazy with me because she knows I can't see past you. Nothing she does means anything to me. For her, it's practice. With Eric, she guessed right. Less is more. It's never occurred to him that he can't get what he wants. I think she wants to bring that reality to the forefront of his consciousness. It's a game and the beauty of it is they both know it."

"Wow. I could never play games like that."

"That's why I love you."

"It's starting to become a little less scary hearing it."

"That's the plan."

"But not a game."

"Not a game."

They stared out across the vast openness, letting the tranquility of the evening sink into them. Near the house, they heard a truck engine come to life.

"I wonder who that is."

"Wyatt. He's probably going to see Pattycakes."

"I hope I get to see her. What has she been up to?"

"She works in some accounting office in Martinsburg."

"Go Pattycakes. When are they getting married?"

"If I had to guess, I'd say not for a while."

"Uh-oh. What happened?"

Holden didn't have any secrets from Cherry. He didn't want any. "The day you left blew a hole in all of us." He smiled at her frown. "It wasn't your fault. We needed a hole blown in us. Bruce set that shit up and Wyatt didn't try to stop him. I lost you, but they caught the backlash. Pattycakes called off the engagement. Eventually, they split. She got a new job and moved on. Just like you." He cut her a hurtful glance, and then surprised her by adding, "Go Pattycakes. Wyatt needed to lose her, at least for a little while. A couple of months ago they started dating again. And I do mean dating. She doesn't stay here and she won't sleep with him." Holden chuckled. He enjoyed having the last laugh in that department.

"Go Pattycakes." She leaned into him, unaware of how at ease she had become. "How does Wyatt feel about that?"

"He's so happy to be in her company again, the rest doesn't matter."

"Maybe he finally got it."

"Maybe. Let's go to the tree house." He climbed down off the fence.

"Okay. Why?" She slid into his outstretched arms.

"So I can kiss you. That's the tree house's purpose."

"You can kiss me anywhere." To prove her point, she brushed her lips across his.

It was her first volunteered act of affection. He relished it. "Yes, but I want to kiss you horizontally," he said, as if his reason was obvious. For him, it was.

She let him lead her by the hand, flashing his favorite dimple.

It was better than the one in his dreams.

"Hey, umm. What was Missy alluding to at dinner, about Bruce?"

"That girl." Holden stopped under the tree house. He opened the trap door and lifted Cherry up through the opening, then hauled himself up behind her. "Missy had been so tolerant of Bruce since they got married."

They spread the sleeping bags and sprawled out side by side.

"Even after she found out about the bunkhouse escapade. That's what Eric calls it."

"Missy? Was tolerant? Missy throws things."

"That was before Missy started screwing around on Bruce."

Cherry's eyes shined bright. "Missy? Wow."

"She had a boyfriend for the better part of their marriage."

"Well now. Didn't see that one coming."

"Neither did Bruce. It almost killed him when he found out."

"Did he try to hurt her? You didn't let him hurt her did you?"

"Don't be absurd. He knew better than to touch her." Holden was becoming distracted by Cherry's lipstick. He cut out the light.

"What happened?"

Holden pulled Cherry into his arms and stopped caring about what happened. "Missy stopped sleeping with him. For a while he walked around here like a dead man. The more Missy flaunted it, the worse he got until he gave her an ultimatum." Holden gave Cherry an ultimatum: Kiss him back or be devoured.

· · · · ·

It was late when they drove back to Cherry's house. Jeanie was in the back seat, on the phone, emphatically telling Eric she was not coming to the farm after work tomorrow.

Cherry rode curled up beneath Holden's arm, content and amazed she could feel that way. "You never finished telling me about Bruce's ultimatum."

"Nothing to tell." He twirled her hair around his fingers, luxuriating in the feel of the silken strands. "Missy chose Austin."

"Austin?"

"I don't like what she did, but I do like Austin. He's a good man. He's good with the kids. He made Missy own up to the relationship. Once her divorce is final, they'll probably get married or something."

"So Bruce walked away scot-free. Missy is the bad guy and you, Eric, Wyatt and Eli are mad at her for hurting Bruce's little feelings?"

Holden shook his head. "You and your opinions. Bruce did not get away scot-free. Nobody is mad at her for hurting Bruce. He deserved what he got. We don't blame Missy. She's as much a Latche as the rest of us. But, we learned the hard way, unfaithfulness is wrong. Missy, on the other hand, thinks it's a good thing. That's the problem we have with her." His hand moved from her hair to her shoulder. It was a wonder that he could do this. He was holding a miracle- his miracle. "As for Bruce. He was kicked off the farm after Eric put him in the hospital."

Cherry sat up.

Jeanie leaned forward.

Holden held his expression. "Because I lost my ability to function, Eric had a lot more responsibilities." He pulled Cherry back against him. "Do you remember how Amy always had car trouble?"

"Amy still has car trouble," Cherry said. "That's why we're here."

"I'll have to reward her for that. Believe it or not, she wasn't always just hearing things. After Amy put a dent in his truck, Eric made it a habit to check her car regularly so she could stop borrowing his. On the days he did the animals he would start her car to make sure it sounded okay before she could complain."

Realization hit. "Did Bruce do something to Amy's car?"

"Eric found him draining her coolant. He tried to kill Bruce. Fortunately, Eric was tired and had his days mixed up. It was Wyatt's morning to do the animals. Wyatt heard the commotion and kept Eric from getting charged with homicide."

"Did Eric get all sweaty?" Jeanie sounded hopeful.

Holden and Cherry exchanged a knowing glance.

Cherry turned toward the back seat. "You should see him ride a bull."

"Ohh baby."

# CHAPTER 39

Back at Cherry's house, Holden made Jeanie promise to call when she got home. While they waited for her call, they made quick work of cleaning up the mess from the night before.

"Shall we go up?" Cherry colored over as soon as she said it. "I didn't mean that like it sounded. I meant, shouldn't we go to bed~No. You know what I mean." She laughed at herself until she noticed Holden hadn't joined in. "What?"

He took the time to weigh his words. "I'm not staying here tonight."

Her countenance dropped.

He pulled her to him. "Don't get the wrong idea. I want to stay. Nothing would give me more pleasure than to wake up and already be here with you." He kissed her. It was chaste, full of reassurance. "If you want the truth, the thought of leaving terrifies me."

"If it scares you to go, why are you leaving?" It scared her, his leaving. If he left, it would be like the day never happened. It might not be real. She might start having second thoughts.

He tilted her chin up, forcing her to look at him. "Yesterday couldn't be helped, but trust me. I've learned my lesson. Sweetheart, I'm not going to play house with you." He gave her another chaste kiss, this one on her forehead as if she were precious. "Sleeping in the same house is just a step away from sleeping in the same bed. I love you too much for that. I'm hoping you'll love me enough not to get spooked and run, because if you do," he smiled to take the sting out of his next phrase, "God help you when I catch you."

In spite of herself, she smiled back. "I can't run. My car won't work."

"I'll fix it on my way out."

"Why would you fix it if you don't trust me?" She didn't say, but it would be easier if he took away her choices.

"Because I want to trust you." He licked her dimple once and claimed her mouth for a real kiss.

· · · · ·

Cherry was jittery all through her shower and preparations. She credited it to the fact that she hadn't slept. How could she sleep? Holden left her with too much to think about. Her mind replayed their week at Deep Creek- the night she told him she was for sale and she wouldn't play house with him. He left her that night, just like he left her last night. Only last night he didn't come back. She waited.

What was she supposed to do with this...these feelings...She was overwhelmed and the only thing that made the slightest bit of sense scared the hell out of her.

· · · · ·

"Go back to bed," Holden said when his twin came down the steps. "I already fed the animals."

"Thanks," Eric yawned. "Why?"

"Couldn't sleep. I figured I may as well be useful." He sipped his coffee.

"She'll be there."

"I'm not so certain."

"You were certain enough to come home." Eric poured himself a cup of the dark brew. He blew on it and gazed out of the kitchen window. "Trust your judgment."

"I'm an idiot."

"Yeah, but trust your judgment anyway...Or not."

"What's that mean?" Holden turned toward his brother.

"She won't be there."

"What are you, psychic?"

"I can see her car. It's sitting in the driveway."

Holden's chair scraped the floor. He bolted out the back door and charged down the steps.

"Way to be cool." Eric watched from the window. "You wouldn't want her to think you were desperate or anything." He sent a quick text – waking up all interested siblings.

Cherry met him halfway across the yard. "Morning."

"How long have you been here?"

"About ten minutes."

"Why didn't you come in?"

"I-I didn't want to disturb anybody." She adjusted her stance, seeming very uncomfortable.

"I don't care what time it is, don't ever not come in." He leaned in for a kiss. Her lips were trembling. "What's wrong?"

"Nothing's wrong." She looked everywhere but at him. "At least, I hope not."

"Cherry."

A tear spilled down her cheek.

"Cherry?"

"Holden, I'm so scared."

He held her. "Scared of what? Did you think I wasn't coming back? I was just getting ready to leave. I was finding it hard to breathe here so I figured I'd wait outside your house until you woke up."

"Guess I beat you to it." She sniffed and wiped at her eyes.

"I guess you did. What did you freak about?"

"Us."

"Cherry, I love you. Only you."

The way he caressed her name made her study him. The mystery hiding in his blue-green gaze. Then it clicked. There was no mystery. She had always been trying to decipher something more, get a better understanding. That was why she ignored the facts, the warnings. She was expecting a mystery where there was none. Holden loved her, wanted her, needed her with a passion too strong to conceal. He meant everything he said. It was always about her. His good. His bad. His need to breathe.

Cherry inhaled and let it out. It felt like the first time. She reached into her pocket and offered Holden the ring box he had placed on her dresser.

He arched his eyebrow and frowned.

His expression was endearing. Her heart melted as she watched his other brow rise to join the first when she extended her left hand, palm down. "Sold."

Holden's understanding was immediate. He let out a whoop that alerted the whole farm.

Eric started across the yard and stopped short.

Holden sank down on one knee and flipped the box open.

Not wanting to miss anything, Amy climbed out on the roof. One floor above her, Missy sat on the window ledge.

"Cherry Nicole Brookfield." Holden took the ring out and touched it to the tip of her nail. "I love you. I want to spend my life with you."

Cherry cried again, too happy not to.

Wyatt draped an arm across Eric's shoulder, having come up behind him. Claire and CW watched from the back porch.

"Will you marry me?" He slid the ring on her finger. "Please."

Yes didn't seem quite big enough. Yes didn't capture the range of emotion she felt, the dreams and hopes and grandeur spiraling through her. But, she said it anyway. "Yes. Yes, Holden. I will marry you." She had been terrified before. Now, nothing seemed easier. Nothing made more sense.

This time his whoop was accompanied by other sounds: cheering, clapping and an identical whoop from his twin.

Holden and Cherry did not pay attention. They weren't aware the entire Latche clan had witnessed his proposal and her acceptance. In that moment they were alone in the world.

Purchase other Black Rose Writing titles at www.blackrosewriting.com/books
and use promo code PRINT to receive a 20% discount.

# BLACK ROSE
## writing ™

CPSIA information can be obtained
at www.ICGtesting.com
Printed in the USA
FFOW01n1355141115
18481FF